LARCENY & LAST CHANCES

---

22 STORIES OF MYSTERY & SUSPENSE

Edited by

JUDY PENZ SHELUK

Superior Shores Press

PRAISE FOR LARCENY & LAST CHANCES

"What a great ride! From a tony Canadian museum to a gritty Texas bar – and everywhere in between – this collection of stories hits in all the right places. The title theme is a throughline, in everything from domestic suspense to international heist to twisty vengeance tales, all brought to satisfying conclusion by these accomplished authors. Sharply written, tightly plotted, and thoughtfully curated by editor Judy Penz Sheluk, this anthology is as good as it gets."— *Kathleen Marple Kalb (Nikki Knight) Derringer and Black Orchid Novella Award Finalist, author of the Ella Shane and Vermont Radio mysteries, VP of the Short Mystery Fiction Society*

"The stories in *Larceny and Last Chances* feature twists that will keep even seasoned readers guessing and characters you'll be hoping to meet again. A superb editor shepherding a stellar group of authors through fun, fast-paced narratives of nimble fingers and desperate chances—what's not to love?"—*Joseph S. Walker, Mystery Writers of America*

"A bevy of beauties! Short, not-so-sweet, and some with a surprise twist, these stories will entertain both the casual and discerning reader alike. Each has its own punch, and picking a favorite is almost impossible. If you put my feet to the fire, I was partial to the Kevin Tipple tale, 'The Hospital Boomerang' and Brenda Chapman's 'The Pool.' Tipple's story was bathed in local Texas flavor and delicious irony. Chapman somehow took a "seen it coming a mile away" premise and made it fresh. Meanwhile, I could easily have chosen any of the entries in Larceny & Last Chances to highlight, as every single outing has its own unique charm. Don't miss out on these quick reads—they truly deliver!"—*Frank Zafiro, award-winning author of the River City series*

PRAISE FOR THE SUPERIOR SHORES ANTHOLOGIES

The Best Laid Plans: 21 Stories of Mystery & Suspense

"Crime doesn't pay, especially for criminals who think they've found a loophole…" —*Long and Short Reviews*

"Killer acting and get-rich schemes…the clever twists are endless." —*Catherine Astolfo, bestselling author and two-time winner of the Arthur Ellis Award for Best Crime Short Story*

Heartbreaks & Half-truths: 22 Stories of Mystery & Suspense

"A memorable collection. Yes, there's heartbreak, but those half-truths will get you every time."—*Crime Fiction Lover*

"Stories that will shiver your spine, tickle your funny bone, and, in a few cases, drop your jaw."—*Robert Lopresti, winner of the Derringer and Black Orchid Novella awards*

Moonlight & Misadventure: 20 Stories of Mystery & Suspense

"What a bunch of misadventures. These twenty authors have created stories where dialog snaps, characters carom, and plots surprise all under the ever-present moon."—*James Blakey, Derringer award-winning author*

"Laced with moonlit suspense, twisty turns, and dark humor, readers will be checking the shadows for murderers and miscreants."—*Rosemary McCracken, Debut Dagger and Derringer finalist, and author of the Pat Tierney mystery series*

CONTENTS

Larceny & Last Chances: 22 Stories of Mystery & Suspense

Collection compiled by Judy Penz Sheluk www.judypenzsheluk.com

All stories, with the exception of The Last Chance Coalition, edited by Judy Penz Sheluk

The Last Chance Coalition edited by Emily Nakeff

Editorial assistance for all stories by Andrea Adair-Tippins

Cover Design by Hunter Martin

Published by Superior Shores Press

ISBN Trade Paperback: 978-1-989495-76-6

ISBN E-book: 978-1-989495-75-9

First Edition: June 2024

"Surely you know that everybody's got a little larceny operating in them."—Bing Crosby, *White Christmas*

INTRODUCTION

If you've read the epigraph, you'll see that I've used a quote from the 1954 classic, *White Christmas*. It's one of my all-time favorite holiday movies and, having seen it at least a hundred times (though full disclosure, I always fast forward through Danny Kaye's "Choreography" number), I can probably cite, verbatim, any number of clever quips. But the one that always struck a chord with me was when Bing Crosby, as Bob Wallace (one-half of the successful singing duo Wallace and Davis), casually informs a not-yet-jaded by the biz Betty Haynes (one-half of the trying-to-be successful singing duo The Haynes Sisters) that "everyone's got a little larceny operating in them." What Bob Wallace meant was, in his world, everyone had an angle, including Betty's own sister, Judy.

I thought of that line when I was trying to come up with a concept for the fourth instalment in the Superior Shores Anthology series. Don't ask me why—it was, as I recall, a hot day in mid-July, but a writer's mind works in mysterious ways (at least, this writer's mind does). Anyway, it occurred to me that "larceny" would make a good theme, or at least, part of a good theme. But what about the second part?

Now, if you haven't already noticed, I'm a big fan of alliteration in titles (*Heartbreaks & Half-truths*; *Moonlight & Misadventure*), and, thinking back to *White Christmas*, I realized that the underlying theme was all about last chances. *Larceny & Last Chances*, I thought. That'll work.

The call for submissions went out November 1 with a deadline of February 15 or 80 submissions, whatever came first. The cap of 80 was made for three reasons:

1) I really didn't want to read more than 80 stories;

2) A cap of 80 would mean each author had roughly a 25% chance of acceptance;

3) I wanted to discourage a flurry of last day, eleventh hour, submissions, which had been somewhat common in the past.

The cap met, submissions closed in early February, with authors representing 34 states and provinces in the U.S. and Canada. I can honestly say there wasn't a bad story in the lot. I am eternally grateful to Andrea Adair-Tippins for her editorial assistance as we debated the merits of including or excluding a particular tale. Her insights were invaluable.

I'm also grateful to every author who trusted me with their story. My thanks go to repeat Superior Shores Anthology authors Tracy Falenwolfe, Kate Fellowes, Edward Lodi, Bethany Maines, and Robert Weibezahl, with a special nod to Susan Daly and KM Rockwood, who make their fourth appearance in as many volumes. It's also wonderful when an author's submission is their first (but by no means last) short story publication, as is the case with Karen Grose, or when new-to-me authors, or authors I've long admired, make the final cut.

But enough of what my husband Mike would call the "blah, blah, blah." It's time to turn the page and find out how 22 authors interpreted the theme. Turns out, there's a little larceny operating in each and every one of them.

Judy Penz Sheluk
June 2024

SUSAN DALY

Susan Daly writes short crime fiction as her way of crusading for social justice. Her stories have appeared in a surprising number of mystery anthologies, and 'A Death at the Parsonage' won the Arthur Ellis Award for best short story from Crime Writers of Canada. She lives in Toronto and hangs out with Sisters in Crime, Crime Writers of Canada, and other known criminal types. Find Susan at www.susandaly.com.

HAIL MARY BLUES
SUSAN DALY

I stood in the spacious upper gallery of the Victoria Conservatory of Music's new wing and tried not to weep.

The state-of-the-art Collections Room lies behind the long glass window that stretches the length of the gallery. Here anyone, staff or student or visitor, can enjoy the sight of the twenty-four treasured instruments that make up the Heath Collection.

Our collection, assembled over the 120-year life of Toronto's Victoria Conservatory is the envy of orchestras, music schools, and acquisitive tone-deaf billionaires the world over. Instruments with history through ownership or performance fame; period instruments no longer in vogue, but still in voice; exquisite representatives of their maker's art.

Not one of these desirable *objets de musique* rests quietly in the collection, to be simply adored in silence. They are taken out and played. Loaned to visiting virtuosi, and to students of promise. They still have their day on the concert stage. They are safe. They are loved. They are heard.

As Director of Collections, I am in charge of them all.

Today, my heart was breaking over the Smith Viola.

A. E. Smith. A plain name for a brilliant luthier. The Anglo-

Australian made many violins, but few violas. Most of which are in the National Museum of Australia. However, some time in the mid-twentieth century, one viola had made its way into the hands of renowned Canadian violist, Cosima di Turi, who, when her fingers had succumbed to arthritis, had bestowed it on indefinite loan to her beloved conservatory. To continue to sing in the hands of younger players.

There was the rub. Indefinite loan. Not permanent. Not a gift. Not a legacy.

When Cosima di Turi died last year, her will was silent on the Smith. Perhaps she'd assumed it would remain with the Victoria. Perhaps her intention was to have it returned to her family. Maybe she forgot. Whatever. It wasn't mentioned. Once probate was complete, and all the questionable matters were covered, there was no doubt the Smith Viola, valued for the estate at $177,000, belonged to the residual heir, di Turi's granddaughter, Elissa Pinkney.

There was also no doubt that once Elissa took possession next week, her husband Walter would sell it to the highest bidder.

I had to hold it again. Inside the Collections Room, I entered the security code for the Smith Viola cabinet and extracted the instrument and its bow.

Tuned it.

Positioned it beneath my chin.

Began to play.

None but the lonely heart can know my sadness...

I played my heart out.

A WEEK HAD GONE. So had the Smith.

Dr. Lucas Hamilton, the Conservatory's executive vice president, sat behind his impressive wooden desk and leaned forward, folding his hands, while I listened—again—to his diatribe.

"She *meant* for us to have it," he said for the eighth (or ninth) time.

"I'm sure she did." I didn't remind him—again—that the law could only go with what was in the will. Or—in this case—not in the will.

"Okay, Tyler..." he leveled a look at me. "What are we going to do about it?"

We? "Short of raising $177,000 to buy it back, there's nothing we *can* do."

"No, no....Wait. Remember that old movie, *The Red Violin?* At the end, this guy made a perfect copy and replaced it moments before the auction began. And no one figured it out."

"That was pretty farfetched. It would have been found out five minutes after the hammer fell."

"Wait, hear me out. 3D printing. I looked it up online. They can produce anything these days. Kidneys, AK-47s. Victims from ancient Pompeii. So why not a musical instrument?" He paused. "Although they probably sound like crap. But those Pinkneys wouldn't notice the difference."

"The buyer would." *Oh, why even bother?*

"Not if it's some moneybags looking for a status symbol. Though a real musician might figure it out."

"In a heartbeat."

He seemed to lose momentum. "I suppose you're right."

"Anyway, Lucas, isn't the whole idea that the Victoria hang onto the real Smith? If we somehow ended up with a Smith back in our world-famous collection, don't you think people would notice?"

"They might..."

"Or were you planning to keep it in a secret vault known only to a trusted few?"

His look told me I might be right. Then his face grew stern.

"You want it as much as I do."

Yeah. I did.

"Visitor to see you, Tyler. No appointment." Cody from the reception area placed a card on my desk.

Joe Romano. Carriage our Specialty.

"Did he say what—?"

"He suggested you might have a specialist's job for him."

Something felt off kilter. I was getting vibes of wariness from Cody, too.

"Okay. Send him in in ten minutes."

"Sure."

I made a call as soon as Cody was gone.

"Lucas, remember when we talked about the Smith Viola last week?"

"Oh. You mean when we, um, joked about how we might...?"

"That's it." Joked, eh? "Lucas, you didn't actually—?"

"*No.* Nothing like that. It was just...just nonsense."

I was fiddling with the card as we spoke. The image on the back hit me hard in the psyche.

"Never mind. I have a visitor. Call you later. Tomorrow."

I hung up and stared at the sketch on the card.

A honeybee.

"*CARRIAGE* IS YOUR SPECIALTY?" I demanded, over beers at the nearby Sinner & Saint. I'd dragged my visitor off the Victoria premises the moment I'd confronted him in the reception area. "Another of your many talents?"

Jesse—*not* Joe—showed no sign of apology. He flashed me his crooked smile. The one that still managed to make my honeybee tattoo buzz with possibilities.

"Oh, Tyler. You know I have gifts beyond even *your* dreams. Never mind that. I heard a rumor you're in need of a particular talent of mine, but I suspect the staff here might smell a rat if my card said *Larceny on Demand.*"

"Heard a rumor *where*?" We'd gone our separate ways a long time ago, and the idea our worlds might intersect was disquieting. Also, intriguing.

"Best not to ask." He leaned forward and dropped into

confidential mode. "Thing is, I understand the Victoria Conservatory has been done out of a valuable and—am I right?—beloved instrument. One we might say morally, if not strictly in the legal sense, belongs to them."

He had it exactly right. "Go on."

Jesse's look was all concern. "Suppose you tell me all about it. Especially the part about the moral right."

I did. As my story unwound, I couldn't keep the heartache out of my voice.

He looked thoughtful for a long minute, then drained his beer and ordered us a second round.

"Okay," he said at last. "The way I see it, you've already missed two—maybe three—chances to stop it falling into the wrong hands."

"You're as bad as Lucas. There was nothing we *could* have done."

"You really should have called me sooner, you know."

As if. "Sorry. I lost your number."

"Oh well, spilled milk and all that. So anyway, now we're down to the last few possibilities, since the farther it moves away from our grasp, the harder it gets. I think our next best chance is before it goes to auction. I mean, I'm good, but I'd rather not go up against the security measures of an auction house. Even worse would be the serious stronghold of some obscenely rich hard-core collector. That would require a real Hail Mary pass."

This didn't make me feel any better.

"So, I figure the granddaughter's house is the place to hit."

"Stealing it won't be any good." I repeated what I'd explained to Lucas, the need for the Conservatory to own the real Smith openly.

He looked wounded at this. "Surely you know me better."

In a way, I did. He was smart, talented, competent (in so many ways) and as far as I knew, he'd never been caught. On the other hand, he remained a mystery to me.

"You're right."

"Thanks. Now, these new owners. Music lovers? Art aficionados? Public benefactors?"

"No. Maybe. And not effing likely. I don't get how Cosima ever came to have a granddaughter as fluff-headed as Elissa. She's a professional socialite and world champion shopaholic."

"And she has the money to support her habit?

"Well, her husband has."

"Car dealership, right?"

"Several. They're high-end, flashy, and make him lots of money. Lots of high-end, flashy friends to match.

"Right. Well, we'll need to pay them a visit."

"We?" Lucas had used that word too.

"Absolutely we. I'll see what I can think up. Meanwhile..." he gazed casually off into the distance, "...you still got that tattoo?"

THE PINKNEYS' house was a monster home, all rectangles with a flat roof. An overblown structure whose creation had clearly involved the sacrifice of a modest post-war bungalow on a quiet midtown street. The houses next door seemed to shrink away in embarrassment from their parvenu encroaching neighbor.

Elissa Pinkney was expecting us, or rather Joe Romano and Melanie Robinson from the (non-existent) Chelsea Auction Galleries. As we entered the cavernous, stark white entrance hall, the chill from the décor—or lack of it—seeped into my bones.

But Elissa herself, like the rosy-pink shades of her flowy dress and equally flowy hair, was warm and welcoming.

"Thank you so much for taking an interest in Grandmother's violin," she said, leading us into a spacious sunroom at the back of the house. Here, the white non-color scheme served as contrast to the multitude of ornaments. Every table, shelf, and stretch of wall held a work of art, an artisan piece, or some cheap and cheerful tchotchke.

"What an amazing collection you have, Ms. Pinkney," I said.

"Thank you dear. Do call me Elissa. Yes, I'm fond of picking up anything that strikes my interest, and Walter never objects to buying me things I love. He always says that worthwhile art will never be worth less than what we paid for it."

Jesse went into his role of auction house representative. I'd almost swear the personal interest and professional knowledge he displayed were genuine. Well, who's to say they weren't?

"You have some excellent pieces here, Elissa." He focused on a simple blue china vase on a stand. "This Shunzhi vase, for example. I'd say you've a discerning eye."

"Oh, thank you. Yes, it's quite the joke among my friends. They're amazed at my sense of taste and judgement. Like this sweet little pair of figurines," She indicated an alcove containing two carved figures. A standing angel facing a kneeling woman.

"*The Annunciation.*" Jesse's surprised appreciation was unmistakable. Or well feigned.

"Yes. The Virgin Mary and the Angel Gabriel." Elissa stepped closer to help him admire them. "I don't know anything about the figures, but look at the nice detail, especially on Mary."

Jesse nodded. "They're about a hundred years old. Copies of the pair made by seventeenth-century sculptor Dante Cavrioli."

"Really?" Elissa was delighted. "That's wonderful to hear. I just loved them the moment I spotted them at a flea market in Naples. Walter paid a lot for them, over 100 euros."

"He did well." Jesse now moved on to inspect a small painting of a river and trees. "This looks like a Tom Thomson."

"It *is*. Walter was able to pick it up as a bargain because there was some dispute about its authenticity. But I'm sure it's real."

She turned to address us both. "Of course, what you really came to see is the violin." She directed us to another alcove across the room.

I couldn't hold back a gasp of dismay. The Smith Viola rested on its stand, wide open to whatever dust and temperature and humidity the room could throw at it, and—greatest sin of all—in full sunlight from the floor-to-ceiling window.

Jesse sent me a look that said *shut up*, but Elissa seemed to hear it as a gasp of awe.

"Yes, I suppose it's impressive, though I'm not really interested in old instruments—"

"Do you play yourself, Elissa?" Jesse cut across her, probably to keep me from reacting again. "Smith violas are prized for their rich, mellow voice."

"Sadly, I didn't inherit my grandmother's musical talent." She sighed. "I'd love to keep it, but, well, Walter insisted. He says it's crazy to keep something *that* valuable just collecting dust. Let alone the insurance costs."

"I understand entirely, Elissa. I think you're wise to be realistic about its future."

She threw him a grateful smile.

"Now, as you can appreciate, we must have it appraised independently before we can offer to accept the consignment. First, we need to hear it played. That's why I brought Miss Robinson along."

Oh, please yes... I could barely keep from shaking with the thrill of playing it one more time. I picked up the bow and the instrument, tuned it, took a long deep breath.

Again, I played my heart out.

"That was *lovely*," Elissa assured me, as the last notes of the capriccio died.

Jesse didn't say a word. He just looked at me. Stunned.

"Je—Joe?"

He recovered himself. "Thank you, Miss Robinson. There's no doubt of its excellent tone."

I remembered my follow-up act and tried to look a little weak and overcome.

"My dear, are you all right?" Elissa asked.

"I'm sorry. Playing Vieuxtemps always affects me like this. I wonder, could I just freshen up in the bathroom, and maybe get a glass of water...?

"Yes, of course. Come with me." She was all solicitude.

"Take your time, ladies," Jesse said. "I'll just continue my inspection if that's okay, take some pictures of the Smith for my report."

"Of course. Take whatever you need. Just this way, dear, down the hall."

I stole a glance back at Jesse. So far, so perfect.

"*Take whatever you need*." Jesse was clearly overjoyed, as we drank to our success back at the Sinner & Saint. "How little she knew. Hell, I could have walked off with Mr. Smith there and then. You did great, keeping her out of the room that long."

"It was easy. Her kitchen was full of things she was happy to talk about." Especially the poster of Paul Newman in a chef's outfit. "But you *didn't* take the Smith. Or anything else, I hope?"

"Just pictures. I've got an app on my phone to scan an object for 3D printing."

"Sounds useful. But like we said before, what could we do with a copy?"

Despite what I'd said to Lucas earlier, 3D printed instruments were making a splash. Though they neither looked nor sounded like the historic originals, nor could they pass for one, they had a surprising quality all their own.

"You never know. I also took videos of the room, and the area outside the window. We'll need them if we make an unofficial return to the scene."

There was that "we" again.

"Oh, and I wiped your fingerprints off the Smith."

My mind went dead cold with the implications.

"Thank you," I managed to murmur.

"It's my job to think of these things." He was silent for a long moment.

"Uh, speaking of jobs, Tyler... I'm sorry. I had no idea you could —you were actually a..."

"A musician?" Okay, how could he know? "Yeah, I play. I earn my living at the Conservatory, but music is my heart and soul."

OVER THE NEXT FEW WEEKS, I heard nothing from Jesse. I had no way of contacting him. No phone number, no email. I didn't know what city, what country he lived in.

Not even his real name.

Was he focusing on the Smith, or on other projects in other countries? I chose not to worry, but kept alert for any hint of news relating to violas or Pinkneys.

It hit us three weeks later. A very nervous-sounding Lucas called me into his office. He had a visitor. Sergeant Michael Kurelek. A six-foot-something wall of uniform and authority.

I might have been dying a thousand deaths inside, but earlier times with Jesse had schooled me to be calm and innocent.

"I'm following up on a break-in two nights ago at the home of Walter and Elissa Pinkney."

I reminded myself to forget I'd ever met Elissa. "The Pinkneys?"

"The people who inherited the Smith Viola." Lucas looked anything but calm. Thank goodness he knew nothing about Jesse's plan. "The sergeant just wants to know—"

"It's fine, Mr. Hamilton. Ms. Dean, your director tells me the instrument was in the Conservatory's possession for the past eighteen years, and that your job includes overseeing the collection."

"That's right." *Don't volunteer. Just answer.* If Jesse had taken it—

"Yes, we hated losing it, but Elissa Pinkney *is* the rightful owner." Lucas couldn't seem to shut up. "Was it stolen?"

"Nothing was stolen. But it looks like that's what the thieves were after. The viola was moved from the alcove where it was kept and was found on the floor near the window."

I couldn't stand it any longer. "How can we help you, Sergeant?"

"We're wondering if there's ever been suspicious activity involving this instrument any time it's been in your possession. Or any other instrument."

I struggled to keep my relief from showing as I assured him that we'd never had any kind of trouble. Maybe because thieves weren't aware of how valuable historic instruments could be. I forced myself to stop babbling.

And that was it. The sergeant left, and after Lucas wondered at length about the thwarted break-in, the thief, and so on, I escaped to my office to enjoy a much-needed bout of asking myself, "What the eff—?" and receiving no answers.

My phone dinged a message.

dont worry its all good

A FEW WEEKS LATER, we heard through the Conservatory's well-connected grapevine that the Smith Viola was going on the block, to be handled by Cormack Fine Arts Auction House. A highly reputable family concern for more than a century.

As the auction date grew relentlessly closer, I found myself increasingly anxious for another note from Jesse. His earlier message had arrived through some internet magic I had no clue about, and had dissolved into the ether only minutes later.

What had Jesse said? He'd infinitely prefer to tackle the job at the Pinkneys' than at the auction house or the Smith's final destination. And yet, any day now, it would be transferred to Cormack, who certainly knew their business, and then sold and shipped to god-knows-where.

I could almost hear the chances ticking down. The antepenultimate, the penultimate, and finally the Hail Mary pass.

Granted, we'd already established it couldn't be stolen, but surely something had to happen. Anything.

Or did it? After all, why should I expect Jesse to swoop in from my past and rescue the Smith for the sake of the Victoria Conservatory? What was it to him, except a bit of fun, a farfetched challenge?

If it didn't happen, so what?

BY THE DAY before the auction, I was a nervous wreck. I haunted the Cormack website, staring at Lot 46.

Viola by Arthur Edward Smith; Sydney, Australia, 1948. Opening bid $75,000. Estimate $125,000-$180,000.

It was like a farewell look at an old friend.

Lucas informed me he and I were attending the auction, which would be held live at the Cormack's premises on Queen Street, with online and telephone bids as well. I couldn't possibly go, having presented myself to Elissa Pinkney as the non-existent Miss Robinson from the mythical Chelsea Galleries. I told Lucas I didn't want to run into the Pinkneys, and, after some persuasion, he agreed to go without me.

"To give our viola the send-off it deserves," he said, waxing surprisingly poetic.

Lucas gave me his report on his return. First, Mr. Smith had brought a hammer price of $230,000.

"No!" Way over the top estimate. "Someone—two people—must have really wanted it."

Lucas nodded. "It was down to two on-line bidders at the end. Some Australian philanthropist. Of course he'd want to repatriate it to Australia. Maybe to add to the National Museum collection?"

"They have enough already," I muttered.

"The other was some anonymous bidder. Apparently some crypto currency magnate with a private collection of expensive toys."

"So, who got it in the end? The gazillionaire, I suppose."

"No. Surprisingly, the Australian. I never thought he'd hold out." Lucas looked mildly impressed. "Anyway, we could never have raised that amount."

"Yeah." At least it was headed back where it would be appreciated. Maybe even loved. I convinced myself I was content.

Until I got another mysterious message.

trust me

THREE DAYS later (and three days of silence from Jesse) I was far from trusting him. Just before the end of the day, Lucas got a phone call from Evelyn Cormack, head of the auction house.

"She wants to meet with us tomorrow morning." Lucas looked even more miserable than at any of our recent meetings. "I swear, I'm beginning to wish I never heard of A.E. Smith and his damned viola."

"It's about the Smith?" Oh god. I was ready to echo his concern. Only I was far more aware of the danger we were in.

"Of course it is. She wouldn't tell me anything, except it was a totally unexpected aftermath and a highly serious matter and completely confidential."

I managed to avoid pointless speculation, made some would-be placating responses for Lucas's sake, and beat a retreat to the Sinner & Saint. Aided by a generous glass of red, I indulged in a serious mental and emotional tailspin towards the worst-case scenario.

The Aussie had discovered the Smith was a fake.

Damn it, Jesse.

How much should I tell Lucas? Everything? To prepare him for what to expect tomorrow? Except I didn't know anything for sure.

No. Let whatever Evelyn Cormack had to say come as a surprise to him.

Either way, I'd be fired by the end of the day. And probably arrested.

I ordered a plate of nachos to help soak up the wine.

I had taken a screenshot of Jesse's second message before it could vanish, and I gazed at it now, looking for some kind of reassurance.

trust me

I was taking comfort from the image of the message, the nachos and a second glass of red when a new message dinged in.

i told you—trust me

And a moment later....

where are you

That's when I noticed this was a regular text. I could respond.

Sinner & Saint

...

15 min

Jesse insisted on waiting until the server had brought him food and drink before letting me say anything other than, "Oh my god, am I glad to see you."

"Okay, now that we're safe from interruptions, let's hear it, Tyler."

Where to start? "The director of the auction house wants to see Lucas and me first thing tomorrow morning. About the Smith."

He looked puzzled. "Didn't she say why?"

"No. She just used scary words like 'serious' and 'unexpected' and 'confidential'."

"And so you think...?"

"They've discovered it's a fake." Even as I said the words, they seemed to lose their power.

He gave me that crooked smile again.

"Yeah. I thought you might think that." He leaned forward and took my hand in his. His look warmed me all over.

"Tyler, it's not a fake. It's the genuine article, and even as we speak it's in secure storage at Cormack's."

"But... when we were at the Pinkneys' home, why did you scan the Smith with 3D software?"

"I didn't. I scanned the Annunciation Mary."

"I'm sorry... what?"

"Despite what I told Elissa, the figure of Mary was *not* a replica of a seventeenth-century carving by Dante Cavrioli. It was the real deal. He carved the pair in 1684. The Gabriel is still in the Chiesa di Santa Giuliana in Montalcino, but the Virgin disappeared sometime during the war. How it ended up in a flea market in Naples is anyone's guess."

He took a long draw on his beer. I gave up thinking.

"I got a perfect 3D reproduction of Mary made, and then I returned to the scene and swapped it out for the real one."

"Okay..." My brain slowly shifted into working mode. "And you moved the Smith as a red herring."

"You heard about that, eh?"

"We had a visit from the police. But you knew that." That's when he'd sent his first message. "So now, Elissa owns...?"

"An impeccable replica of the Cavrioli Annunciation Mary, worth about $350, and a third-rate copy of the Gabriel, worth maybe $20 on a good day."

"But if they bought the real one—"

"Well, to use your favorite argument, she never had any moral right to it. Stolen property. She's happy with believing they're good reproductions. And don't forget, she got the hammer price for the Smith Viola—minus commission."

"So where is the Mary now?"

"I sold her. After all, she was still hot. Stolen from Montalcino eighty years ago. Stolen by me two months ago. And god knows how many times in between."

"And you sold her to...?

"Oh, just a man I know. One of those collection-crazy billionaires you have no use for. But he was the one with the money."

Jesse paused. He seemed to be waiting for me to connect the last dots.

"So I guess this means our final last chance is gone? Now that the Aussie is the legal—and moral—owner, he'll take Mr. Smith home to Australia. And they might even love him—it. I suppose I can live with that."

Jesse's jaw dropped. Just a little.

"My god, Tyler, you're slow. There was no Australian."

"Then who bought—?"

"I did, of course. The Aussie persona was a mask. I could have bought it three times over with what Mr. X paid me for Mary. I had to go higher than I expected, since there was some super-billionaire who didn't want to give up."

Just like that, everything shifted.

A million lights of joy fluttered all around me.

He grinned. "That's what the Cormack woman wants to meet with you about tomorrow. Though why she had to go all secretive about it I don't know. She's going to tell you that the anonymous buyer is donating the Smith Viola to the Victoria Conservatory. In memory of Cosima di Turi."

I couldn't help it. I burst into tears.

"Oh, Jesse..." I sniffled and grabbed a handful of paper napkins.

"Ironic, isn't it?" he went on, politely pretending I wasn't a mass of dripping emotion. "You do know, right, that the Annunciation is the source of that number one Catholic prayer, *Hail Mary, full of grace...*"

FOUR WEEKS LATER, the Victoria held a gala reception to celebrate the return of the A.E. Smith Viola. I sat on the podium with the others, thrilled to see all the musicians, students, and alumni in attendance, sharing our happiness. Evelyn Cormack was here to make the presentation, in the absence of the actual donor and their hidden identity. Even she had no idea who it was.

Lucas had wanted to invite the Pinkneys, but I pointed out

they'd washed their hands of the Smith when they'd sent it to the auction block. Lucas argued—half-heartedly—that they were within their rights, but I stood firm.

Jesse was gone from my life again. He'd left me with the endless joy of having the Smith Viola back where it belonged, and the memory of the handful of nights we'd shared over the course of our adventure. We both knew we belonged in different worlds, worlds that could never do more than cross on the rare occasion when one of us needed the other.

Lucas finished his recap of the Smith's history, and Evelyn was ready to present it. As Director of Collections, I had the honor of receiving it.

Which I did with a heartfelt speech of gratitude to the anonymous donor. Sadly, I couldn't so much as hint at Jesse and all he'd done.

One further honor was mine.

The audience hushed, while I straightened the Schubert score on the stand and my colleague stepped up to the piano beside the podium.

I positioned the viola beneath my chin, positioned my bow.

The piano intro began.

Ave Maria.

I played my heart out.

ROBERT WEIBEZAHL

Robert Weibezahl is a two-time Derringer Award finalist whose stories have appeared in *Mystery Tribune*, *CrimeSpree*, *Beat to a Pulp*, *Yellow Mama*, *Futures Mysterious Anthology Magazine*, *Kings River Life*, and the anthologies *Moonlight & Misadventure* and *Deadly by the Dozen*. He was twice nominated for the Agatha and Macavity Awards in the nonfiction category. Author of two crime novels, *The Wicked and the Dead* and *The Dead Don't Forget*, he is also an award-winning, internationally-produced playwright. Robert is a member of International Thriller Writers, the Short Mystery Fiction Society, and the Dramatists Guild of America. Find Robert at robertweibezahl.wordpress.com.

ARTIFACT

ROBERT WEIBEZAHL

FRUSTRATED AND TIRED, Sebastian has just settled on a bench on the otherwise deserted outer deck of the ferry when his phone rings. It's his mother, and though he's in no mood to talk, he takes the call. He always takes the call when it's his mother.

"Hi, Mami. I'm on the ferry…What? Not so good. I'll tell you when I get home…No. No, they didn't…I said I'll tell you when I get home…*Sí*. Forty-five minutes."

That is when he spots the boy. Fourteen, fifteen years old, maybe. A white kid in his private school uniform, wine-colored blazer, dark gray slacks. The requisite earbuds. A backpack slung over his shoulder. Manhattan kid. Maybe Brooklyn Heights or Park Slope. Not the kind of kid you normally see heading to Staten Island. Certainly not the kind of kid Sebastian normally pays much attention to. But something is off. The kid seems agitated, furtive, up to no good. He's gripping a plastic Duane Reade bag, and Sebastian watches as he approaches the railing. The kid hesitates. Sebastian realizes his mother is saying something on the other end of the line.

"Sorry, Mami. *¿Qué?*"

But Sebastian doesn't hear what his mother repeats, because at that moment it dawns on him what the kid is up to. The privileged brat plans on tossing the Duane Reed bag over the side of the boat into the water below.

"Hey, don't do that!" Sebastian calls out reflexively. "Stop that!"

Whether absorbed in the music pulsating from his earbuds, or just alone with his thoughts, the kid doesn't seem to hear.

"Mami, I've got to go." Sebastian ends the call, makes his way quickly to the boy. But when he gently touches a shoulder to get his attention, the kid recoils, startled.

"What the hell, man?"

"What are you doing?"

"What?" shouts the boy, his earbuds still in place.

Sebastian impatiently tugs one of the buds from the kid's ear. "I said, what are you doing?"

"Hey, leave me alone, dude, okay? You some kind of perv? Don't touch me."

Sebastian takes a step back. "Okay, sorry. I shouldn't have…But what are you doing? You can't throw stuff into the water."

"What's it to you?"

"Hey, don't be a dick. Freakin' prep school boy should know not to throw trash into New York Harbor."

"Who says it's trash?"

"Don't start with me, *Pendejo*."

"Mind your own business."

"It is my business. I live here. I don't like assholes throwing trash in the harbor. Which, by the way, is illegal."

"You a cop?"

"Do I look like a cop?

"You look like a douchebag." The kid takes back his earbud, ceremoniously replaces it in his ear, and begins to walk away.

"Nice," Sebastian says flatly. "Hey, hold on."

The kid keeps walking, his head bobbing slightly to the beat of his music. This time, Sebastian's grip on his arm is firmer.

"Hey, I said don't touch me!" The boy shouts with a vehemence that takes Sebastian by surprise.

"Where do you think you're going?"

The kid spits out, "Anywhere you're not." For the first time Sebastian looks more closely and sees the damage in the boy's face.

"What's in the bag? Why throw it in the water? There's a trash bin right over there."

"I said, mind your own business."

"Give me the bag."

The boy signals his refusal by clutching the bag tighter. Sebastian tries cutting the tension with a joke. "Whaddya got in there, body parts?"

The kid seems to consider his options, then thrusts the bag into the older man's chest. "Don't be stupid."

Sebastian takes the bag and looks inside with caution, as if it might indeed contain fresh body parts. He finds only a single item, a small decorated sack made of some kind of animal skin.

"What's this?"

"Be careful. It's old," the kid says, suddenly a pillar of responsibility.

"I can see that." Sebastian sighs. "What is it?"

"It's a Native tobacco pouch. Very rare. Couple of hundred years old, I think."

"Sure it is," says Sebastian, not hiding his skepticism. But the thing he is now holding is unquestionably fragile and distinctly beautiful. The leather is dry and brittle in spots, but the beadwork is exquisite, even to the untrained eye.

"It is," the boy counters, petulance rising. "Iroquois. Or maybe Shoshone."

"I don't know much, but even I know Iroquois and Shoshone are not remotely the same thing."

"Whatever. That's not the point."

"No, the point is—what are you doing with a two-hundred-year-old Iroquois tobacco pouch?"

"It's mine." The boy says it with unpersuasive conviction, snatches the pouch and the plastic bag back from Sebastian.

"Okay, okay. If you say so. Jeez. Just be careful with it."

"It *is* mine. Well…my father's." Then, as an afterthought, "My *step*father's."

"Assuming that's true…and I'm not," Sebastian says, "why would you throw your stepfather's two-hundred-year-old Iroquois, or possibly Shoshone, tobacco pouch into the harbor?"

"'Cause I hate the bastard and I want to watch his precious crap float out to sea. Or, even better, get chewed up by a ship's propeller."

"Hold on. Did this 'bastard' do something to you—"

"He's gonna crap himself when he finds out it's gone."

Sebastian looks at the boy. Vengeance in watery blue eyes that by rights should be filled with youthful brightness. He knows the answer to his next question, but asks it anyway. "How'd you get it?"

"I just took it. He keeps it in his study, in a cabinet with all his other so-called priceless artifacts. But he never locks it."

"Priceless artifacts? What are you talking about?"

"He collects old Indian stuff. Native. Indigenous. Whatever. Pays way too much for it, I'm sure. Thinks it's part of his heritage."

"He's Native?"

"Nah, he just claims he is. One-sixteenth something or other. Load of crap."

"Maybe he is."

"He's a freakin' ginger. He's no more Native than you or me."

"Well, I'm Puerto Rican," Sebastian interjects, "so actually I could have some Taino blood."

"Sure. Everyone's an Indian nowadays."

"I didn't say I was."

"That's cool," says the boy. "I couldn't care less."

"So, you just lifted your father's two-hundred-year-old Iroquois…Shoshone—"

"—*Step*father—

"—tobacco pouch thing, and you were going to throw it in the harbor."

"I still might."

"Why don't you just sell it? If you hate him so much."

"'Cause then he might get it back."

"But money, hey. You called it priceless."

"That's, like, just a saying, you know? It's probably only worth twenty thousand."

A shock-fueled whistle inadvertently escapes Sebastian's lips. "*Only* twenty thou?"

"The asshole spends that on a golf weekend in Bermuda."

"*Ay dios mío.*"

"All that matters is he never gets it back. It's all he cares about. His freakin' artifacts."

"Hey, man, there's something else going on here. You wanna talk about it?"

"Hell no," the boy responds, a little too quickly. A moment later he says, "He doesn't even care about my mother, really. Certainly not me. He'll be glad I'm gone."

"Gone? Where you going?"

The boy shrugs. "I just wish I could be there and see the veins pop out of his ugly face when he realizes it's gone."

"Where are you going to go?"

"I'll figure that out when I get off the ferry."

"Have you ever even been off Manhattan Island?"

"Don't be a douche."

"I mean, on your own."

"I'll figure it out," the kid says again.

"What are you gonna do, take an Uber to Bayonne?"

"I said I'd figure it out!"

Argument spent, the boy looks out over the railing and says nothing more. Sebastian joins him in the moment of companionable silence. The eternity of a minute or two passes.

"So, that's freakin' Lady Liberty, huh?" the boy says at last. "You know, I've never…This is the closest I've been."

"Yeah. New Yorkers. We don't do the tourist thing."

"You?"

"What?"

"Been up inside? In the crown?"

"When I was a kid. With my *papá*. He liked that sort of thing. Be proud, he used to say. *Somos americanos. Todos juntos.*"

"I don't speak Spanish."

"No?!" Sebastian says with feigned, but good-natured, shock.

"How soon before we dock?" the kid asks after another silence.

"About ten minutes."

"You ride the ferry a lot?"

"Now and then."

"You from Staten Island?"

"Yeah."

"What's that like?"

"What do you mean, what's it like?" Sebastian makes no attempt to hide his annoyance. "It's like…I don't understand the question."

"So why were you in the city? Job?"

"No."

"Some girl?"

"What is this, the third degree?"

"Well, I told you what I was doing."

"Yeah, well, *I* wasn't throwing trash off the boat.

"Not trash," the boy says. "Treasure."

Sebastian focuses on the Jersey skyline in the distance. "I had an appointment. With a bank."

"Exciting."

"For a loan. A business thing."

"Like I said, exciting."

"Yeah, well some of us can't just steal stuff from Daddy when we need money."

"He's my *step*father. And I didn't steal from him for the money."

"Splitting hairs."

The kid persists. "So, what do you want a loan for?"

"To open a business."

"What kind of business?"

Sebastian hesitates before he answers, "A cheese shop." It gets the anticipated laugh from the kid. "It's not funny."

"It kind of is."

"Now who's being a dick? *Gourmet* cheeses. People like that kind of thing in your bougee part of the city, don't they?"

"Sure, I guess."

"So, folks in Staten Island deserve good cheese, too. Give me a break."

"It's cool." An airhorn sounds, announcing the ferry is approaching the St. George terminal. "So, did you get the loan?"

"Hell, no."

"Why not?"

"Because my name is Rodriguez, not Rockefeller."

"That sucks."

"Sucks?" Sebastian laughs ruefully, anger rising. "I'll tell you what sucks. I don't have enough money in the bank to borrow more money from the bank. Or own a house. I'm gonna be thirty-six on my next birthday. I'm a *man* for chrissake. I've worked hard. Time is running out. Don't I deserve the same break as some trust fund baby?"

"I don't have a trust fund."

"I didn't say you did."

"It sounded like you meant—"

"Let it go, kid."

The kid contemplates the faded pouch he holds in his hand. Gently placing it back in the plastic bag, he offers it to Sebastian. "Here, take this."

"What? What are you doing?"

"For your shop. For the money."

"I'm not taking your stolen artifact."

"Why not? I'm just going to throw it away…one way or another. I'm not giving it back to that bastard. You might as well have it."

"You stole it."

"I'm sure you can find somewhere to sell it. Put the money toward your shop."

"I'm not a guy who fences stolen goods."

"Just this one time. It'll help you get what you want."

"No."

"I'm telling you, it's either you or the deep blue sea."

"That's ridiculous."

"Why? It should do some good. It's probably more rightfully yours, if you think about it. You might be Taino. You said so yourself."

"I'm not Taino. Even if I am—"

"It's like…your birthright."

"That's a stretch, even if—"

"More than his. Or no less."

"I don't want it." Sebastian tries to return the bag, but the kid puts his hands behind his back, out of reach.

"Take it. Come on. I'm just going to throw it away if you don't."

"I'll turn it in to the police."

"Don't do that! Please. Anything but that. *He'll* get it back if you do that."

The grinding hum of the engines shifts to a higher pitch and the boat begins to slow.

"I think we're about to dock," the kid says. "Hey, nice meeting you. Thanks for the advice."

"Advice?"

"About the Uber to Bayonne."

"Don't be a douche," Sebastian says, mimicking the boy in a good-natured way. "Give me your phone for a second."

"Why?"

"Phone." Sebastian extends his hand. "Trust me."

The kid hands the phone over. Sebastian glances at it and hands it back. "Unlock it."

After the boy enters his passcode, Sebastian takes back the phone and adds his number to the contacts.

"That's my number. Listed under Sebastian. You can call if you ever need to. You know, if the Evil Ginger ever goes too far."

The boy covers his emotions with a feeble joke. "Or if I ever have a craving for gourmet cheese?"

Sebastian swipes the back of his hand toward the boy, a joking gesture that he should go away. "Get the next ferry back to the city, okay? Promise?"

"I'm Zachary, by the way," the kid says. Then, "Zach," before disappearing into the crush of commuters and tourists making its way ashore.

Sebastian stands, momentarily frozen, bag in hand, as impatient passengers push past him on their way off the boat. Weighing his options, he glances at the bag, then over the railing, but immediately dismisses carrying out Zach's original intention. Trash cans dot the deck, and there will be more inside the terminal. But how can he throw away a valuable artifact like yesterday's garbage?

He can't, of course. He knows that the minute he is off the boat, he should beeline to the first police officer he sees and hand it over. Say he found it abandoned on a bench. Let the chips fall. But would that lead to trouble for Zach? Likely. He could send it, anonymously, to some Native museum out West. Would they be able to trace it? Send it back to the Evil Ginger? What kind of records did they keep of this stuff?

Or…

No. He couldn't do it. Could he? It wasn't right. Wasn't legal. Or ethical. It wasn't his to profit from. True, Zach *had* given it to him. But Zach had stolen it himself. Still, how many times had it been stolen, bartered, illegally sold, over the last two hundred years? Whose was it to sell, really? Wouldn't the Evil Ginger just put in an insurance claim and buy something else for his collection?

Sebastian's phone rings. His mother again. He wishes he could ask her advice. He lets the call go to voicemail. He hears the coarse voice of a deckhand telling him and a handful of other stragglers to get off the ferry. Holding the Duane Reade bag tightly against his chest, he joins the disembarking crowd.

KM ROCKWOOD

KM Rockwood draws on a varied background for her stories, including blue collar jobs in steel fabrication and glass making, and supervising inmate work crews in a large state prison. Now retired from working as a special education teacher in correctional facilities, inner city schools, and alternative schools, she spends her time writing and caring for her family and pets. Published works include the Jesse Damon Crime Novel series and numerous short stories. KM is a member of Sisters in Crime National, Chesapeake, and Guppy Chapters, and the Short Mystery Fiction Society. Find KM at www.kmrockwood.com.

THE CONSTELLATION NECKLACE
KM ROCKWOOD

"Shrimp cocktail for the lady," Roger told the waiter. He turned to me. "Would you like some wine, Hannah?"

We were seated on the terrace, and the cool night air, carrying the scent of the ebbing tide, danced on my bare shoulders. I drew the soft cashmere shawl closer. "No thank you."

I was eighteen. The humiliation of being carded in such a nice place. And then being refused service.

What were we doing here? Roger operated a ferris wheel on the boardwalk.

No way could we afford this classy restaurant.

When the waiter left, I leaned forward. "Roger. This place is expensive."

He reached over and stroked my hand. "You're worth it, my dear. Once this little venture of ours is complete, we'll move to Mexico. Then I'll be able to treat you like you deserve to be treated."

"About 'this little venture…'" I started to say.

"Now don't tell me you're getting cold feet." Roger gave me that sad smile. "We've been planning all summer. This weekend might be our last chance."

Roger may have been planning all summer. I had to admit I shared the guilt a bit, too. Although I'd never agreed to participate, I'd let myself be carried away with his talk of whisking me away to an idyllic life as wealthy ex-pats. I'd murmured only vague objections to his plan.

I should have put my foot down weeks ago, but who would have thought Roger would ever have the means to actually go through with it?

Twisting my napkin—fine cloth, no paper napkins here—between my fingers, I asked, "How can I *steal* from Daphne?"

Daphne was my employer. The job as her personal assistant paid better than anything else available. And was much more pleasant.

"You're not stealing," Roger soothed. "All you have to do is turn off the alarm to let me in and show me where the wall safe is. I'll take care of everything else."

"Daphne loves that necklace. Her father got it for her sweet sixteen birthday."

"What's not to love?" Roger straightened the several spoons next to his plate. "The Constellation Necklace. An exquisite bib necklace in sterling silver with a brilliant array of sapphires and diamonds surrounding the internationally-renowned Starlight Diamond. Last sold for a little over two million dollars."

That sounded like the description from an auctioneer's catalog. It might have been.

"She'll be heartbroken," I said.

"She'll never even know. You've seen the replacement. You couldn't tell the difference. And you've handled the real thing a dozen times, helping Daphne get ready for events."

"Yes, but…"

"No buts. I already have an overseas buyer lined up, a Saudi prince who's planning to present it to his favorite wife. So it will never be on the open market, and since this guy doesn't let his wives go out in public, no one else will ever see it."

"Sooner or later they'll take it for an insurance appraisal…"

"Okay, then they'll find out they have a replica instead of the real thing. But it might not be for years. They'll have no idea when the substitution was made. No way to trace it back to this summer. Or us."

I shivered again despite the cozy shawl. Like most of my wardrobe, it was a cast-off from Daphne. When she tired of her clothes, she tossed them in my direction.

I was grateful for them, and we were nearly the same size, but somehow the clothes never looked quite the same on me. Drooping in the bosom where Daphne filled them out. Snug across the hips where they gently hugged Daphne's curvaceous form.

"I can't do that to Daphne," I objected. "She's my *friend*."

"Some friend." Roger snorted. "Daphne's at the end-of-the-season gala with a bunch of the rich folks from the yacht club. Did she even invite you?"

Of course she hadn't.

Daphne was "summering" in her family's "cottage" overlooking the ocean. Her father was busy in his office in Manhattan. Her mother enrolled in a "luxury spa" for the summer. Daphne had confided to me that it was really a fancy alcohol rehab.

In the fall, Daphne would be off to a small exclusive college where she wouldn't have to worry about money or work too hard. While I had been hoping to use my summer earnings to start at the community college. But things were tight at home, and an awful lot of my money seemed to have gone to electric bills and mortgage payments on my parents' house.

How would I even get to classes? I didn't have a car.

Off-season jobs were few and far between.

When Roger heard that I'd have tonight off, since Daphne would be at the gala, he had invited me out to this fancy restaurant.

I was thrilled. Usually, we got hot dogs and fries and sat on benches on the boardwalk to eat.

Lately, he'd been hinting about us getting married. Maybe it wasn't all a fantasy. Maybe tonight he was planning to propose.

A shiver of anticipation quivered down my spine.

If it hadn't been for this invitation from Roger, I would have been sitting in the tiny living room of our tiny house with my morose father, watching TV. That was the only room that had an air conditioner.

But Roger wasn't proposing. He was talking about his plan to steal Daphne's necklace.

"Daphne gave me this job for the summer," I protested. "Probably because we were besties when we were kids. She didn't have to do that."

Roger sighed. "I'm not saying it's not an okay summer job. Or that you didn't have a good time with her when you were kids. But it was hardly really *friends*, was it? Your mom was the cook, and you tagged along. Nobody wanted to have to pay attention to Daphne, so they were happy she had you to play with. I bet you always ended up doing whatever Daphne wanted to do."

I had to admit that was true. Head to an amusement park? Go horseback riding? Rent jet skis? If Daphne wanted to do it, no expense was questioned, and the chauffeur was available to take us anywhere she wanted to go.

She'd always been a little bossy and impatient with me. Now that I was her employee, not her playmate, it was even worse.

I'd met Roger one afternoon when I'd decided to splurge on a ferris wheel ride. He let me stay on for a second ride without paying.

We began to spend time together whenever we could. I knew I wasn't exactly pretty, or even cute. I'd never had a boyfriend and I was flattered by his attention.

Gradually Roger turned to talk of running away to Mexico.

It sounded like a lovely pipe dream and I went along with the fantasy, even when he started saying we could finance it by stealing Daphne's necklace.

The entire scheme sounded so ludicrous that I didn't take it seriously until he showed me the replica necklace he'd somehow managed to acquire.

It was a good copy. My inexperienced eye saw no differences between it and the original.

Of course, it probably wouldn't fool an expert for a minute.

Roger made the whole idea sound almost like a victimless crime. Even if someone discovered the substitution, it would make no difference in Daphne's life. Insurance would pay for it, and her father would just buy her another necklace.

The Constellation Necklace was Daphne's favored piece of jewelry this summer. Prominent on the bib of the necklace was the famed Starlight Diamond. It was surrounded by smaller diamonds and blue sapphires spread on a bib of delicate silver chains. As Roger noted, it had been sold at auction for a little over two million dollars. Undoubtedly it was worth more than that today.

The purchaser had been one Harold Remingford. He'd bought it as a sixteenth birthday gift for his daughter. A newspaper article quoted him explaining, "It matches Daphne's eyes."

Daphne had arranged for a famous fashion designer to create a form-fitting dress in sapphire blue, reflecting both the necklace and her eyes. The neckline of the dress enhanced the necklace as it lay on the creamy skin above her ample bosom. A pair of sparkling silver spiked heels and a tiny silver purse completed her outfit.

She looked stunning.

I'd been surprised when she wore the dress with the necklace on multiple occasions this summer. She usually tired of clothes quickly, which was a tremendous benefit to my own wardrobe.

Despite the enormous difference in our social and economic status, Daphne and I were friends. Sort of.

For years, my mother had been their cook. My father ran a cotton candy stand on the boardwalk until a hurricane washed it away. Although the original stand was grandfathered-in, it no longer met zoning standards and Sea Cliff wouldn't authorize construction of a replacement.

That was when I tagged along with my mother. Daphne, who came without siblings or friends, was just about my age. Naturally, we ended up playing together.

But this year Mrs. Remingford was staying at her luxury spa. Mr. Remingford continued his daily commute to his office from their winter home on the Hudson River.

After graduating from her private high school, Daphne came by herself to Sea Cliff for the summer. She certainly didn't host receptions and parties as her mother had, but she spent most of her time with the yacht club crowd, crewing on sailboats and attending social events in the evenings.

The yacht club had several formal dances over the summer. I would help Daphne get ready for those occasions. Daphne always wore her designer dress and the Constellation Necklace.

The jewels sparkled and twinkled in the evening light. With her long dark hair caught up in an elaborate swirl and her blue eyes flashing, she looked like a fairy-tale princess.

Besides me as Daphne's personal assistant, the only staff left was the resident caretaker couple, who lived in an apartment over the garage.

This year, the chauffeur was nowhere to be seen, but Daphne had a car of her own. In a brief fit of interest in outdoor living, she'd acquired a tricked-out Jeep with serious off-road capabilities.

One camping trip and Daphne decided outdoor living was not for her. The Jeep had never been off-road.

Since Daphne's mother hadn't come for the season, my mother hadn't been hired for her usual summer position as a cook at their mansion. Mom had recently landed a job in a greasy spoon on an alley two blocks away from the boardwalk. It wasn't the type of place that appealed to tourists. It didn't pay as much as her old job and she found it exhausting. She came home late every night with a throbbing headache and swollen ankles.

I could have gotten any number of poorly-paid, menial jobs.

But Daphne offered an astounding pay rate for my services as "personal assistant."

It felt weird. I guess we could no longer be considered "friends." But aside from taking care of her personal needs—picking up after her, doing her laundry, running errands—I didn't have much to do.

We certainly didn't run in the same social circles. And she was usually gone for most of the day.

Tonight, after I helped her get ready for the end-of-the-season gala at the yacht club, she told me not to wait up for her. Just show up about ten the next morning.

I told Roger. That's when he invited me to this dinner.

I knew it didn't make much sense, but I was obsessed with

Roger. No one had ever paid attention to me like he did. Was this love? I didn't know, but I'd never experienced anything like it before.

He joked about being "friends with benefits," but the "benefits" never materialized. My dad was always home, and Roger shared a studio apartment and a car with his sister Jeanette.

Jeanette manned the ticket booth at the amusement park where Roger operated the ferris wheel.

As we left the restaurant, Roger put his arm around my shoulders and murmured into my ear that Jeanette was staying elsewhere tonight. We could go back to his place for a drink.

My skin tingled at his touch. I doubted the evening would end with a drink. I was ready. Even if this didn't lead to marriage.

Roger was offering a possible escape to a better life.

All I had to do was betray my old friend and current employer.

Who would not really suffer any loss.

And who probably didn't care much about me anyhow.

We headed for his car. Roger opened the door for me and leaned in to plant a sweet kiss on my forehead.

Just as he was closing the door, I heard a shrill voice.

"Roger! Roger! I need a ride home."

He turned and looked. His sister Jeanette was dashing toward us.

"Jeanette!" he said. "What are you doing here?"

I could see her shake her head of brassy blond curls. "I need a ride."

Roger leaned against the car. "I told you I wanted the car tonight."

"Yes. And you've had it, haven't you?" she said.

A harsh tone slipped into Roger's voice. "Did you follow me here?"

"Follow you?" She tossed the curls. "Of course not."

"I thought you were staying out tonight."

"I changed my mind."

Sighing deeply, Roger opened the back door.

Jeanette slipped in. "Hi, Hannah," she said brightly. "Have a nice dinner?"

The magic tingles had faded. "Yes, thank you."

Roger climbed into the driver's seat.

"It's got to be tomorrow, Hannah." He didn't even look back at me. "You said Daphne wanted you to pack her things. She could be leaving any time. Right?"

"Yes."

"I'll be in the car, waiting in the alley. Call me when the coast is clear."

My stomach lurched.

I SHOWED up for work the next morning at 10 a.m.

Daphne must have had quite a night. She lay sprawled in her bed, covers sliding half off, onto the floor. She was clad only in her underwear, the lacy red panties tangled around her shapely hips and the matching bra unhooked and skewed over her chest.

She lay inert, apparently deeply asleep.

I tiptoed over and pulled the blanket up to cover her. She didn't move.

Then I surveyed the room.

The glittering silver shoes were abandoned just inside the door, the spike heel broken off one. The gorgeous blue gown had been ditched on the floor next to a chair. A shawl was tossed over the back of the chair.

And there, right out in the open, the Constellation Necklace lay in a jumbled heap on top of the dresser.

My throat closed.

If I just took it, I wouldn't have to sneak Roger into the house. He wouldn't have to break into the safe.

Could I do that? *Would* I do that?

Decision time.

Leaving the necklace where it was, I crept out of the room and down the hallway, stepping into an unoccupied bedroom. I pulled out my phone.

Roger answered on the first ring.

"Daphne didn't put the necklace in the safe last night," I whispered. "It's right out in the open."

"Can you get it?"

"I think so. If Daphne doesn't wake up."

"Great. You take the necklace. Meet me in the alley. I'll give you the replacement."

I felt dizzy. "When?"

"I'm there right now."

Quietly, I made my way back to Daphne's bedroom. Moving closer, I peered at her sleeping face.

She lay very still.

How much had she had to drink? Had anyone given her any drugs?

Was she even breathing?

Reports of nightmarish alcohol poisonings and overdoses flashed through my mind.

I put my hand under her nostrils to see if I could detect a breath.

My hand brushed her nose.

With a sudden snort, she tossed her head and jerked her shoulders sideways.

Okay. She was alive.

But did I wake her up?

If I were going to take the necklace, I should have done it before I took a chance on disturbing her.

Maybe I should just stay here until Roger got tired of waiting and left.

But that would end the dream of Mexico with Roger. And he'd be mad.

I tucked the covers closer around Daphne. She lay motionless, her breathing now louder and perfectly even.

Feeling as if I were a disembodied observer, I watched my hand reach for the necklace.

I closed the bedroom door quietly behind me, crept down the back stairs to the kitchen and out the door.

When I rounded the hedge along the back of the yard, I could see Roger's car in the alley.

He was too close to the garage. Suppose the caretaker saw his car and remembered?

Roger was in the driver's seat, with Jeanette next to him.

Why had she come along?

He rolled down the window and held up a cloth bag. "Here's the duplicate. Take it back and put it just like you found the real one." He reached for the sparkling heap in my hand.

I clutched it, almost unable to loosen my grasp.

"Come on, let go," he said impatiently, leaning out of the window.

My gaze traveled over the interior of the car.

Suitcases and boxes jammed the back seat.

When I tried to say something, my voice quivered and I had to clear my throat.

"Why are you all packed up like that?"

"Once we have the necklace, I thought it would be best to get out of here and hand it over ASAP. After that, no one will be able to trace it to us."

"But if I don't stay to help Daphne get ready to leave for college the way I promised, she'll know something's up."

"Of course." Roger was staring at the necklace. "I'll be back for you in a week or so. Just hang tight. I'll call."

His finger stroked the Starlight Diamond. "We'll go to Mexico like I said. And live like kings."

I looked into the passenger seat. "Is Jeanette coming with us?"

"Of course." Roger couldn't tear his eyes away from the necklace.

"I didn't know that."

"Well, she's my *sister.* I couldn't leave her here."

Jeanette lifted her chin and smirked at me.

Some of my mental fog lifted abruptly.

Why hadn't I seen it before? Jeanette was *not* Roger's sister. She was his girlfriend. Or maybe even his wife.

They would not be coming back for me.

I had just stolen a multimillion-dollar necklace for a cheating creep. From someone who had been my best childhood friend. And, although she was a spoiled rich kid and could be pretty thoughtless, she was still my friend. My best friend.

Roger started the car and drove away.

I stood there, feeling like I was going to throw up.

But what could I do about it now? Admit to Daphne that I'd been part of a plot to steal her necklace?

The mental fog may have lifted briefly but now my mind was swirling. I needed some time to think this through.

First thing, I would go put the substitute necklace back. It would give me time to think.

Maybe a solution to this horrible dilemma would come to me.

Yeah, right.

Daphne was in the bathroom when I came slinking back in with the replacement necklace.

Had she noticed its absence?

I laid it on the dresser. I still couldn't see any difference between it and the original. But I'm not an expert.

Daphne wasn't, either.

I had barely gotten it in place before she opened the door.

"Do you like that?" she asked.

No way could I pretend that I wasn't looking at it.

"It's…it's *magnificent,*" I stuttered.

"I've been thinking." She rubbed her wet hair with a towel. "The Jeep isn't the right car for college. I told Daddy I needed something more comfortable."

"Oh?"

"Yes. And I told him I was going to give the Jeep to you, so you wouldn't be stuck here when the season's over. You could use it to get to your classes."

I swallowed hard. "Daphne, I don't see how I could accept that…"

"Nonsense." She dropped the damp towel on the floor and reached for another one. "It's your bonus. We *always* give a bonus to the help at the end of the summer."

Tears stung my eyes. Needing to hide my face, I bent down to pick up the wrinkled dress from the floor.

Daphne glanced over. "I've worn that a half dozen times this summer. You can have it, if you want it."

"Not your designer gown," I protested.

"Yes. Everybody who's anybody has seen it. Too many times. I'm not going to take it with me."

I held the dress at arm's length. "It'll clean up nicely. It goes so well with the necklace."

"Oh. You can have that too, if you want."

I stared at her. "The Constellation Necklace?"

She laughed. "You don't think Daddy would let me bring the real Constellation Necklace down to the shore, do you? That's a knock-off. He had it made when I said I wanted to wear it this summer with the blue gown. The real one is in his safe deposit box in the bank."

And the Saudi prince would be getting a knock-off. He would *not* be happy.

I could almost feel sorry for Roger. He might never even get to see Mexico.

CHARLIE KONDEK

Charlie Kondek is a marketing professional and writer from metro Detroit. His work has appeared in *The Saturday Evening Post*, *Mystery Tribune*, *Hoosier Noir*, *Yellow Mama*, *BULL,* and elsewhere. Kondek is a member of the Short Mystery Fiction Society. Find Charlie at CharlieKondekWrites.com.

UNCLE RANDY'S MONEY
CHARLIE KONDEK

PROBABLY THEY WERE JUST men and women like you or I, but in my imagination and memory the desperadoes and sunflower maidens of the late '70s and early '80s strode denim-clad, slender and calibrated as dancers, through the sidewalks and driveways of my childhood. Every man looked like an ad for leather coats and cigarettes, every woman like Linda Ronstadt or Toni Tennille, my parents, aunts, uncles, and their friends, including, or perhaps especially, my Uncle Randy. He was my mother's brother, returning to Michigan after a long absence and amidst much murmuring because my grandfather, their father, was dying.

It was August, when my return to school in September hung resented and ignored over the last of my summer vacation. Uncle Randy slept on our couch for a few days, and we had a party for him that seemed to stretch for two or three of them. Actually, I don't think it was planned. More like, assorted family members dropped by to see him, my grandma, some aunts, uncles, and cousins, great-aunts and great-uncles, and still others who just heard Randy was in town. The next thing you know, being Polish and prone to enlarge a visit into a gathering, I was being sent to accompany my dad to the corner store for ice and more beer, and whiskey was on the table, and ashtrays, and bags of pretzels, and my mom and one of her sisters were counting heads and ordering pizza, or making kielbasa and pierogi in the kitchen with *busia*.

I really don't know how we crammed everybody into our little bungalow in Royal Oak. We must have simply overflowed. The kids played in the yard, throwing a football with some of the grownups, while others played board games or raced Matchbox cars on the tiled basement floor. When we ran out of things to do, my mom corralled us in front of the VCR. The grownups went on drinking, smoking, and talking over us. Among the topics of conversation— that year's cars, the Tigers—were solemn questions about the state of my grandfather, old Butch Padorchek, laying in his bed in hospice, his big, burly body diminished by cancer. Looking back on it, it occurs to me this was a strange occasion to have a party, these Polenickis and Pardorcheks, these Wozniaks and Kreslewskis. But maybe that's a Polish family's natural response to a problem, especially one in which you can only stand around and wait. Crack open a beer and talk about baseball.

While it's true this kind of happy chaos was natural for us at that time, I have no doubt my Uncle Randy contributed somehow to the energy of it all. I can picture him at or near the center of a lot of laughter with a can of Schlitz and a cigarette in his hand, yellow hair touching the shoulders of a tight black t-shirt, horseshoe mustache likewise yellow and framing a mirthful mouth from which issued a voice like the grinding of a garbage disposal. He was thin and muscular in faded jeans taut across thighs that had ridden a motorcycle out of Detroit a couple years before. He'd returned in an olive-green Bonneville and an atmosphere of anxious suspicion, because no one was quite sure what he'd been up to besides my mother, who got the occasional call and card from him in Chicago. And because he had never reconciled with his father after the last bitter argument that resulted in his flight. I got a chance to ask my dad about his brother-in-law shortly after he arrived.

"Oh, Uncle Randy was an outlaw all right. Probably still is. I remember when things were getting serious between me and your mother, Randy pulled me aside one day and showed me the gun he was going to kill me with if I ever broke his sister's heart. He was laughing while he said it, said he liked me and thought I was a good guy, but that he'd absolutely put me down if I ever did wrong to Nancy. I have no doubt he meant it. With guys like him, you can't be too careful."

"Well, where has he been?"

"I guess Illinois mostly. After bumming around America and Canada on that bike. Your Uncle Randy was not a biker, meaning he wasn't part of a gang, or I guess you'd call it a club, a motorcycle club, but he was friendly with all those dudes and God only knows what he was doing before he settled in Chicago. Probably the same kinds of things he was doing when he lived in Detroit."

"Like what?"

"Well, son, I find it's better not to ask too many questions about that. Let's just say making deliveries of things that could get him in trouble with the police and made your Gramma Padorchek a nervous wreck and your Grampa Padorchek angry as hell."

"Is that why they don't get along?"

"They never did see eye to eye. I guess they're both pretty stubborn. *Jaja* was a serious, spiritual moral dude who didn't appreciate his kids being flippant about the law."

"You mean 'is.' Not 'was.' Grampa 'is' a serious dude."

"You're right, son, I shouldn't have said it like that. But yeah, I think Grampa respected…respects…rules, the rules of the world, very much. Whereas Uncle Randy thumbs his nose at them, which always drove Grampa right up a wall."

"Has Grampa been able to talk to Uncle Randy?"

"I don't know. I don't think so. As you know, when Grampa is awake, it's hard for him to focus and understand what's going on. It makes your uncle very sad. I think he very much wants to talk with his father before he passes. Let's pray for that."

"Okay."

Sometime after that, maybe as that first weekend of Randy's visit was winding down, I was able to overhear (okay, eavesdrop on) him and my mom talking in our back yard. I think they may have been smoking a joint, and my mom didn't know I was perched near the open window of the back bedroom instead of watching TV. I can't remember if all this occurred in one conversation or if I am piecing it together with others, but it went a little something like this.

Randy: "He looks terrible."

Mom: "I know."

"Level with me, Nance. How long has he got?"

"Could be days. Could be weeks. We just don't know. How long can you stay?"

"I don't know. Couple of weeks, I guess. I have to consult with my business partners."

"You have business partners? I thought you were a bartender."

"Among other things."

"Wanna tell me a little bit more about what you been doing out there? You never say much about it over the phone."

They had three other siblings, but my mom and Randy were always closest to each other. It didn't surprise me he'd be more candid with her. Maybe he was even bragging a little. "You won't believe this, Nance. Your brother's practically a cop." A phlegmy chuckle. "Well, not quite. So, I am a bartender. But I got a hustle on the side selling info to the police. Not kidding. You know I've always had a talent for keeping shady company. Now, I find out what they're doing, and drop the dime on 'em. The cops pay me. How you like that?"

"Randy, what the hell…"

"I know. Don't it sound like *Starksy & Hutch* or something?"

"You could get hurt."

"Nah, kid, you know me. Those morons will never find out, and even if they did, they ain't tough enough to take me. And I'm making a nice bundle. Wonder what the old man would say if he knew."

"His head would burst into flames."

Like Ghost Rider, I thought.

"Anyway, that's why I never say much about it on the phone. I've probably said too much already."

My mom did Sgt. Schultz from *Hogan's Heroes*. "'I know nuh-thing.' Anyway, even if pop did hear this, he probably couldn't comprehend it. But I think he knows you're here, Randy. I think he at least knows that."

"Yeah. I hope so. I can't stand to see him like this. Guy fought his way across Europe being eaten alive by his own body. Reduced to that."

"I know. I know."

"He was a mean old cuss. Too quick with a slap upside the head. Dumb. A bigot. But he doesn't deserve that."

"I know."

Is, I thought. *Not was*.

I CAN'T REMEMBER, or don't know, exactly where Uncle Randy stayed while he was in town. I believe he slept in his old room at my grandma's for a few days, but also at the homes of a friend or two. Eventually he moved into one of the motels on Woodward because he didn't want to come home late from a wild night and disturb anybody. "Plus," he explained with a satyr's leer, "someone might want to spend the night."

In between visiting family, catching up with friends, and whatever invisible errands he performed, he was up at Beaumont at my grampa's bedside, part of a near constant vigil of family that attended him. My parents didn't take me or my sister up there much. I think after the first couple times they decided it was too frightening and sad for us. I remember being at home with my dad for a lot of these evenings, and the one vision I have of my grandfather in his hospice bed is of his body propped up but collapsing beneath what seemed like a thousand machines and tubes.

I kept thinking about what Uncle Randy had said privately about *jaja*. That he was "mean," "dumb," "a bigot," and "too quick with a slap." This was not the man I knew at all, the quiet foreman with jowls and dark eyes partially concealed by glasses, and a bony brow that seemed to take in everything around him in a kind of mute amazement, his grandchildren most of all. I was old enough to imagine Grampa Butch was different as a father than a grandfather, but I also wondered if Randy provoked something in him. I resolved to ask my mother about it someday, if I could find a way to bring it up.

One afternoon, I rode my bike around our neighborhood off 12 Mile looking for someone to play with and, finding no one available or interested in doing what I wanted to do, pedaled downtown. I was headed to the drug store to feed a few quarters into the Galaga machine when I spotted my uncle's Bonneville, or one just like it, parked outside Tiernan's Bar & Grill. I'd never been inside, and wondered if kids were even allowed, but as I pushed open the door to its dark interior and was greeted by soft rock played at just the right volume to enable conversation, and the scent of thousands of beers and cigarettes that lived permanently in the walls, I saw my uncle sitting at a table. I joined him before anyone could chase me out.

"Well, look who's here," he exclaimed. "Teddy Polenicki. My kin. Take a load off, son. Set a spell. Whatcha doin', just getting off work?"

Uncle Randy was drinking a beer, and he bought me one—well, not a real beer, a root beer, but it felt grownup just the same. Even so, it seemed too early in the day for Randy and the few other patrons to be drinking. Then again, Uncle Randy was on vacation, sort of, and maybe the others, old men, were retired. I couldn't help feeling this was a fortuitous occasion, and my uncle seemed to feel that way, too. "We got time to shoot the breeze, so tell me more about yourself, nephew. What kind of stuff are you into?"

"Stuff?"

"Yeah. You like sports or cars or what?"

"Yeah, I like those things, I guess. Uh, I like imagination stuff mostly. You know, *Star Wars*. Comic books. Dungeons & Dragons."

"That's cool. Got a girlfriend?"

I chuckled, embarrassed but liking the attention. "I went with a girl this year named Stephanie but didn't kiss her or anything."

Randy laughed, loudly, a sound like sandpaper. "Well, you'll have plenty of time for that."

"How about you, Uncle Randy?" I ventured. "Got a girlfriend?"

"Got a thousand girlfriends. They ain't tied old Randy down yet."

Uncle Randy was easy to talk to, maybe assisted by the endless supply of beer and smokes and the soft sounds of Poco and James Taylor over our heads. He didn't just listen, but responded, took me seriously and treated me a little like a peer. When he asked me what I wanted to be when I grew up, I told him I wasn't sure, but that I thought I wanted to travel the world, like an explorer in *National Geographic*, and that I thought I'd start out by joining the army and then going to college.

He didn't like that so much, said, "Think carefully about that G.I. Joe stuff. The problem with it is you gotta go wherever they send you, and you could get shot. And for what? So some guys can get richer? I'm not telling you what to do, Teddy, just think about it, you got time. My opinion, the only thing the army will teach you is how to say yes. There's lots of times in life where you gotta say no. Like if they'd tried to get me into Vietnam? I would have told them to kiss my ass and you'd have seen my exhaust pipes headed straight for Canada."

We talked about religion. I said I guessed I'd be making my Confirmation in a couple years and that I'd need a sponsor. Maybe Randy could come back to Michigan for that?

His laughter boomed in the bar. "That church would get struck by lightning if I set foot in it. Geez, if I went to Confession I'd be there for a year. But seriously, Teddy. Your spiritual life is a good thing. Stick with it, son. It may not seem like it, but I'm a spiritual person, too. I guess I just always had a problem with church, as maybe you can tell. Anywhere they try to control you too much, that's always been a problem for me. But I've met God. Yeah. I talk to Him all the time, and I've seen Him, deep in the forests, in Oregon, first thing in the morning. Or coming down a winding mountain road in Utah, when you're just trying to keep your wheels on the pavement, and you can see the whole valley spread out in front of you, for miles, like you didn't even know you could see that far. There is God. Perfectly clear. But, uh, yeah, you don't want me for a Confirmation sponsor, man."

This created an opportunity to ask about him and Grampa Butch. Randy took a deep breath and sighed. "Keep in mind, I love and respect my dad, okay? But him and me? Oil and water." He shook his head. "Growing up, I loved him, but I didn't like him. Do you know what I mean?"

I nodded, but I didn't. At that point in my life there were people I loved to whom I was indifferent, but I'd not yet loved someone I disliked.

"He's a perfect example of what we were just talking about, of someone that's always gotta have 'yes.' Like, he sees everything in black and white. Government. Religion. He couldn't stand any fluid concepts about anything, and he was one of those people that always has to be in control. And like I said, if you wanna try to control me, we're gonna have a problem."

The talk between us having flowed so easily, the space in the bar in the music and the smoke having grown so intimate, I felt encouraged to take a risk.

"Uncle Randy, don't be mad but I heard what you told my mom about what you do in Chicago. You know, about working for the police? Gathering information? Does that make you, like, unofficially an undercover cop?"

Randy guffawed and declared, "Damn, son! Maybe you got a little of me in you after all, you little sneak." He laughed and laughed, then he leveled his blonde mustache at me. "Well, listen, man. Since you got the guts to ask about it, I'll tell you something. Something Grampa Butch could never understand. The cops are the thieves. See, when they make a bust, they are supposed to round up all the contraband and keep it for evidence. Drugs, guns, money, merchandise, all that stuff is supposed to be carefully counted, writ down and catalogued. But what they do, they help themselves to some of it. Yeah, they bag it up, separate it, put it in someone's trunk and make off with it. So that's where me and my partners come in. I'm not just dropping the dime on these busts, I'm telling a certain group of cops where the big scores are, the dope, the cash.

So they can know ahead of time, and help themselves, and then pay me off. There's your law and order. There's the black and white."

Randy leaned back, but he kept his voice lowered. "Actually, me and my partners been told we gotta cool it for a while because someone is starting to think something's up. But I got a duffel bag full of money I've been stashing here and there for whenever I need it. It's best if you don't tell anyone about this, Teddy. I probably shouldn'ta told you this much. But someday I'll find a way to let you know some of the hiding places. That way it'll be there if you or your mom and dad ever need it. It'll be our secret. It's the least I can do after not being around the last few years, watching you grow up."

"Don't be silly, Uncle Randy. You don't have to give me money or anything like that."

"Well. It's an uncle's pleasure to give money to his nephew." He seemed to be thinking. "Anyway, living away from home, it just costs you something."

ALL IN ALL, I think Randy stayed about two weeks. The minutes and the hours in hospice ticked by like small eternities. My dad went to work. My mom made us lunch. When he wasn't with family, Randy piloted his Bonneville to secret places—in Michigan? Ohio? Indiana, Ontario? Burying, I imagined, his treasure. Anonymous keys to bus station lockers. Steel boxes in the ground at the base of broad trees.

At my grandfather's deathbed he watched the labored rising and falling of his father's breathing which were like the aftermath of sobs. Went to the smoking lounge. Came back. No change. Huddled in a room full of siblings, his and his father's, he went on waiting in that place divorced from time. I, meanwhile, slipped between the black lines that marked the borders of squares on the parish calendar that hung on our refrigerator, each day crossed out with an X falling like a portcullis, blocking my retreat from the oncoming year.

On one of them, I again rode my bike downtown, on a similar

mission as before, this time with my eyes out for my uncle's car parked near Tiernan's. It was there. I went inside hoping for another root beer session. Randy was at the same table as last time, but he was not alone. I got a fairly good look at the man sitting with Randy as I approached. He was massive, with a large round chest and bulging biceps in a short-sleeved sports shirt, wore a crewcut and black mustache, and I could clearly hear Randy say as I drew near, though he kept his voice low, "At least let me wait 'til my old man is in the ground."

The big man started to say something in response, but then noticed me. Following his companion's gaze, Randy turned in his chair, found me, and said, "Well, hey, sport. Jimmy, this is my nephew, Teddy. My sister's kid. Teddy, this is Jimmy, a buddy of mine from Illinois."

"What's going on, young man?" Jimmy said, extending a hand that engulfed mine.

We bantered for a while, and then Randy said, "Teddy, I hate to brush you off, man, but Jimmy and I are talking some important business. Do you mind? Tell your mom I'll drop by the house later. I'll see you there."

"Nice meeting you, kid," Jimmy said, his deep voice effortlessly loud.

Randy did come to our house that afternoon with a six pack and some groceries in his arms, and he helped my mom make dinner before my dad got home. After dinner he watched TV and played games with me and my sister. I wasn't there for the talk he had with my parents in our basement that night—more like, I wasn't allowed to listen this time. I am reconstructing this from what I was later told.

My uncle asked my dad how much, if anything, my mom had told him about what he'd been up to in Chicago. Turns out, not much. When he explained it, he also told them some of what he told me, that the cops he worked with weren't just paying him as an informant, that they were cutting him and his partners in on what they took.

"The thing is," he said, "my associates in blue have found out there's some heat on. I'm pretty sure one of them is in the district attorney's office. They have asked me and my partners to get lost for a while."

"Get lost?" my mom asked. "What does that mean?"

"It means disappear, Nancy. Leave the state. Leave your known whereabouts. And most of all don't talk to any attorneys or investigators."

"For how long?"

"Unknown. For a while. Until the coast is clear. A year or two, maybe. But the thing is, me and these guys are having a disagreement about how long I can delay. I told them I want to stay here 'til my dad passes, but, uh, they are starting to get anxious." He explained about the visit he'd had from Jimmy. "I guess what I'm saying is, I might have to clear out soon. I hate to do it, but I might have to."

I don't know how that conversation ended. Maybe my mom asked Randy if he was in any danger. Maybe he tried to reassure her he wasn't.

WE MAY NEVER KNOW exactly what happened next, unless my uncle is apprehended, or new evidence is discovered. What we do know is that shortly after this there was a shootout at Randy's motel, and a man was killed. I can't remember if we learned about it first from the morning news on TV or from neighbors who called to ask if we'd seen the police cars and crime scene tape on Woodward, but I remember my mom paced the floor for a couple hours, then called my dad—who never listened to the news on the way to work— and asked him to come home.

Apparently, she was uncertain whether to volunteer any information to the police, but after some discussion, they decided to come clean because they didn't trust themselves to stay consistent under questioning, and they wanted to help Randy. They didn't know if was alive, dead, wounded, being hunted by his fellow informants, crooked cops, or somebody he had ratted on. Besides, they were religious. They told everything they knew.

An aunt came to sit with me and my sister while my parents went to the police station. They were there until late at night. That's where they learned someone had been killed, but not my Uncle Randy, whom some witnesses described as trading shots with a dark-haired man and fleeing the scene in his car.

The dead man was named James Antonin Ionescu, and I recognized his face when I eventually saw it in the newspaper.

Jimmy from Illinois.

I sat on my information about seeing Randy and Jimmy at Tiernan's for a few days until I got the idea that I, too, should say what I knew. I don't think it much mattered by then. The cops had an idea what had happened.

Somewhere in the middle of this my grandfather died. I do not know the hour or remember, without looking it up, the day, or who may have been with him when he passed, a final silent pronouncement on the proceedings. His wake was a weepy, boozy, joyous affair, what is now popularly known as a "celebration of life." Every Polish funeral I've ever been to has been that way. Remember what I said about how we respond to problems? But even so, in the VFW hall with us was the specter of uncertain doom and deep worry for Uncle Randy, his absence like a gaping hole in the floor. I didn't know it then, but we might as well have mourned the withdrawal of two Padorchek men from our lives.

The FBI got involved. They continued to ask us questions for more than a year. My mom thought they might be tapping our phone. Eventually they must have realized we didn't know anything else and weren't in contact with Randy, and it all stopped. Then it was our turn to ask questions, which they didn't always answer.

What we did learn was that Jimmy Ionescu had a record for robbery and possession with intent to distribute, and that he was a known associate of my uncle's.

Were there other people that were part of the gang Randy had described, people like Jimmy they could question? The police wouldn't say.

Was he really involved in helping police steal evidence? Was he in danger from them? Was someone looking into that? Again, they wouldn't say.

Did they think Randy was alive? Did they have any idea where he might have gone? Yes, they thought he was alive, maybe. If we received word from him, we were to contact them right away. And no, they didn't have any ideas where he might be, or how he got there, wherever it was.

A year after that, I was confirmed in the Catholic church at Shrine of the Little Flower. Another uncle was my sponsor. I have remained a Catholic ever since, not a very good one, earnest, sincere, but hopelessly compromised and compromising. Maybe there's a little of my uncle in me after all.

A few years later, when I was in college at Wayne State, we got a call from the FBI saying they'd found my uncle's Bonneville in an old barn in Azalea, Michigan, stripped of its plates. They asked us if we knew anything about the barn or the owners of the neglected property. We didn't.

I never did travel the world like a *National Geographic* explorer. I became a reporter and worked at newspapers in small cities across the Midwest, eventually seeing the writing on the wall and becoming a corporate communications manager at a car company. Over the years I have tried to find out more about what may have happened to Uncle Randy. I tried to request the report of the investigation of the motel shootout from the Royal Oak police and Oakland County Sheriff's office. The request was denied because it was still considered an active investigation.

Next, I tried to get Randy's record as a confidential informant from the Chicago PD but was informed that I wasn't adequately describing what I wanted. I wrote to the lead investigator at the FBI Detroit office, explaining I was just seeking some kind of closure for my family, and was told that officer had retired, but that the case, though unsolved, was still active. They were sorry, but they didn't have anything more for us.

I made a friend at the *Chicago Tribune* who worked the courthouse beat and asked if there had ever been an investigation into cops stealing evidence around the time my uncle went missing. He said if there had been, a curtain had been dropped over it. He'd keep asking around, but I shouldn't expect much.

I am now in my fifties and my parents are old. It may strike you as strange that I, a purveyor of facts, should be a little imprecise in relating this story. I could hide behind the notion that I am an unreliable narrator and a doctor of spin. Or I can admit that I prefer these things live partly in my memory, partly in my imagination. That way, I can imagine how my Uncle Randy escaped, how he lived, swapping his Bonneville for a motorcycle, and riding off to Mexico, or catching a boat to the Caribbean, where he resides among forgotten outlaws. I can imagine how he had wanted to contact us to tell us where he'd hidden his money but couldn't take the risk of giving his pursuers a clue.

I have to imagine these things. It's the only way I can see him again.

BETHANY MAINES

Bethany Maines is the award-winning indie and traditionally published author of romantic action-adventure and fantasy novels that focus on individuals who know when to apply lipstick and when to apply a foot to someone's hind-end. She also holds numerous screenplay awards and a short film—*Suzy Makes Cupcakes* (from her script and short story)—is now listed on IMDB. Bethany participates in many activities, including swearing, karate, art, and yelling at the news. She can usually be found chasing after her daughter or glued to the computer working on her next novel. Find Bethany at www. BethanyMaines.com.

THE RAGE CAGE

BETHANY MAINES

I GOT MARRIED so I wouldn't have to date anymore. I do realize that dating is an opt-in experience and I could have taken up crochet instead, but I wanted someone to snuggle.

It's 11 a.m. on a Tuesday, so I'm in the Hang On Saloon with my third Bloody Mary and my dog, Beau, curled around the base of my barstool. Dogs, for the record, are champion snugglers.

Four years ago, I picked out the best of my candidates—Nathan Miguel Colton—and went for it. I figured how bad could the whole marriage thing be? Turns out I should have gotten a pet earlier because now I'm the manager of an anger management store and trying to figure out how things went so wrong.

My boss thinks therapy might have benefits but takes too damn long, so he opened a Rage Cage right across from the Saloon. Come on in, Monday through Saturday, from 12:30 p.m. until 3 a.m., and you can bust up the best that online storage unit auctions have to offer. Grandma's china? Random VHS tapes? Precious Moments figurines? We got 'em. You can even bring in your own items. As long as it won't catch fire or cause cancer when broken, we will let you bash it with the hammer, bat, or scary apocalypse toy of your choice.

Tammy, the sixty-five-year-old bartender who doesn't chitchat with me anymore because she disapproves of my lifestyle, looks up from her phone.

"Delivery's here," she says, jerking her head toward the door. Through the angular empty slices in the poster-covered glass, I can see the truck with the latest purchase pull up across the street at the Rage Cage.

"I don't suppose you'll let me take the rest of this with me?" I ask, making sure not to wobble as I step away from the bar.

She skewers me with her drop-dead stare. "Amber, you're better than this. Your father would be so disappointed."

Bringing my father into it is a low blow.

"Yeah, well, it's his fault I'm an alcoholic."

Tammy turns her eyes back to her phone. "Nobody is making you drink but you."

"Whatever," I mumble and head out the door, Beau at my heels. I'm a thirty-year-old woman with no kids or college degree who couldn't even stay married to the loser I picked out. I don't know why Tammy thinks I could do better—I was never going to amount to anything. My father drank himself to death by downing a twelve-pack and then driving off the road on the way to Stevenson. I was seventeen at the time and immediately tried to copy him. After one too many nights I couldn't remember, I finally figured that maybe I didn't have to do the *exact* same thing.

So now I don't drive.

I did give up drinking for a while. But it didn't stick. The first night I picked up a beer again, I got pulled over for going through a stop sign. The cop, an old high school classmate, said I blew a point one six, which is equivalent to about ten drinks. I only remember the one, but there are a lot of nights when I only remember one, so what do I know?

It was the last straw for my husband. He got the house, the car, and almost got the dog. But Beau kept on running away until Nathan gave up. I ought to feel smug about that. Instead, I feel sorry for Beau that he has such poor judgment. He's a smart dog otherwise, I swear.

I walk to the curb and pause for traffic. My husband pulls up in our champagne-colored Landcruiser and rolls down the window. He's got facial hair now—a goatee—and the same Superman swirl on his forehead. I used to feel like he rescued me. Now I feel like the pet who shit the rug one too many times.

"Don't jaywalk, Amber. You don't want to get arrested for being drunk in public. Again."

"Drop dead, Nate," I say, but he's already pulled away laughing and probably didn't hear me. The Bloody Mary feels like acid in my stomach. I ignore it, and go to open the doors at the Rage Cage.

The delivery is our latest purchase from the online auction site— three storage units worth of items to smash.

I work my way through the boxes. This shipment has all kinds of crap. Furniture, clothes, jewelry, knickknacks, VCRs, old VHS tapes, computers, kitchen utensils. I sort it into three piles—sellable, smashable, and garbage. I want the third category to be *reusable*, but my driver's license is still suspended and the nearest Goodwill drop-off is two towns away.

I'm on the last box when I start to freak out, lifting a chiffon pink Le Creuset Dutch oven out of the box with shaking hands. That's *my* Dutch oven. Nate never wanted to put it on the gift list, but I figured if he could include the whiskey subscription, then I could get a $420 Dutch oven. Each item that came out after that was something I had personally selected for our wedding registry. He'd put it all in storage and then forgotten to pay the bill. At the bottom of the box was a pile of thumb drives clipped on a lanyard. They clack against each other, tangling like Christmas lights as I lift them up. I knew exactly what they were.

Nate saved recordings off his laptop because he didn't want to get caught with anything embarrassing at work. I knew for a damn fact that we had a couple of sex videos that I didn't want floating out there. I hesitate for only a second. Revenge porn was out. He hadn't done that to me, so I wouldn't do it to him. But at three Bloody Mary's into my day, a lot of other things were on the table.

The guy I've got running the evening shift comes in. Usually, that's when I clock out, take Beau for a walk, make dinner, and then head back to the bar. Tonight, I don't do that. I plug a thumb drive into my computer. Then another. And another. Watching clips of my old life flash before my eyes. Beau is starting to look at me funny. We're way off our usual schedule.

As the next video starts, my eyes drift down to the bottom drawer where everyone knows I hide the vodka underneath a box of junk I never gave back to Nate—his favorite Stanley thermos, the remote control to the TV, the spare car keys. Each one reminds me of a fight we had.

"You could pull her over any time," says Nate's voice, and I look up. The video keeps playing, turning my life upside down. When it's all over, my stomach is a roiling mess, and I feel like puking. Unable to sit still, I grab my Dutch oven and hurry toward the front, intent on getting to the safety of the Saloon and the bottom of a glass. Anything to get away from where I was.

At the front desk, I nearly crash into Walker Trivette Gage. He gives me a weak smile, eyes dropping immediately, as he heads to the cage. I've known Walker since elementary school. He's been coming into the Rage Cage a lot lately.

I carry the Dutch oven out the door, across the street, into the Saloon, and plunk it down on the sticky wooden bar. Beau sits beside me, looking confused. It's nearly midnight, but on a weeknight, it's a pretty mellow crowd.

Walker Trivette always wanted to become a doctor, but his girlfriend—Stephanie—got pregnant right after high school. They got married, and he became a paramedic. After the baby turned two, she went back to school and became a cop.

"What's up, Amber?" asks Tammy, eyeing the pink enamel pot.

Stephanie was the one who arrested me. The look on her face that night still haunts me—there was no pity or empathy, only contempt. Funny how some things stick with you.

I look up at her deeply lined face. "Do you really think I could do better?"

"Yes."

I can feel the prickle of tears starting behind my eyes. But Beau doesn't like it when I cry. He gets worried and tries to bring me stuffed animals and potatoes he steals from a bin in the pantry. No, we don't know why.

"You're smart. You always were. Too smart for this bullshit." She waves around the bar. "But it doesn't really matter, does it? You're still going to order something, and I'm still going to pour it."

My mouth is dry. I really want a drink. I look down at Beau. His Rottweiler eyebrows are just brown dots, making him look like an anime character. Beau believes in me. No, we don't know why he does that either.

"Can I have a glass of water?" I ask, my voice wavering.

Tammy stares at me. Then she slowly pulls a glass from the stack, pours it with a sharp hiss from the gun, and slides it across the bar. I chug it in one long gulp. All the phrases from the twelve-step meetings are thrashing through my head like tumbleweed across an empty street. I used to say them. I used to cling to them. That was before I forgot how to stop. Before I met Nate.

Courage to change. Pray for strength. Correct your mistakes.

"The help I have received, I shall pass on to others," I say, thumping the glass down.

"Uh… okay." Tammy looks as confused as Beau. I heft my Dutch oven under one arm and return to the Rage Cage.

I kick open the door to the smash room, and Walker Trivette, his blonde hair poking through the top of the safety mask, freezes, hockey stick above his head.

"Suzy says you're getting divorced, and Steph's taking the kids."

He lifts the mask up, wiping his nose with the back of his hand, and nods miserably. He looks like Beau after he upchucked on the carpet.

"I've got something to show you," I say.

My hand shakes as I open the door to the office. Walker Trivette looks around the office like he doesn't understand how the Fireman's shirtless calendar goes with the nodding kitten and the samurai wall hangings. It's the found-in-a-dumpster aesthetic that really speaks to my life. I don't expect him to get it.

I wake the computer up and hit play.

"You could pull her over any time," says Nate as the video starts.

He's setting up to film, and his nose is enormous. He steps back, squinting at the camera, red silk boxers making a statement next to a folded laundry pile.

"That's my house," says Walker Trivette.

"I've been spiking her mocktails for weeks." Nate says it casually, as if he's not concentrating on what he's saying.

"How does she not notice?" asks Stephanie, laughter rippling through her voice—like my sobriety is a joke.

"I said her new allergy medication was interfering with her taste buds. And she bought it!" Nate laughs.

I hadn't bought it. Not exactly. I had just chosen to believe Nate. I liked feeling a little giddy in the evenings—it took the edge off living with him. "Anyway, we can pull the trigger anytime."

"No," says Stephanie, from off-screen. "It has to be way over the limit, and people have to see her drinking. This has to be ironclad. Your house is way bigger than mine, and I'm not losing it over a technicality."

"The house, huh? Yeah, for me, it's the car. There is no way I could have got that Landcruiser with my credit score, and I'm not giving up heated leather seats and four-wheel drive."

"Champagne is your preferred color?" Stephanie asks drily.

"It's beige metallic," he says defensively. Then grins in her direction "And I like expensive things."

"Yeah, well, I like when you give me something I can work with." Stephanie must be close to the camera because her voice is crisp on the audio.

"Well, the anniversary of her dad's death is next week. She always gets emotional. Although, seriously, it's been over ten years. Can we get over it already? But yeah, by the time I have someone offer her a drink, I'm sure she'll take it. But you have to be ready to pull her over. There won't be much time between when I text you and when she heads for home."

"I'm *always* ready." Stephanie steps into the frame then. She's wearing red lingerie.

"Uh-huh," says Nathan. His boner says he likes what he sees, but his tone is still serious. "Have you filed yet?"

"I *just* got him to sign up for night shift. I need him to do it for at least six months to show a pattern of neglect. Then I can file."

"That's exactly what she did," whispers Walker Trivette.

On-screen, they start to make out, and I stop the playback so Walker Trivette doesn't have to have the rest lodged in his brain like I do.

"This is..." He gapes like a fish, gasping for words like they're water but finding only air. "You can take this to the police."

"Nah. I'm a lifelong screw-up with a long-term hangover. Stephanie's not getting arrested for this. But you can take it to the judge."

He's already shaking his head. "You don't understand. I've got Judge Herald Arbenz."

I groan.

Judge Arbenz is so notoriously pro-cop that it's a town joke, and he's recently thrown his hat into the ring for Sheriff. The endorsements had flown in so fast you'd think he and the police chief slept in the same bed.

I look down at the bottom drawer. "This would be a lot easier if I'd had a drink."

"You quit?" Walker Trivette looks worried and grabs for my wrist, trying to take my pulse. I yank my arm back.

"I think, at this point, the best we can say is that it's been twelve hours since I've had a drink. If I make it to tomorrow at 11, I'll be on day one."

"Twelve is pretty good!" I give him a look. "Right. Sorry. Just trying to be encouraging."

I try to think it through logically. There has to be another option. I look at the bottom drawer where I keep all the things I hate but can't let go of. I pull it open. Yeah, I see the vodka, but it's the spare set of car keys I pick up.

"How badly do you want to keep your kids?"

Thirty minutes later, we're walking up the driveway of my old house. Beau is in the passenger seat of Walker Trivette's truck, waiting down the block.

"Are you sure about this?" whispers Walker Trivette.

"Did you ask your mama that when she tried to get a statue of Chuck Norris in front of city hall?"

He gives me a look. Apparently, that's a sensitive issue.

"We know Judge Arbenz won't rule against cops, so we need to give him a personal reason to hate her and Nate. If you've got something else, I will take it."

"Okay, but do we need that?" He gestures to my apocalypse weapon. It's a Rage Cage special—a baseball bat wrapped in barbed wire and nails.

"Um…" I take a few steps to the right to get a better look behind the shed. "You tell me."

The Landcruiser is in front of us under the carport, but behind the adjacent storage shed, I can see Stephanie's discreetly parked police cruiser.

"She said she couldn't watch the kids tonight because she was working," says Walker Trivette, anger rippling through his body.

"She's working something, anyway. Come on."

I use the spare keys to unlock the Landcruiser, then slip it into neutral, and we coast down the drive to the street. Getting it back up the hill is going to be a bitch, but that will be a problem for later.

We drive to the judge's house and pause on the dark street.

"I'm doing this, aren't I?" Walker Trivette asks as he pulls a ball cap low on his head.

"Yes. You have to get close enough so the car shows up on the doorbell cam."

He posted on social last week about the newspaper guy deliberately dropping his paper into a puddle, so I know he's got one.

"Crank the radio, blast through the stupid fake wishing well he put up for his wife, drive across the lawn. Then we take the car back to Nate's place, and when your lawyer turns in the tape tomorrow, the judge will recognize the car's description and Stephanie's toast."

That's the first time I haven't thought of it as *my* house.

"Okay," he says, taking a deep breath. "I'm doing it."

I crawl between the front seats so I can hide. It's an awkward thing for a grown woman to do, and I can feel him looking at my ass as it goes by. That's probably the most action either of us has gotten in a while, so I don't mind.

Walker Trivette cranks the volume on whatever Nate has on the sound system. It turns out to be Ted Nugent. I sink down into the wheel well out of sheer embarrassment that I had sexual relations with the owner of that music. Walker gives it a second and then hits the gas. He whoops like a good ol' boy when the wooden boards of the wishing well explode like confetti over the windshield, and I can't help laughing. The Landcruiser skids across the lawn and into the street, then we haul ass back to Nate's.

Pushing the Landcruiser up the drive sweats whatever alcohol I still have left in me out of my system.

"Okay," I say, pulling the baseball bat out of the back, "time to take care of Stephanie."

"Uh..." says Walker Trivette, his eyes going big.

"Her *car*, dumbass."

"Well, you looked scary," he says, following me to the parked police cruiser. "What are you going to do?"

"I'm going to pop two of your wife's tires."

"Two?"

"She's only got one spare. She'll have to call it in and get it towed. Everyone will know she was here."

Walker Trivette grins. "I would offer to hold your beer, but you're at thirteen hours and counting. I'll just buy you water in a can when we're done."

"Thanks." I think he really means that, which is weird.

I've never been much into vandalism or baseball, but an entire year at the Rage Cage has brushed up my skills. The first swing lands with a solid thump and an audible hiss. It takes a moment to unstick the bat, and then tire two goes the same way. I thought about stopping there, but Stephanie's expression as she put me in cuffs pops into my head, and I swing like I'm Babe Ruth. Then I line up on four.

"Stop," hisses Walker Trivette. "Four isn't believable."

The bat hovers over my head. I need to quit while I'm ahead.

In the distance, I hear a muffled bark from Beau, who can probably see me from the cab of Walker Trivette's truck.

Was that what I was—a quitter? Dad never quit—not once. Except on me.

This might be my last chance. Beau and an imported water are waiting.

"God grant me the strength to know when to stop," I say to myself and put the bat down.

JULIE HASTRUP

Julie Hastrup grew up in the Appalachian region of Ohio, but her home now alternates between South Florida and a small fishing village in Denmark. Her writing stems from her travels and business career prior to becoming a fulltime writer. Julie's work has been published by *Shotgun Honey* and *Mystery Magazine*. Julie is a member of Sisters in Crime, International Thriller Writers, the Short Mystery Fiction Society, and Mystery Writers of America. Find Julie at https://hastrup.com.

SKEETER'S BAR AND GRILL

JULIE HASTRUP

Rounding the bend in the road, Jim—Sarah liked to call him James —caught sight of the enormous slate-gray shelf cloud barreling toward him like an alien ship going into battle. It blotted out the sun and the last remaining shreds of happiness in his soul. His fingers brushed the chilled leather of the passenger seat, searching for his phone and the directions it held. It couldn't be that many more miles to Key West. The slim red line on the screen's battery icon warned him his GPS instructions were about to end.

He'd made it 420 of the 470 miles from St. Augustine, only stopping twice. Once for gas and once to use the bushes along the side of the road. His hands cramped from gripping the steering wheel like a vice for most of the last eight hours. His eyes burned from squinting into the sun. And from crying. The gurgles in his stomach reminded him he hadn't eaten since last night's rehearsal dinner. Time to pull over. But where? All the places he'd passed since leaving the mainland had been boarded up. A road trip during the forecasted storm of the season probably wasn't the best idea. Then again, he hadn't chosen the timing.

The swampland and scrub on either side of the desolate road gave way at last to a gravel drive marked by a faded white and red sign belonging to Skeeter's Bar and Grill. Tacked to it was a makeshift poster. The flapping cardboard said, "Open," in black Sharpie.

Jim's borrowed Subaru bumped its way through the slalom course of mosquito-filled potholes and pulled up next to the back of a lemon-yellow building badly in need of a paint job. It was bordered on one side by massive unpruned seagrape bushes and on the other by a covered porch made of an imaginative combination of corrugated metal, warped plywood, and cinderblocks.

Surfacing from the air-conditioned confines of the car, Jim tumbled into an invisible blanket of humidity. Simply breathing made him sweat through his white dress shirt. He pushed some overgrown ferns out of his way, stepped onto the porch, and followed the floorboards as they wrapped around the building to a breathtaking view of the vast Florida Straits.

The first plum-sized drops of rain darkened the perimeter of the open-air establishment, and Jim backed instinctively toward the bar in the middle of the otherwise empty structure. The blackness of the quickening storm blotted out the view he'd just enjoyed.

"Ya runnin' to or runnin' from?"

Jim jumped and turned to face the molasses-laden voice seeping toward him through the thick air. "Excuse me?"

"Ya gotta be runnin' either to or from, 'cuz ya ain't from 'round here." The speaker, a willowy man with a salt and pepper beard, pulled a stained rag from his shoulder and wiped a glass before setting it on the bar as an invitation.

"How do you know I'm…" Jim's voice faded as he glanced at his reflection in the mirror covering the bar's back wall. Even after the day he'd had, his short blond hair was still perfect. He closed his lips over the whitest teeth modern dentistry could provide. Even the tuxedo he'd been wearing all day remained uncreased, with barely a smudge. "I'm not running."

"Are too. Might as well admit it. No tourists come 'round here in the dead o' summer, an' the locals know to stay home when a storm's brewin', though this one's gonna pass on by. Sit." The bartender took his time getting the words out, unlike Jim's coworkers back in DC. There, every conversation felt like an assault by a jackhammer.

Like a good dog, Jim sat on one of the stools, its foam padding held together with duct tape. He'd been following orders his whole life. First from his father, the Loudon County Sheriff, and then from Sarah, his fiancée, for the past year.

"I'll take a Yuengling." Jim pointed to the only choice of draft beer. The Bud and the Miller Lite pulls had a clear plastic cup over their handles marking them as empty.

"Comin' right up."

Jim's phone vibrated once and then died. "And could I borrow your phone charger?"

The bartender handed Jim the business end of a long white cord. "They call me Skeeter. Just holler when you need a refill."

"I'm Jim. And thanks." He clicked his phone onto the charger, then took a long pull on the ice-cold beer.

Skeeter disappeared into the back leaving Jim on his own with his thoughts, solitary when he should have been surrounded by friends.

Angry rain poured down in thick sheets. Pounding the roof and spattering the floor, it created an opaque barrier between the porch and the outside world. No one would be joining him at the scarred and scuffed bar any time soon. Jim took a deep breath and opened his messaging app to see what had kept his phone buzzing since leaving the church. Alone.

The first message was from The Sheriff. "Dad" was an honorific his father didn't deserve.

> Knew you weren't man enough to keep her around

Jim tried not to let the self-doubt that had dogged him since the morning start up again. Who was he kidding? The seeds of insecurity were sewn the moment Sarah accepted his ring. He scrolled through a few more texts.

> Cn't Bleve she left U @ da altar. She's crzy.

That was from his best man.

Various messages from her bridesmaids all said roughly the same thing.

> She'll come back. 4give her.

Jim didn't believe she'd come back. They didn't know her like he did.

As the timestamps progressed from morning to afternoon, the messages shifted to concern.

> Where R U? U OK?

There was nothing from Sarah, herself, since her text yesterday informing him he couldn't tell time because he was five minutes late to their rehearsal dinner.

The phone vibrated again in Jim's hands.

> You'll never find her. You're too weak.

He didn't need to look to see who that was from. Jim concentrated on releasing the fist that came automatically whenever he interacted with the man.

The Sheriff prided himself on his tracking capabilities. In all his career, he'd only ever lost one suspect. Samuel Riley. The name stuck in Jim's head because the newspaper clippings and The Sheriff's notes were never cleared from the study of Jim's childhood home. Most fathers had framed pictures of their children on their desk. The Sheriff had one of Samuel Riley's BOLO description.

According to The Sherriff, Samuel Riley had beaten his girlfriend and her boss to death with a baseball bat before doing a runner. The Sheriff, long retired, still took his evening whiskey while parked at his desk, trying to find the one who got away. Samuel Riley consumed more of The Sheriff's attention than Jim ever had.

If it was up to Jim, the old man wouldn't have been invited to Florida, but Sarah had insisted her future father-in-law attend their wedding.

The *thunk* of a full shot glass being set in front of him drew Jim's eyes from his screen.

"You need more than a beer. Not like you're going anywhere in this weather." Skeeter had silently reappeared. He leaned his forearms on the bar and stared until Jim squirmed. "What's got you looking like you ate bad fish?"

Jim shot the clear liquid and savored the tequila's burn snaking down his throat.

Skeeter moved left and right but never took his eyes from Jim's face. "Get stood up?"

"How'd you—?"

"You come in here dressed in that there penguin suit with no ring and no posse. What else could it be?"

"Let's just say I was at the church, and she wasn't." Jim put the glass down on the bar, and the tequila-fairy masquerading as a bartender refilled it.

"Running from… What I thought. It's what most do down here. Where you running from?"

"I started out in St. Augustine this morning."

"So, you were supposed to have a morning wedding. My LaVonda always wanted a morning wedding. Said we'd be forgiven by God the night before and not have time enough to sin again before bowing to Him as man and wife." Skeeter rubbed his eyes before focusing on Jim again. "St. Augustine, huh? You must be hungry. Lemme see what I got in the fridge. Didn't get any food delivered this week because of the storm, but Bert down the road brought me a plate when he closed up after lunch."

As Skeeter turned toward the refrigerator, Jim studied the photograph next to it. A much younger version of the bartender stood with his arm around a woman while posing beneath a bright red maple tree. She was about to his shoulders and slightly lighter complected. They were both wearing what looked like their Sunday best.

Skeeter placed a mound of fried chicken on the bar between them. "Help yourself."

"What about you? Where did you run from?" Jim asked.

Skeeter pointed over his shoulder. "That picture there was taken at LaVonda's family's farm just outside Purcellville the day she said she'd marry my sorry ass. That's about two miles from where I grew up."

"That's in Loudon County, Virginia, isn't it?"

"You know Purcellville?" Skeeter gave Jim a skeptical look.

Jim thought about how to answer without pinning himself to The Sheriff. "I've heard of it. I work in DC. Well, used to work in DC, until I quit my job to join my future father-in-law's company after the wedding. Guess that's not happening either."

"Yeah, lots of you rich White folk used to come out to Loudon County."

Jim laughed, surprised he remembered how. "Don't include me in the 'rich DC' category. Copy editors don't exactly bring in the big bucks. This," Jim drew a circle in the air in front of his upper body, "is all Sarah. She's the one with the money. I was a scruffy guy in secondhand clothes when she met me."

"Nothing like a woman's touch."

"At least my father liked what Sarah was able to do. He wasn't exactly proud of what I'd become."

Skeeter refilled Jim's beer glass. "Daddies are never happy. What'd he want from you?"

Jim placed a second picked-clean chicken leg next to the one he'd already devoured and took a drink before answering. "I'm not quite sure, but whatever I did wasn't it. After each of his beatings, he told me to toughen up. The belt didn't get put away until I was six inches taller and twenty pounds of muscle heavier than him."

"Did you wallop him back?" Skeeter wiped at the already clean counter.

"Nah. He had enough bully in him for both of us."

"I know the type."

Jim didn't want to think about The Sheriff or Sarah any longer.

He'd had enough sadness for one day. He nodded at the picture on the opposite wall.

"So, did you and LaVonda get married? I don't see a ring on your hand, either."

"Ah, now that's a story." Skeeter poured himself a shot of tequila and downed it before leaning against the wall. "Where to start?"

"How'd you meet?"

Skeeter smiled at the memory and pulled the rag from his shoulder. He ran it through his hands a couple of times before speaking. "It was the church picnic about twenty-five or thirty years ago. I didn't want to go, but you didn't say no to Mama. You still got a mama?"

"No. She died when I was twelve." Jim's thoughts took him to the time he called *the change*, when everything good in his life soured. He shook himself back to the present. "But you were telling me about LaVonda."

"LaVonda… Now she was a beauty. And smart, too. She was a secretary for old Rev' Whitcomb." A look of hatred flitted across Skeeter's face, and he spit on the floor next to his feet. Regaining his composure, he continued. "Hate saying the man's name. Anyway, LaVonda was selling raffle tickets at the picnic for some fancy cake I didn't even want, but I bought ten dollars' worth just so I could spend time with her. She must've seen something in me because we started stepping out not long after. How'd you meet your girl?"

"I was working a second job as a waiter in Georgetown. Sarah and a bunch of her friends from grad school stopped in one night. And, well, she and I spent most of my shift in the supply closet."

"Ah, love at first sight." Skeeter nodded.

"Something like that. I thought she'd be bored with me in two seconds, but she made me her project until I made her my fiancée. Guess it took a little longer than two seconds. So, what happened with you and LaVonda?"

"We didn't have no supply closet, so I saved and saved until I could rent the little blue house next to where LaVonda worked at St. George's. You know, she wouldn't step foot in it until I put a ring on her finger. Guess she knew what would happen when she did. What a fine woman." Skeeter's chuckle dwindled into silence, but his eyes continued to sparkle.

Jim waved a drumstick to get the barman's attention. "What happened?"

Skeeter began twisting the rag in his hands. "The day after that picture was taken, LaVonda spent her first night in the little blue house. I didn't have no coffee, no milk, nothing, so the next morning I hightailed it down to the corner store to get something for her to have for breakfast. When I came back… Well, that's when all hell broke loose."

Jim sat on the edge of his barstool as Skeeter poured himself another shot and downed it.

"I walked in the door to hear a man screaming. And my LaVonda, she's crying. I could tell the sounds were coming from the bedroom, so I grabbed the baseball bat I kept by the door and went to see what was going on.

"There was old Rev' Whitcomb standing with his pants down around his ankles and pounding my beautiful LaVonda with his fists. Did I tell you he wore a great big ring on his left hand? That ring broke my girl's jaw. He was yelling about how God wanted *him* to be the one who took her for the first time."

"What'd you do?"

Skeeter ran his hands over his head. "LaVonda was bleeding mighty bad, so I took that bat to the rev's head. Just needed one swing, and the old man went down hard. I wrapped my LaVonda up in the sheet and ran with her to the hospital. That's where I was when I heard the sheriff and his men outside her room. They was hollering at the staff that they was letting a killer hide there. I knew that sheriff hated people like me, so I ran and hid at my cousin Shawn's."

"Holy shit…"

Skeeter sniffed and rubbed at his nose. "That's where I was when I found out LaVonda didn't make it. When the sheriff came pounding on Shawn's door, I hightailed it again. I kept on going until I wound up here working for Skeeter."

Jim frowned. "Wait. I thought *you* were Skeeter."

"I can see how that could be a might confusing. Whoever owns the bar is Skeeter. I'm actually Skeeter number three. Skeeter number one gave the place to his son, and that's who I worked for. Skeeter number two didn't have no kids, so when he passed, he gave it to me. My Christian name is Samuel Riley."

"Samuel Riley." Jim shook his head in disbelief and held out his hand. "Nice to meet you, Samuel Riley."

Skeeter stepped away from the wall and shook the offered hand. "No one's ever called me that but my mama. I was Willie before I was Skeeter."

"Willie?"

"As in Willie Mays, the baseball player? After a while, I started introducing myself as Willie M."

"I'm sure that helped keep that sheriff off your tail." Jim inwardly smiled at the irony.

"Probably did just that."

Skeeter cleared the chicken bones and tequila glasses from the bar and took them to the back while Jim got up to stretch his legs.

"Looks like the rain's letting up." Skeeter had silently emerged from the kitchen, but Jim had gotten used to the man's quiet entry and didn't startle.

The sky outside the covered porch was lighter now. Blue herons, cranes, and frogs greeted one another from beyond the tree canopy encircling much of the building. An air horn blared somewhere in the distance. The confessional atmosphere disappeared with the cool breeze wafting through.

Jim pointed to an outcropping of trees a few hundred yards away, visible for the first time now that the weather was clearing. "What's that over there?"

"That's Jake's Point. You can't really see it proper from here because of the trees, but there's a little beach. It's where folks put their canoes and paddle boards into the water. Won't be good for a couple of days because of the current, but if you stick around, it's a good spot to start from. Then you can come back and have another beer with old Skeeter."

Walking over to the bar, Jim checked his phone. The battery was nearly full, and the clock told him he needed to get moving if he was to finish what he intended to do. "How much do I owe you?"

Skeeter waved the question away. "It's on the house. It's not every day a man gets asked to tell his tale."

Jim slid a twenty under his beer glass. The story was worth at least that much.

"So you ain't got no woman, ain't got no mama, ain't got no job. What you going to do now?" Skeeter asked.

Some plans weren't meant to be shared. "I'm going to keep on driving."

"Well, you're in the right place to disappear for a while and figure yourself out."

Jim waved farewell and walked away from The Sheriff's lifelong quest. He scrolled through his contacts and pulled up the man's number. He so badly wanted rub The Sheriff's nose in who he'd found but decided it would be better to let him go to his grave as a failure. Besides, if he was worried about his son, he could follow the cell tower ping of his last message. Jim would say goodbye but not yet.

The Subaru crept toward Jake's Point, bouncing and splashing through the pockmarked parking lot. Jim did a three-point turn and backed up as far as he could to the water line without going in. Walking around the rear of the car, he recoiled as part of a towering gumbo limbo tree crashed into the tributary three feet from where he stood. The current was so fast, the branch was gone after only one blink.

Jim had thought he'd do this from a boat he'd booked leaving for Cuba from Key West in a little over an hour, but now was just as good. Better even. He popped the trunk and grabbed the bright yellow elbow-length cleaning gloves he'd used that morning. Old Spice cologne wafted from the heavy-duty garbage bag he'd hauled all the way from St. Augustine. He was staggered by the rehearsal dinner memories the smell conjured: The waiter in his black vest hovering in a cloud of cologne before pulling Sarah's chair out for her as she left the table, Jim going to look for her. Between the grunts and the aroma coming from the janitor's closet, Jim had suspected what he'd encounter. There was Sarah with her skirt hitched high, her legs wrapped around the waiter, his hands on her bare ass, and the reek of Old Spice.

Jim heaved the dark green sack out of the trunk. Inhaling the cologne, he shook his head. *She could've had the decency to not have another go with him while in her wedding gown.* On an internal count of three, he launched the bag into the current. It quickly sank taking Sarah with it down into the depths as it rushed toward the Straits. Jim opened the driver's door and looked over his shoulder at something in his peripheral vision. A white veil had bobbed to the surface. It swirled as if to say goodbye, then floated away.

GREGORY MEECE

Gregory Meece's passion for creative writing was first recognized in high school when his English teacher challenged him to produce a novel as an independent study project. Following his career as an educator and retired head of school, Greg's stories have found homes in anthologies such as *Love Letters to Poe: Tales Torn from the Heart* and Malice Domestic's *Mystery Most Traditional,* and in magazines including *Black Cat Weekly, Bristol Noir, The Yard: Crime Blog, Kings River Life,* and *Thriller Magazine.* He lives in Southeastern Pennsylvania and is a member of the Short Mystery Fiction Society. Find Gregory at twitter.com/GRMSenior.

ONCE A THIEF
GREGORY MEECE

GEMMA SAT QUIETLY AS the prosecutor presented the jury with the mountain of evidence against her. He told them Gemma admitted to being at the victim's home when he was killed. He held up her apron, directing the jury's attention to where the victim's blood had stained it. He brandished the murder weapon while citing the forensic report that showed Gemma's fingerprints were found on its handle. He told them how Gemma lied when investigators asked her to explain why the stolen gems were hidden in her apartment. What hurt Gemma the most was the prosecutor's summation: "We will demonstrate that Gemma Garcia has been a chronic, compulsive thief her entire life."

The jury stared at her as if she were a circus freak on display for their horror and amusement, and Gemma remembered the schoolgirl she'd once been, the one described by her teachers as shy, polite, studious…

And a thief.

As soon as Gemma spied the object on her teacher's desk, she knew she had to make it her own.

The girl seated on the other side of the classroom was going on and on about how the main character in the story they were reading had traits that paralleled some of today's powerful leaders. Mrs. Jamison, Gemma's English teacher, listened attentively as the girl continued to rack up brownie points.

Gemma peeked at the wall clock, feigning nonchalance. She would take the object from Mrs. Jamison's desk when the class dismissal bell rang. She played it out in her mind. The teacher would turn her back on the students and proceed to wipe today's notes from the board in preparation for her next lesson. The controlled chaos of students traveling to various locations within the permitted four-minute transition time would present her with the opportunity to slip the object into her backpack and dissolve into the congested hallway traffic.

Gemma knew that she couldn't afford to get caught. Not again. She also knew she had no choice. She didn't need the object. She just needed to take it.

Timing was essential. Gemma silently counted, "Five, four, three…" Like a signal from a starter gun, the bell buzzed loudly. Gemma watched as her classmates quickly closed their books, stowed pens and notebooks, and rose from their desks, almost in a single motion, like a flock of startled blackbirds reacting to a sound in the woods.

The students brushed past Mrs. Jamison's desk as the teacher turned to locate her markerboard eraser. Gemma dropped back to the end of the line of exiting students. She was experienced; all she needed was a couple of seconds. Without taking her eyes off the student in front of her, she grasped the object and quickly deposited it into her unzipped backpack. That familiar rush washed over her. Suddenly, she felt a firm hand gripping her elbow from behind. As Gemma's head swiveled, she saw the look of disappointment on her teacher's face.

ALTHOUGH ACCOMPANIED by both of her nervous parents, one on either side of her, Gemma looked all alone sitting at the expansive conference room table. Her hands were folded demurely in her lap and her sitting posture was perfect. The innocence in her eyes showed through her wire-rimmed glasses, the very image of the conscientious young girl she had always strived to be. Though this was her third appearance before the school's Review Board, she couldn't have looked more out of place.

On the other side of the room sat an array of administrators, teacher representatives, and board members. A school secretary was poised to type every spoken word into her laptop. The imbalance in the room made the outcome appear almost certain. So did Gemma's disciplinary record.

The high school's principal, Mr. Abernethy, began by explaining the purpose of the meeting. When he was through, he seemed to be searching for what to say next. The secretary stopped typing; her fingertips hovered over her keyboard as she waited for him to continue.

Abernethy held up a red, plastic, ashtray-shaped apple. It was meant to hold paper clips.

"This? This is what you stole?" he asked with incredulity in his voice.

"Yes, sir," Gemma said.

"But why, Miss Garcia?" His tone of voice reflected just how confused and frustrated he felt. "I mean, you could probably find these at the dollar store. Why in the world did you risk your enrollment at Westbury School for something so—so worthless?"

"I don't know, sir. I just wanted to have it."

"May I speak at this time?" Gemma's father asked.

Abernethy placed the evidence on the table in front of him. "Certainly, Mr. Garcia."

"You all know about my daughter's condition," said Mr. Garcia. "Her impulsivity—taking things that don't belong to her—it's well documented in your guidance counselor's records."

"It's like the time Gemma took a book about diabetes from the school's nurse's office," Mrs. Garcia added. "She didn't need it. She doesn't even have diabetes and, if she did, the nurse would have given her a copy for free. It's just that, at that moment, she simply had to have it. We taught Gemma that stealing is wrong. No one feels worse about it than Gemma herself. She just can't resist when the impulse comes over her. It has nothing to do with the value of the item."

"We understand about Gemma's…condition," said one of the teachers on the Review Board.

"It's called kleptomania," Mr. Garcia said.

Several of the Review Board members winced upon hearing the medical term spoken out loud. The teacher cleared his throat and spoke again.

"As I said, we understand her condition. However, Westbury is known for its high standards for student behavior and decorum. That's why parents choose us. Our students agree to uphold those standards. How can we allow Gemma to keep on stealing things—even if she does have some…some personal issues?"

The others on the Board nodded.

"The fact is, this was Gemma's last chance," Abernathy said. "Our school policy is quite clear. Three strikes and you're out. This is Gemma's third Review Board hearing." He turned his attention to Gemma. "Do you have anything else to say on your behalf?"

The secretary entered two final words into the minutes after Gemma replied.

"I'm sorry."

"I DON'T KNOW why we hired you," said Paloma Jackson, the woman seated beneath the Favorite Housekeepers sign. "You don't even have a high school diploma. And now this?"

Gemma was prepared for what was coming. Before she had even given anyone a reason to fire her, she knew it would come—because she knew the reason why.

"I'm so sorry, Ms. Jackson," Gemma said. "It was just a small wooden box for holding tea bags."

"And you didn't give it back."

"I gave it away as soon as I got home—I donated it to the local thrift shop. I don't even drink tea."

"You stole something you can't even use, and then you got rid of it—you are some piece of work, Miss Garcia. Look, Gemma, you do good work, but you know how this kind of thing gets on social media, and there goes our company's reputation. I should terminate you right now. The only reason I'm not firing you—yet—is because Millie, the girl who cleans our biggest client's home, just left the company for another position. You're all I've got right now. Here's the address. Mr. Swanson is an older man who lives alone, so you know what to expect—lots of dusting and vacuuming. And the bathrooms are probably a mess. He expects someone there first thing tomorrow morning."

Gemma smiled and reached out her hand. The woman stared at her open palm. "One more thing, Gemma," she said. "If you're caught stealing anything...I don't care if it's a crumb from the kitchen floor. Assume that it will be your last day here at Favorite Housekeepers. No more chances."

When Gemma stole things, she hoped the items wouldn't be missed. It was the act of stealing itself that fueled her compulsion. Afterward, feeling self-disgust and shame, she would tend to discard the items. Sometimes, she would throw them in the trash. Other times she would drop the item in the donation bin at the Goodwill store. Either way, it was her attempt to erase the deed. She knew stealing was wrong and she understood the consequences of her actions. Kleptomania might be a disease that could be explained, but it could not be excused, either in school or on the job.

Gemma arrived promptly at the address she was given. It was hard for her to imagine that just one person lived in such a large and elegant house. After she rang the doorbell a man with white hair and a Colonel Sanders-style goatee came to the door. He was wearing a cashmere cardigan over a white button-down shirt, with corduroy trousers—casual chic. He looked like a man who enjoyed retirement but wasn't about to give up his sophistication.

Gemma introduced herself. "Pleased to meet you, Mr. Swanson.

I'm Gemma, from Favorite Housekeepers. I brought my things. Where would you like me to start?"

"Where's Millie?" asked Mr. Swanson.

"My boss, Ms. Jackson, told me Millie left our company. I'm her replacement." Remembering her boss's warning, and so many of her previous posts that turned out to be short-lived, she added, "At least for today."

"Very well, then. Come inside, Gemma," said Mr. Swanson. He motioned her into a spacious foyer, crowned with an ornate chandelier. "You can get started in the kitchen." He pointed down the hallway. "I have some work to do in the study. Come and get me if you need anything."

Just off the foyer, a set of French doors opened to a room lined with built-in bookshelves. Gemma watched as Mr. Swanson took his seat behind a large, cherrywood desk. Then she hoisted her bag of cleaning supplies and headed down the long hallway toward the kitchen.

Gemma looked for a good place to start. There were dirty dishes in the sink. It wasn't necessarily part of her cleaning routine, but she needed to transfer the dirty dishes to the dishwasher so she could scrub the sink and countertops. She opened the dishwasher door and found rows of sparkling clean dishes inside.

At first, it was hard for her to determine which cabinets and drawers were meant for the various items she removed from the dishwasher. The first cabinet she opened held spices and canned goods. The next one was filled with coffee cups and saucers. On the top shelf, she saw several water bottles.

Most of the water bottles were made of plastic, some bearing logos—giveaway items. One appeared to be metallic. That was the one Gemma couldn't take her eyes from. The uncomfortable feeling began to coil like a snake inside her. She couldn't explain it. The only thing she could compare it to was her grandmother's constant battle to quit smoking. All it took was one whiff of cigarette smoke and the urge to resume her old pack-a-day habit would return.

Gemma assumed that most people wouldn't store items they use every day so high up, where they might need a stool to reach them.

Mr. Swanson was not much taller than she was, and he walked with a slight stoop. She supposed that he seldom used the bottles, if at all. And no one needed so many. One bottle wouldn't be missed. Even if was made of stainless steel, it couldn't have been worth more than a few dollars.

Gemma already had several water bottles of her own, but that had nothing to do with her desire to take this one. The urge inside her was too hard to resist. Adrenaline pumped through her blood. Before she knew it, she was climbing onto the countertop to reach the top shelf. The bottle disappeared into her cleaning supply bag, and she was quickly back at work.

Gemma heard what sounded like Mr. Swanson talking to someone in the foyer. She hadn't heard the doorbell. Perhaps he had seen someone approaching by looking through the window in his study and he opened the door for them. The two voices were growing louder, but Gemma was unable to discern what was being said. She continued polishing the countertops and wiping the kitchen island clean. After a few minutes, she heard the front door close abruptly. Then there were no more sounds coming from that end of the hallway.

Not having had an opportunity to consult with her predecessor, and absent any specific instructions from Ms. Jackson, she needed to check with Mr. Swanson to see what areas she should clean next.

Gemma lifted her bag of supplies and proceeded toward Mr. Swanson's study. When she reached the foyer, she noticed a stain on the oriental hallway runner. It appeared to be wet. She crouched and pressed the corner of her apron against the liquid to absorb what it could before spraying the area with a carpet cleaner. The color that appeared on her apron was deep red. "Is this blood?" she wondered. Looking around to check if there were any other droplets, her eyes caught something on the carpet, just sticking out from behind a floor vase filled with soft pink flowers. Without thinking, she reached for the object and pulled it away from the vase. Gemma gasped. It was a knife, and there was blood on the blade.

The doors to the study were closed. Gemma shouted for Mr.

Swanson, but there was no reply from within. She pressed against the doors to see if they were locked. The doors moved inward, so Gemma opened them the rest of the way and walked inside. She almost stumbled over a body lying on the floor beside the desk.

It was Mr. Swanson, blood matting in his goatee and streaking his white button-down shirt. Gemma screamed, backing out of the room, and tried to avoid stepping on several books strewn around the floor. They appeared to have been thrown from the bookshelves. A wall safe, with its door hanging open, was embedded where the books had been removed.

Gemma didn't even realize she was still holding her bag of cleaning supplies in one hand and the knife in the other when she flew out the front door to her car and reached for her keys. She shook the knife out of her hand as if it were something that had suddenly caught fire. She tossed her cleaning bag onto the passenger seat and got inside. As she tried to catch her breath, she thought that she should call the police, but she didn't own a cell phone, and she wasn't about to go back inside the house to use the phone on Mr. Swanson's desk. And so, she just drove.

When a neighbor noticed that Mr. Swanson's front door had been left wide open for some time, he decided to make sure everything was alright. His elderly neighbor had taken some falls recently, and he had been using a cane when he went outside to retrieve his morning newspaper. When he came upon the bloody knife lying on the front lawn, he immediately reached for his cell phone and dialed 911.

The police observed the telltale signs of a break-in, robbery, and homicide. One of the members of the forensics team carefully placed the knife in a plastic bag. It would be taken to the lab to check for fingerprints and to see if the blood on its blade was a match with Mr. Swanson's. They took pictures of the appointment book on the desk in the study. It was open to today's date, with the words, "Favorite Housekeepers, 9:00 AM" written on the page.

After the police spoke with Paloma Jackson, they had the name and address of the cleaner who was sent to Swanson's home that morning. And they had more than that. An angry and upset Ms.

Jackson told them that she planned to fire Gemma because she had been stealing things from the homes where she cleaned.

With a search warrant in hand, Lieutenant Dobbins knocked hard on Gemma's door. It didn't take his men from the homicide division long to comb through her tiny apartment before they found the blood-stained apron and a peculiar-looking water bottle nestled among Gemma's cleaning supplies. Lieutenant Dobbins had seen this type of container before. When asked about the bottle, Gemma told him it was hers because she knew that she would be fired if she admitted taking it, and she didn't see how it could have anything to do with a homicide investigation or whatever had been stolen from Mr. Swanson's safe.

Turning the bottle upside down, the Lieutenant screwed off its false bottom. "They call these things 'diversion safes,'" he said to one of the other officers. "People use them to hide their valuables in places a robber wouldn't think to look—books, cans of food, and even water bottles." When he removed the bottom, he found what he expected to see inside—a small, lockable safe. What he didn't expect to see was its contents—an envelope filled with rare South African diamonds. At Gemma's trial, someone from the insurance company would testify that Mr. Swanson had insured them for over a million dollars.

THE PROSECUTOR WAS RENOWNED NOT ONLY for his track record of winning cases, but also for his ability to connect with a jury. It wasn't just that he was handsome, charming, and self-confident. He had a special talent for simplifying complex cases in a way that made the outcomes seem obvious. In his opening remarks, he described how the crime was committed, by whom, and why. Means, motive, and opportunity. Open and shut.

"Miss Garcia may have entered the Swanson residence with the intention of housecleaning," the prosecutor began, "but when she saw her opportunity, she couldn't restrain her impulses. Isn't that the story of her whole life? You and I see lots of things we'd like to have.

Right? But we don't just take them. Yet, when Miss Garcia sees what she wants, there's no stopping her. When she saw the homeowner open his safe in the study, she had to have what was inside. After slashing the defenseless, elderly man's throat, she removed the contents and fled.

"The defendant wants us to believe that 'someone else' did the crime." The prosecutor used his fingers as air quotes every time he mentioned, "someone else." "Did she see this 'someone else'? No. Were 'someone else's' fingerprints on the knife? No. Can she tell you what she heard 'someone else' say? No. Did she even hear 'someone else' knocking or ringing the doorbell? No.

"We don't know whether Mr. Swanson kept his diamonds hidden inside the bottle—the diversion safe—as an added security precaution or whether Miss Garcia uses the item to conceal the things she steals. What you and I know for certain is that Gemma Garcia is a chronic thief."

Gemma's defense, by contrast, sounded muddy. To the jury's ears, it sounded something like, "She says she didn't do it, but even if she did, it was part of her 'condition.'"

Gemma wanted to crawl under the table when the psychiatrist hired by her defense attorney discussed kleptomania using terms such as "illness" and "mental health disorder." "Kleptomania is a disease, not a crime," the doctor said convincingly.

But would the jury see it as an excuse for what occurred at Mr. Swanson's home that morning or the cause? "Do we let off the fellow who kills someone while driving drunk because he says he's an alcoholic?" the prosecutor had asked rhetorically.

On the witness stand, Gemma admitted under oath that she took the water bottle, but from the kitchen—not from the safe in the study. She had no idea at the time that there were diamonds inside the bottle. She explained about picking up the knife before she knew what it was, and that she used her apron only to clean a spot on the carpet. It was not blood spattered on her while she committed murder.

As the prosecutor was making his summation before the jury, Gemma's eyes wandered. Her eyes landed on her attorney, sitting beside her, jotting notes on a yellow legal pad. But it was the silver pen in the lawyer's hand that held Gemma's gaze.

She probably has several just like them in that briefcase, Gemma thought.

Had Gemma looked at the jury during the prosecutor's closing argument, she would have seen skepticism on the faces of some of the jurors. Empathy on others. Her trial was coming to an end, the crossroads that could change her life forever.

And still, she couldn't take her eyes off the shiny object. Her attorney put down the pen and assembled her papers, preparing to rise and present her rebuttal.

The prosecutor rested his case with one final denunciation of Gemma: "Once a thief, always a thief," he shouted, pointing his finger directly at the accused. The members of the jury turned their heads to follow where he was pointing—just as Gemma was making her move.

For her, there was no other choice.

CHRISTINA BOUFIS

Christina Boufis is a San Francisco Bay-Area writer whose short fiction has appeared in *Pulphouse Fiction* and *Kings River Life Magazine*. Under C.B. Peterson, she's the author of a domestic thriller, *I Want Him Dead*. A former academic with a PhD in Victorian literature and Women's Studies, she spent eight years teaching women inmates at the San Francisco County Jail. She has recently published the first novel in a jail mystery series, *The Cruelest Month*. Christina is a member of Sisters in Crime and the Alliance of Independent Authors. Find Christina at www.christinaboufis.com.

HIT-AND-RUN

CHRISTINA BOUFIS

Marcy told no one. Ted insisted nothing had happened and there was nothing to tell. But this didn't stop Marcy from imagining what she should have done, could still do. She could go to the police. *Confess everything.*

They were driving. *No,* she reminded herself. *Not they. Ted was driving.*

The night was foggy and dark. One of those pea soup nights in the Bay Area where the thick fog swallowed the road and everything else.

Ted had been drinking. They all had. Samantha and Jonah were known for their dinner parties—and their wine. They owned a goddamn vineyard, so of course the wine was very good, and they'd drank more bottles than they could count.

They should have called a car service, but Ted insisted he could drive back to San Francisco. "That's one reason I got a manual," he'd told her more than once. "If I can drive the stick, I'm not too drunk to drive."

Marcy didn't argue. They couldn't afford a car service and she didn't want to cause a scene. They'd been arguing a lot lately and

Ted didn't like to be challenged. The dinner party guests, aside from Samantha, weren't really her friends.

Though Sam suggested they spend the night, Marcy declined. The two women had been known each other since sophomore year of college. But in the nearly two decades since graduation, while Sam's life had risen sharply upwards on the prosperity curve, Marcy's had gone south in the opposite direction.

Unlike Sam and her crowd, she and Ted didn't own a multi-million-dollar home in the Marin hills. Nor did they have a winter ski cabin in Lake Tahoe. No. They lived in a one-bedroom rent-controlled apartment in San Francisco's Inner Sunset district, where the fog didn't burn off until late afternoon, and the N-Judah train rattled their windows as it screeched by. They were a high school teacher and a basketball coach living in an expensive city and accumulating more debt than savings.

Even after being recruited by a private high school on the peninsula to coach the basketball team and run the physical education department, Ted didn't bring home all that much more than Marcy did on her public school teacher's salary. Ted had successfully brought his former high school team to two state championships, and the private school promised him more money—if his coaching could turn their team around as well.

Though she hated to admit it, Marcy had grown increasingly envious of her friend, her perfect family with her handsome husband and two teen twins, and her money. How was it that Marcy's life hadn't quite turned out the way she expected? Marrying Ted hadn't made it any easier.

Marcy's steps were unsteady as she called goodbye and made her way to the car. But she was lucid enough to feel fear as Ted drove down the long winding road away from Sam's house. The two-lane highway snaked down from the hills and was full of sharp twists and turns. Take one too fast and you'd plunge over a steep embankment.

There were no streetlights. *What is it with rich people?* Marcy wondered. *Can they see in the dark?*

They'd hardly driven more than a few minutes when they came upon a parked car, half blocking the road that appeared out of nowhere. To avoid hitting the car, Ted swung widely into the other lane. Miraculously, there was no oncoming traffic. But when he avoided hitting the parked car, Ted overcompensated and drove onto the opposite shoulder. Marcy saw something out of the corner of her eye, heard a large thud, and a human cry. Or was it an animal?

Ted didn't stop the car. Instead, he sped away.

Marcy turned her head around, scrutinizing the darkness behind her. But the road was inscrutable, and she could see nothing through the fog.

"Aren't you going to stop?" Marcy's voice was high and shaky. "I think you hit something back there."

"Probably just a raccoon." Ted's eyes were fixed on the road ahead. "Or a deer. Besides, it's too dangerous to turn around."

Marcy accepted the logic. Ted would never pass a breathalyzer. And it was true there was no place to turn around. It had all happened so fast anyway. Marcy couldn't be sure the shape she thought she saw was human. Was it a deer?

Though she said nothing, Marcy's mind was busy with what ifs. *What if they hadn't gone to the party? What if she'd called a car service?*

She cursed herself. Why had they gone to the party in the first place? She dreaded those dinner parties. How could people her and Ted's age, barely forty, have so much money? Where did it come from? How could they afford nice houses when she and Ted were barely scraping by?

At home, Ted stopped in the driveway before pulling into the underground garage to let Marcy out. This wasn't chivalrous on his part. The garage was so narrow it was difficult to open both the car doors without scraping them.

Marcy got out of the car on wobbly legs. She was tempted to examine the car to see if there was a dent. Or worse yet, blood. Instead, afraid of what she might find, she walked towards the apartment building, fished out her keys, and went inside without saying a word.

By the time Ted came upstairs, Marcy was in bed.

"Any damage?"

"Not much." Ted shook his head. "Probably a deer. I'll have Sergio fix it tomorrow."

Marcy couldn't sleep. She'd been plagued with vicious insomnia her entire life, and tonight the voice in her head was relentless. *It's your fault. You shouldn't have let Ted drive. Why didn't you stop him?*

The next morning, Ted was up, showered, and gone by the time Marcy woke. She'd fallen asleep just after 4 a.m., sheer exhaustion overriding her brain.

Ted had left a Post-it note on the coffee pot. *Didn't want to wake you. See you later xx*

It was Saturday, Ted wasn't coaching any games this weekend, so there was no reason for him to be up so early. Marcy knew he'd gone straight to his mechanic in the Mission. She wasn't sure if she was relieved or annoyed that he hadn't mentioned it in the note. Maybe he was being careful and covering his tracks? *Now you're thinking like a criminal*, the voice told her.

Marcy poured herself coffee that had gone cold and didn't bother to microwave it.

She stared out the window holding her cold coffee. She was disoriented. Had last night been a bad dream? Then she sat on the couch and opened her laptop. She couldn't help herself. She googled, "Hit-and-run Marin."

To her surprise, there was nothing recent. An article from several years ago, but that was it.

Then she googled "California hit-and-run penalty" and skimmed the results. If they'd hit the car itself and caused property damage, fleeing the scene was just a misdemeanor, remedied with a $1,000 fine, a six-month jail term, and perhaps probation for three years—assuming you were caught.

More troubling was when a driver caused serious injury or death and left the scene. That was a felony. *Not to mention the injury or death to another person*, the voice in Marcy's head told her.

A hit-and-run felony could mean three years in prison and a large fine. *For Ted*, the voice told her. *Not for you.*

Marcy then searched Facebook and other social media sites, but nothing came up. Perhaps they'd gotten lucky and hit an animal after all? She doubted it. She and Ted were not the lucky types.

Ted came home just before noon and went to bed. He had a headache, he told her. Marcy didn't ask about the car. The less she knew, the better.

As a high school English teacher, Marcy looked forward to Saturday and Sunday almost as much as her students. Not this weekend. Time seemed to drip by tortuously and slowly as she and Ted stayed holed up in the apartment. Marcy didn't want to go anywhere with Ted. Besides, they were carless.

When Sunday night came, Marcy felt relieved. Usually, she dreaded the piles of student essays she had yet to grade. Tonight, she was glad for the distraction.

Monday morning, and there was still nothing online about a hit-and-run. She'd googled and searched social media sites all weekend, trying not to let Ted see what she was doing. He hadn't asked.

When she entered the faculty lounge, a windowless room with a few round tables and two communal computers, Marcy felt lighter than she had in days. Maybe Ted was right about the raccoon or the deer.

She settled in at one of the computers to check her work email before first period. There were the usual requests from students asking for extension and several from the principal about cell phones in class and vaping (both forbidden). She was about to log off when a new email popped into her inbox. She read the subject line.

I saw what you did

The sender's address was a bunch of random letters and numbers, not a recognizable name. Marcy's index finger hovered over the delete key. The bell rang indicating the start of first period. The other teachers filed out of the lounge, chatting and shuffling books and papers. Marcy sat at the computer her finger suspended in midair over the keyboard.

She had less than a minute to get to class.

You should have stopped

Two sentences. That was it.

Under the text was a video link. Marcy knew she shouldn't click on unsolicited links, but she did it anyway. If she hadn't been there, Marcy isn't sure she would have recognized the road from the video. It was foggy. Dark. Hard to see. But then she saw approaching headlights. Ted's car. Then a screeching sound as his car veered into the other lane and onto the narrow shoulder. A human shape on the other side. Ted's car swerved into it. Then a loud thud, and a cry, a very human cry. The video ended.

From the camera angle, it looked like the video was filmed by someone sitting in the parked car they'd swerved to avoid. Had there been someone inside that night?

Marcy's hands were shaking as she dragged the email to the trash and emptied it. Then she turned off the computer. As she walked to class, the only sound she heard was the blood rushing in her ears.

Somehow, Marcy got through her first three classes. At lunch time, she texted Ted.

I got an email

she wrote. Ted texted back immediately.

Me too. Talk later.

Marcy found it difficult to get through the rest of her classes. She changed her lesson plans and had her students do group work, so she didn't have to stand in front of the classroom, but instead could pace around, her mind on the video.

Ted didn't get home until after ten—a big game, he told her, one as head coach he couldn't miss. By that time, Marcy had exhausted herself. She'd done endless google and social media searches, looking for anything that mentioned hit-and-runs or accidents in Marin.

"There was a witness at the scene, maybe in the car," Marcy told Ted before he'd even put down his school bag.

"Do you have to call him the witness?" Ted asked, defensive. "What did he really see, anyway? The footage wasn't that good. Did he even get our license plate number?"

"He or she has our work emails, Ted. Whoever it is knows a lot more than our license plate. They know who we are and where we work."

Ted shook his head. "We still don't know exactly what happened. I don't think we should overreact and get hysterical."

"I'm not hysterical, Ted. I'm just stating facts."

"As you see them," Ted shrugged and walked towards the kitchen to make himself a sandwich for dinner. Marcy still hadn't eaten.

Ted's laissez-faire attitude was unbelievable. He was the one who got them into this mess and then he called *her* hysterical and overreactive? *Well, screw him*, she thought. Marcy went into the bedroom and slammed the door. She hoped he'd take a hint and sleep on the couch.

The next morning, they both received another email. It was before work. The two of them were sitting facing each other at their tiny kitchen table when their phones pinged simultaneously. The subject heading and strange email address were the same. No body text this time. Just another attachment.

"Don't open it," Ted said. "You never know. It could be some kind of malware."

"You're worried about malware? I think we've got bigger problems than that."

Marcy clicked on the attachment. It was a PDF newspaper article from the *Mill Valley Sentinel*, a local, small-circulation paper.

POLICE SEEK INFORMATION ABOUT HIT-AND-RUN

The Mill Valley Police Department is seeking the public's help in a serious hit-and-run accident. The incident occurred on Lucas Valley Road on Friday, April 6th, at approximately 1:30 a.m. A teenage girl, whose name is being withheld because of her age, was walking on the shoulder when she was struck from behind by a white or light-colored car, possibly of foreign make. The young woman and a male friend had pulled off to the side of the road due to engine trouble. Anyone with information about this incident is asked to call the 24/7 hotline at 800-555-4444.

Marcy was too stunned to speak.

"It has to be the boyfriend who sent the emails," Ted said. "But if he knows who we are, why didn't he go to the police?

"I don't know. But for crying out loud, Ted, you hit a girl. A teenager. Did you take in the part about her being seriously injured?"

"Yes, Marcy." Ted's tone was icy. "But why not just turn us in?"

Turn you in, Marcy thought. But Ted had a point. Also, for all her searching, Marcy hadn't found this story herself. Granted, the Marin paper was a small, local publication, but why hadn't it been picked up by other news outlets? How could she have missed it in her google searches?

They didn't have to wait long for an answer. An hour later, they both received another email.

If you want your hit and run kept quiet, pay $25,000 by Friday. If not, the video will go viral.

The email also included instructions on how to transfer the money. It involved downloading a particular cash app that neither Marcy nor Ted had ever heard of, let alone used.

"What are we going to do?" Ted asked. For the first time, he looked scared. That made two of them.

"I don't know," Marcy said. "I think we should go to the police."

"And tell them what? That we left the scene? Think about it, Marcy. We'd lose our jobs. Our careers would be over. I'd never coach again. Who would trust us around kids? We'd be pariahs."

"What if we paid?" Marcy asked.

"With what? Where are we supposed to get the money?"

Marcy didn't know. They still paying off Ted's student loans from college and grad school. There were credit card bills and a car loan. Debt, they had. Money, not so much.

Neither Marcy's family nor Ted's had money either. They'd paid for their own wedding a few years ago, a small affair at San Francisco's City Hall. They'd never taken a real honeymoon.

Finally, Ted said, "I might be able to borrow from someone at school."

"Who?"

"Maybe one of the basketball parents?" His students' parents were wealthy. The tuition was higher than at many colleges. Maybe Ted could borrow from a parent on the basketball team. Everyone loved him. He was their great white hope of getting the team to the playoffs.

"Well, you'd better do it soon," Marcy said. "We only have until Friday."

On Thursday, Marcy took a $3,000 cash advance from a credit card and deposited it into their joint checking account. Ted still hadn't done his part and gotten the rest of the money.

Time was running out. They had less than twenty-four hours.

The dinner party felt like another lifetime. They were a different Marcy and Ted now. She was no longer envious of Sam and her friends. In fact, Marcy would give anything to go back in time and be the couple she'd previously found so wanting.

Friday afternoon. Marcy paced their small apartment wondering where the hell Ted was. The banks were closing soon. She heard his key in the lock and looked at him expectantly when he came in.

"I got it." Ted looked pale, and sunken, unlike his usual athletic and confident self.

Marcy pulled out her phone and pulled up their banking app. The balance showed $25,873.59. They'd never had so much money. In few minutes, all of it would be gone.

Ted had downloaded the cash app and linked it to their bank account, but it took him a few tries to sign in. Marcy cursed at him under her breath. What if after all this trouble, Ted couldn't send the money because he'd forgotten the password?

When he finally logged in, entered the staggering amount of $25,000, and hit send, Marcy felt both relieved and nauseated. Ted got a beer out of the fridge and asked Marcy if she wanted one. How could he drink? They weren't celebrating. Had he forgotten that there was an actual person, a teenage girl, in the hospital fighting for her life?

She thought about this young woman constantly. What was she like? Was she an A student or an athlete? Did she play the flute or volleyball? She never told Ted how much time she spent thinking about her. He wouldn't understand.

By the following Monday, with no new emails, Marcy began to breathe easier. She could see a way that their lives could move on. They'd have to teach during the summers and take on extra jobs to pay back the debt, but they could do it. She'd take on freelance editing. Ted could do private coaching. They'd make it work.

Ted had gotten the car back from his mechanic, though he had to go into their overdraft to pay the repairs. Marcy didn't ask how much it was.

The next email came on Wednesday afternoon while Marcy was in the teachers' lounge. This time there was another newspaper clipping pasted into the body of the email.

HIT-AND-RUN DRIVER KILLS MILL VALLEY TEEN

The Mill Valley police are still seeking information about a fatal hit-and-run on Lucas Valley Road, Friday, April 6th at 1:30 a.m. A young woman, 17, whose name is being withheld at the request of family, died Tuesday of injuries sustained in the incident. The police urge anyone who may have heard or seen a light-colored car that night, possibly of German make and model, to come forward with any information.

Marcy started to heave as if she were going to vomit. She quickly signed out of her account and bolted to the bathroom.

She texted Ted. He'd gotten the email as well. Marcy left school, claiming she had a stomach bug.

Now they were felons. *No, he was a felon*, the voice inside her head told her. *You were just an accomplice.* Was that any better?

Marcy called in sick at work the next day as well. She couldn't eat. She hadn't slept. She and Ted had fought long into the night about what they should or shouldn't do. His position was that they do nothing. They'd already paid the money. "We paid our dues," he'd said, as if killing someone and paying the blackmail money was good enough. She thought they should get a lawyer and go to the police.

"Absolutely not," Ted said. They didn't have money for a lawyer.

Marcy curled in a fetal position and stayed in bed.

The next email demanded another $50,000 payable in two days.

The stakes have changed. Pay if you value your freedom.

"What are we going to do?" Ted asked. He was near tears.

Marcy could hardly move. She hadn't left their apartment, which, like their lives, had become a place of unspeakable dread.

What are you going to do, Ted? Marcy wanted to say out loud, but she didn't. She was just as guilty. Maybe a little less guilty than her husband, but she too had a role in a girl's death.

Suddenly, Ted looked up at her.

"You can ask Samantha," he said. "She and Jonah have tons of money. They can spare it."

"I couldn't do that." Marcy was horrified. "What would I tell her? I need to borrow money because we killed someone the night of your dinner party and fled the scene?"

"You can make up something. You're an English teacher. You'll think of something."

"I can't," Marcy insisted.

"You have to," Ted said. "There's no other way."

As much as she loathed the idea, Marcy didn't see any way out of asking Sam. She decided she'd make up a story about her mother needing money for cancer treatment. Marcy was disgusted with herself, but there was no other way.

Ted, meanwhile, was busy with work with long practices to get his team ready for an important game.

Marcy wished it was Ted who had the fictional cancer. Would she ask Sam for the money if it were him? *Probably not*, the voice told her.

Marcy didn't want to drive Ted's car to Marin, but her options for public transit (too long and not direct) or car service (too expensive) were limited.

To avoid passing the scene of the crime, Marcy asked Sam to meet her for lunch at a quiet café in downtown Mill Valley. Her treat.

But Marcy's phone pinged as she drove across the Golden Gate Bridge. It was Sam texting her to ask her to come to her house instead. She'd forgotten it was a half day at the twins' school and they'd invited friends over.

Marcy's hands were shaking when she drove past the scene of the accident. Irrationally, she felt as if she might be arrested enroute to Sam's house, and tried to take deep breaths and steady herself.

Marcy was dismayed to see Jonah's car in the driveway, an electric Porsche. She wanted to face her friend alone.

Sam's dogs barked when she rang the bell. Jonah opened the door and smiled when he saw her, pointing to the kitchen with one hand and holding his cell phone to his ear with the other.

Sam's house was a chaos of noise and family, a stark contrast to the sullen, tense air at Marcy's. Sam called from the kitchen, and Marcy passed through the large foyer and headed to the back of the house. The kitchen was Sam's domain: a bright cheery space, with a large marble island and shiny stainless-steel appliances.

Sam kissed her on both cheeks—she'd recently adopted this European greeting after her family had vacationed in France—and then poured them both large glasses of white wine.

Garden doors led from the kitchen to a patio and a heated kidney-shaped swimming pool. Music and teens' voices drifted into the kitchen. If only Marcy had married someone successful like Jonah. She could be living here instead of her foggy, cold apartment with Ted.

Marcy settled in at a kitchen stool, while Sam chatted and prepped a large salad with poached salmon. "Leftovers," Sam said, "nothing fancy."

Marcy silently compared the contents of her own refrigerator, with its rotting vegetables, then told herself to snap out of it.

"Shall we eat outside?" Sam asked, taking the plates and moving towards the patio. "We can sit away from the kids."

Marcy followed her out with her wine and the large salad bowl. She'd gulped her wine hoping it would give her courage to say what she needed. But it was getting harder by the minute. What was she thinking? How could she lie to her friend and ask her for money? *This is Ted's problem*, the voice in her head told her. *Let him deal with it.*

But she felt responsible, too. A girl was dead.

"You're so quiet today." Sam looked at her with concern. "Are you feeling okay?"

Marcy took a deep breath. "I need to ask you something."

Sam put her down her wineglass and yelled for her twins to turn down the music.

This was the last thing Marcy wanted. She was about to tell the story about her mother and the cancer and…she couldn't do it. Instead, Marcy told Sam the entire story, omitting the fact that she'd come to ask for money.

It was such an unexpected relief to share this burden.

Sam didn't interrupt. She listened and shook her head when Marcy said she was thinking of going to the police.

"She's not dead," Sam said.

"Who?"

"The girl you thought you hit. She's not dead. I would know."

"What do you mean? There's a video. Evidence. Emails. It was in the paper."

"It's a prank. I heard the twins talking about it."

"A prank?" Marcy bristled at the word.

Sam nodded. "There's this thing on social media. Some kind of dare. Kids park and pretend they've broken down. Then they wait for someone to show up. See who would stop. But then they started taking it further."

Marcy sat with her mouth open. Sam told her how the prank evolved. She'd heard the twins saying something about a sandbag and blackmail, but they clammed up when she'd asked them. She told them never to do something that stupid. They assured her they wouldn't, and, in the way of these things, Sam explained, she thought that was the end of the prank. Apparently not.

Ted and Marcy had walked—or driven—into a trap.

"But how did they know who we were? We didn't stop."

Sam shrugged. "License plate?" Her tone was maddeningly nonchalant.

Marcy's fear turned to relief, then anger. "Do you know who they are? We need to go to the police. They've made our lives a living hell."

"And what would you tell the police?" Sam asked. "That you and Ted thought you hit someone, but didn't report it even after you knew a girl was dead? You don't think that would ruin your careers? Both of you involved in a hit-and-run of a teen, even if it was a prank?"

Sam had a point. It was a perfect crime in many ways. She and Ted were the perfect victims. Even if it was a scam, who would trust her and Ted now? She'd never get another teaching job. Who would hire Ted to coach and mentor young players?

"I need to know who these kids are. We need to get our money back."

Sam called one of the twins, Chloe, over and told her to tell Marcy about the prank.

Chloe stood there in her tiny bikini, gooseflesh on her arms, twisting her long hair, and looking back towards her friends.

"I already told you." Chloe refused to meet either adult's eyes.

"Is it any of these kids?" Marcy motioned towards the pool and the half dozen teenagers now in the hot tub.

Chloe shook her head.

Sam called Aidan over next. He looked at his sister and shrugged his shoulders.

"Chloe knows them. I don't." Then he walked away to join his friends.

"Chloe, we're going to find out who's behind this prank." Marcy unsuccessfully tried to keep the anger out of her voice. "We could go to the police right now, but it would be better for all involved if you'd just tell us who these kids are."

Chloe's bottom lip quivered.

"Everyone will hate me. They'll know I told." She looked at her mother imploringly.

Sam stood up. "I'll get your father, and you can explain it to him."

"No wait." Chloe put her hand on her mother's arm.

She whispered two names, Sara and Milo. The names meant nothing to Marcy, but Sam nodded.

"Thank you, Chloe. You did the right thing."

Chloe took off as if she'd been sprung from prison.

Marcy drove home with a wave of emotions ricocheting through her. First relief that there was no dead teen. Then outrage at how she and Ted had been targeted. Then she felt another emotion that at first she couldn't identify. It felt…it felt like…possibility.

Marcy told Ted nothing of her conversation with Sam. Instead, she said that Sam and Jonah were facing financial hardships themselves and couldn't spare any money right now. Ted would just have to ask another parent for help.

Ted left the apartment without a word, slamming the door on his way out.

"I got the money," he hissed at Marcy later that night when he crawled into bed. Marcy rolled over and went back to sleep.

A week later, there were no additional requests from the blackmailers. Could this be the end of it?

Friday night, she and Ted were sitting on opposite ends of the sofa in the icy silence that had become their norm, watching TV when their buzzer rang.

A man identified himself as Detective Suarez and asked if he and his partner could come up and ask them a few questions. Marcy buzzed them in.

"What's this about?" Ted asked.

There were two detectives, both wearing suits. One blue, one brown. Suarez, the shorter detective introduced his partner as Phelps, and asked if they could chat.

Marcy offered them coffee. When they said yes, she went into the kitchen to make a pot.

"Don't you want to talk to her too?" Ted sounded confused.

"Let's start by asking you a few questions first," Suarez said.

From the kitchen, Marcy could hear Ted's voice getting louder and more emphatic.

She stayed in the kitchen long after the coffee had brewed, listening to Ted's denials, muffled through the kitchen wall.

When Marcy brought the tray with coffee into the living room, Ted was standing over his computer. The two detectives flanked him on either side, also looking down at his laptop screen.

But the emails were gone. Ted shook his head.

"They were right here. Marcy show them. You got them too."

Marcy took out her phone and scrolled. She shook her head. They weren't there. Ted checked his phone. He was telling them about the cash app they'd used to transfer the money. He couldn't find that either. It had been deleted.

Marcy wasn't surprised when the two detectives arrested Ted on suspicion of embezzlement. She had to force a look of concern on her face as they escorted her husband out of the apartment.

Embezzlement was a felony, punishable by up to three years in prison, Marcy knew.

Ted hadn't asked the students' parents for loans. He'd taken the money from the basketball team, and then raided the school's building improvement fund.

Marcy had a hunch where Ted had gotten the money. She'd checked his computer and made a phone call to the school. Then she met with the detectives and told them Ted would make up a story about a hit-and-run and being blackmailed. She assured them there was no such event.

Marcy had also tracked down the two blackmailing teens and used her scariest teacher tactics when she confronted them. She'd go to their parents. Then the principal. They'd be expelled. Any hope of getting into a good college would be ruined. Their reputations would be destroyed. She might even turn over her evidence to the police. How did a stint in Juvenile Hall sound?

Marcy got all but a few hundred dollars back. There was no point in returning the money to Ted's school without explaining how she got it. Anyway, she'd need some of it to divorce Ted. And when the money ran out, maybe she'd have another conversation with the blackmailers—or their parents.

And that feeling of possibility that had filled her when she'd driven home from Sam's? It had bloomed and was growing every day.

EDWARD LODI

Edward Lodi has written more than 30 books, including six Cranberry Country Mysteries. This is his third story in a Superior Shores Press anthology. He is a frequent contributor to *Mystery Magazine*. His short fiction has also appeared in anthologies published by Black Beacon Books, Cemetery Dance, Murderous Ink, Main Street Rag, Hungry Shadows Press, and Black Widow Press. Edward is a member of the Short Mystery Fiction Society. Find Edward at www.goodreads.com/author/show/275844. Edward_Lodi.

THE PURLOINED PARCHMENT
EDWARD LODI

Dr. Arnold shook his head. "I'm sorry you traveled all the way from Central Asia on a wild goose chase, Professor Chana. I wish I could help you, but there's nothing I can do." He tapped his fingertips against the desktop. "The Kayla Parchment legally belongs to the museum."

Professor Chana smiled. "And yet, I have proof that it does not." She held up a large manila envelope. "I will demonstrate that the parchment was stolen from our national archives sixty years ago. Whatever documents you may have, are forged. The real proof lies here."

"May I see what you have?"

"It would help if you could have the parchment brought in so that I can point out salient features. Is that possible?"

Dr. Arnold nodded. "It's the least I can do since you've come halfway around the world. This is the last time, I'm afraid, that anyone will be able to see the parchment for a long time to come. It will go back into storage next week." He took the phone from his desk and made the necessary call.

"It will arrive shortly, with two sets of gloves so that we may both handle it. You, Professor Chana, are much too young to have ever seen the original."

"Only photographs. It will have been worth my journey to hold the parchment in my hands, if only for a moment. The beauty, the delicacy, can only be truly appreciated when viewing the real thing."

"I agree. I myself saw it for the first time only when it went on public display last month." He again tapped nervous fingers on his desktop. "But where are my manners? Can I offer you a beverage? Tea? Coffee? Juice?"

Professor Chana smiled. Her plan to restore the painting to its rightful owners might yet succeed. What happened in the next few moments would determine the fate of the parchment, a tiny pastoral scene painted centuries ago by an unknown artist—a precious artifact of her people's cultural identity.

"Coffee please," she said, "but only if you join me."

"My pleasure." Dr. Arnold picked up the phone and made another call. "The coffee should arrive before the parchment, which is far too delicate to be exposed for long periods to the open air. We display all our fragile pieces in climate-controlled cases."

True to the curator's word, the coffee arrived within minutes, wheeled in on a cart by a young man, who promptly left.

The fate of the parchment is now in my hands, Dr. Chana thought. She surreptitiously removed a tiny vial from her purse while her host poured the coffee, stirring in cream and sugar.

They sipped their coffee, facing one another, the professor relaxed in her chair, as Dr. Arnold, behind his desk, relaxed in his. Professor Chana knew she had only moments to act; the parchment would arrive at any moment.

"Now, that's an interesting painting." She pointed to one of several pictures that hung on the wall behind Arnold's desk. "I don't believe I've ever seen anything quite like it."

As the curator swung his chair around to see which painting she referred to, she emptied the contents of the vial into his cup.

"The primitive cityscape? That's by an unknown artist."

Professor Chana listened politely as Dr. Arnold went on to

explain the painting's provenance and why he had selected it for his office.

"Please don't let your coffee grow cold," she said, when he concluded.

The curator obligingly brought the cup to his lips and drained it. At that moment there was a knock on the door, followed by a middle-aged woman carrying a storage box, which was roughly the size of the professor's manila envelope. She carefully handed the box to the curator, along with two pairs of soft white gloves. Dr. Arnold thanked the woman and she left.

Professor Chana rose from her chair. "Allow me to clear these cups from your desk so that no harm may come to the parchment." She carried the now empty coffee cups over to a glass-topped display table and dawdled a few moments before returning to her seat.

Dr. Arnold, who had politely waited, removed the lid from the box, and sheathing his hands with the gloves, gingerly lifted out the parchment. Professor Chana found herself trembling as she beheld the painting, a bucolic scene of sheep in a meadow and a shepherd asleep in the grass—and in the distance, the sinister approach of armed men on horses.

The colors seemed as vibrant as the day the painting had been completed. "May I?" She slipped on the gloves provided for her and took the parchment from the curator's hands.

"I feel guilty gloating over it," Dr. Arnold said, his words ever so slightly slurred. "It's a shame, you came all the way…" His voice trailed off.

"Believe me, it is I who should feel guilty, Dr. Arnold," Professor Chana replied.

"Such a long way…"

"Do you mind if I slip the parchment into my envelope for safe keeping?" she asked.

Dr. Arnold appeared not to hear.

She slid the parchment into the envelope, then removed the gloves and placed them on the desk, while Dr. Arnold stared vacantly. Having ascertained that he was positioned in the chair in such a manner that he could not fall and injure himself, she tucked the envelope under her arm and left the office, closing the door behind her.

She walked slowly through the museum, nodding to each of the guards she encountered along the way. Outside, she hailed a taxi, instructing the driver to take her directly to her hotel, located three blocks from the museum.

As she handed him the fare she requested, in an exaggerated accent, that he wait until she had safely entered the hotel before driving off, even though it was broad daylight, and they were in the city's safest neighborhood. "First time America," she explained. "Many gangsters, no?"

The driver shrugged but waited as requested.

In the lobby, she lingered at the reception desk, pretending to examine brochures, then walked slowly to the elevators. She rode up to the ninth floor and, again slowly, walked to her room. Pressing her key card against the electronic lock, she entered room 930.

It wasn't until midafternoon the following day that the professor heard a knock on her door.

"Who is it, please?"

"Police."

She peered through the peephole. Several forms crowded the hallway. She released the security latch and opened the door.

"Professor Anna Chana?" The man who asked the question wore a business suit. The woman standing next to him wore a police uniform.

She nodded. "May I ask what this is about?"

"Detective Marino." He presented his identification. "This is Detective Tsu. We have some questions we'd like to ask."

"Come in." Marino and Tsu entered. Three others, a woman and two men, remained in the hallway. "As you can see, I can offer only one of you a seat."

"We'll remain standing."

"Aren't the others coming in?"

"Not at the moment."

The questioning lasted half an hour. Detective Marino asked the questions. Tsu took notes. The questioning went something like this:

Yesterday morning, around 10:45, had the professor visited Dr. Lambert Arnold at the Museum of Folk Art?

She had.

During her visit, did the curator send for a rare painting on parchment for her to examine, a painting which she claims was stolen from her homeland?

He did. It was kind of him.

When she left the museum, did she take the parchment with her?

Of course not. That would be stealing. Legally, though not morally, the parchment belongs to the museum. Dr. Arnold would never allow such a thing.

Dr. Arnold claims the professor stole the parchment.

How could that be possible? He never left his office while Professor Chana was there. But wait. The poor man did seem, well, ill perhaps. That is to say, disoriented. Or perhaps he was simply tired from overwork. He seemed to have trouble keeping awake.

So, the professor denies having the parchment in her possession?

Of course. The professor is not a thief.

Why did the professor, traveling by herself, book two connecting rooms?

The transportation system in the professor's homeland is primitive. She spent a full day traveling under difficult conditions from her home to the airport, only to find her flight delayed. She spent an uncomfortable night in the airport lounge. She had to make several connections before finally arriving in America. She was exhausted. It was worth the extra money to book two connecting rooms, to ensure that she be able to rest in peace and quiet, with no noisy neighbors, to prepare for the long—very long— return journey home.

As Detective Marino was wrapping up his questioning a knock came at the door. Marino answered it and was handed an official document.

"Professor Chana, I have here a warrant to search your rooms."

Professor Chana smiled. "A warrant is not necessary. I would have granted you permission without it. Do you want me to leave while you conduct your search?"

"No, I want you to remain right where you are."

One of the individuals the professor saw standing in the hallway was the hotel manager. He now let the detective and uniformed officer who had been waiting with him in the hallway into room 932. The two teams searched the rooms simultaneously. The team searching room 932 was the first to complete their task. Detectives Marino and Tsu took longer, because their search entailed not only room 930 itself, but also the professor's luggage and clothing, as well as her person.

After hours spent taking the room—and many of Professor Chana's belongings—apart without result, Detective Tsu escorted her into the bathroom to make certain the purloined parchment was not somehow concealed under her clothing.

The body search proved fruitless. Finally, the searchers left, Detective Marino first having instructed Professor Chana not to leave the city, and to make her whereabouts known at all times.

The manager phoned from downstairs and offered to move the professor to another room, since those she'd engaged were in total disarray. She thanked him for his consideration but assured him she could make do where she was. She then ordered a full-course meal with a bottle of wine from room service. She spent the evening watching television. Around ten she made up the torn-apart bed as best she could and fell into a peaceful sleep.

THREE WEEKS later Detective Anthony Marino and his partner, Detective Cheryl Tsu, were explaining the case to their colleague, Detective Roberto Gonsalvez, over drinks in The Second Chance Saloon.

"Arnold claims to have no memory of what happened after the parchment was brought to his office," Tsu said. "Tony thinks she slipped some kind of date drug into his coffee, and I agree."

"Unfortunately, there's no way to verify she used a drug," Marino added. "Arnold's assistant removed the cups and washed them while his boss was still confused and unaware that the parchment had gone missing."

Gonsalvez studied the head on his ale before bringing the glass to his lips and downing half its contents. "Ah, nothing like a hoppy IPA to sharpen the wits." He wiped away the foam mustache with his finger, pondering the problem.

"Let me get this straight," he said after a few minutes. "Security cameras show this professor entering the museum carrying a manila folder. An hour and ten minutes later she leaves the museum with the same envelope, and nothing else. The temperature that day was in the eighties. She wore a blouse and a short skirt. If she carried out the parchment, it would have to have been in the envelope."

"We figured she might have hidden the parchment somewhere in the museum with the intention of having someone retrieve it later," Marino said. "But we don't see how she could have. Three guards remember her walking casually through the museum. One actually saw her leave the curator's office. Nothing on camera. The museum staff also made a thorough search. Nada."

Tsu eyed Gonsalvez's IPA with distaste. "How can you drink that stuff?" She took a sip of her gin and tonic and sighed. "Now *that's* refreshing. Anyhow, getting back to our impossible crime. The video feed from the cameras shows her leaving the museum. She remained at the front of the museum, without speaking to anyone, and hailed a taxi—even though her hotel is a short walk from the museum and the weather was fine. She got into the taxi. The driver—a Haitian immigrant who's been in the States ten years and has a clean record, not even a traffic ticket—swears he took her directly to her hotel."

Tsu paused to take another sip of her drink. "Now this part is interesting. She makes a point of having him wait until she enters the hotel lobby. Like she was setting up an alibi."

"Like she's taunting us, ahead of time," Marino said.

"She goes into the lobby," Tsu continued, "kills time at the desk, gets into the elevator, and goes to her room. Surveillance cameras show that she met no one on the way to whom she could have passed the parchment. The hotel has a state of the art security system. Their computer keeps a record of every time a room key is used. Hers was used just that once. She never left the room until we searched it. She ordered from room service. She declined housekeeping. No one else entered or left either of the two rooms."

"She claimed she rented two rooms because she was tired and wanted absolute quiet?" asked Gonsalvez.

Tsu nodded.

"Connecting rooms?"

"Yes."

"And you each searched a room?"

"With experienced uniforms who are pros at it."

"You entered both rooms from the hallway?"

Marino nodded. "Just in case an accomplice was hiding in the spare room. I also wanted to keep an eye on her at all times."

"Where is Chana now?"

"Back in her homeland. We tried to keep her in the States, but her embassy intervened. We didn't have any probable cause to detain her. Only the curator's word, and even he's not sure what happened."

Gonsalvez finished his ale. "I think I know where the parchment is."

"Where?" Tsu asked.

"In Central Asia. I'd bet my pension she took it with her on her flight home. Another round? Or would you rather have me show you where she hid it?"

THE HOTEL MANAGER on duty that evening let the detectives into room 930, which was currently unoccupied. "I'm afraid 932 is taken," she apologized.

"No problem," Gonsalvez said. "This room will do."

When the manager left Marino said: "Gonzo, you're wasting our time. If the parchment was in either of the two rooms—930 or 932—Cheryl or I would have found it."

"I agree. You guys are thorough. The trouble is, it wasn't in either room."

Tsu frowned. "What are you talking about?"

"This." Gonsalvez pointed to the door in the middle of the wall which connected to room 932. "If I understand correctly, you never opened this door during your search."

"No reason to," Marino said. "Both rooms were thoroughly searched by us and our team, nothing left unturned or untouched."

Gonsalvez unlatched the door and swung it open.

"There's another door behind it," Tsu said, surprised.

"Yes, double doors, back-to-back. For privacy. When two hotel rooms connect, each has its own door. You open your door, then knock on the other one for someone to open it. Say, for example, that a couple has one room, and their kids have the other. They might not want the kids walking in on them, you know?"

Marino groaned. "The space…she hid the parchment in the space between the two doors. There's just enough room."

Gonsalvez examined the door he'd opened. "She taped the manila envelope here, on the inside. See the marks, the tiny bit of adhesive residue? She took a gamble you wouldn't open the adjoining doors. A gamble that paid off."

"I guess we should be philosophical," Tsu said. "Work this job long enough, you see everything,"

"And sometimes," Marino said ruefully, "you don't see anything at all."

WENDY HARRISON

Wendy Harrison is a retired prosecutor who turned to short mystery fiction during the pandemic. Her stories have been published in numerous anthologies. After Hurricane Ian destroyed her home in Florida, she moved to the Pacific Northwest. When she isn't writing, she is weaving, reading, or walking the steep hills around her new home. She is grateful to have traded devastating hurricanes for potential wildfires, volcanoes, and earthquakes. Wendy is a member of Sisters in Crime (SinC) national, SinC chapters Columbia River, Guppies, and Desert Sleuths, and the Short Mystery Fiction Society. Find Wendy at www.wendyharrisonwriter.com.

RED INK

WENDY HARRISON

Tattooing is an intimate art.

It requires close proximity to strangers as you penetrate the skin that holds them together. You may never see them again, but they will carry a permanent mark of your own creation. Those of us who take our profession seriously respect the trust these strangers put in our hands. We are artists.

The Tattoo Studio in downtown Portland was my greatest achievement. Keeping it alive during the pandemic had taken every cent I had, but business was slowly picking up. At my age, on top of worrying about paying the bills, I was facing a future of hands and arms that would no longer tolerate the abuse of the vibrating tattoo machine. I lived with constant pain. Ibuprofen helped at first, but when I found my work deteriorating, I switched to oxy, sometimes trading my tattoo services to keep a supply on hand. I knew where this road would end, probably sooner rather than later. Without being able to work, I'd end up in a doorway on Commercial Street.

When I arrived at the studio the morning that changed everything, I performed my usual inspection to make sure there was no graffiti on the outside walls or windows and no trash to clean up.

Satisfied no damage had been done overnight, I turned the key to open each of the three locks and stepped inside.

I still felt a rush of joy, getting to spend my days here. The walls were covered with framed flash, my own tattoo designs. Up front was a counter which served as my desk and drawing table. Behind it, a tattoo client chair was placed in front of shelves holding supplies, an autoclave, and a stencil paper machine. A sink was off to the side. I worked alone there. Coping with my own eccentricities was hard enough without another artistic temperament in the room.

I turned on the lights and spotted an envelope on the floor under the door's mail slot. My stomach clenched when I read the return address. It was from the real estate company that owned the building. I tore it open, knowing what it was going to say. I saw the words "end of lease term" and "increase," followed by a number that doubled my current rent. Life in that doorway just became a real possibility.

I tossed the letter into the wastebasket. Nothing I could do about it. It was time to check the schedule and pretend this was just another day.

Clients booked ahead, sometimes months in advance. A tattoo from me was a three-step process. First, we discussed what they had in mind so I could make alternative suggestions when they asked for the impossible. Next, I created the design, and finally they returned to get the work done. My specialty was tackling the big tattoos, the full sleeves covering the arms, back pieces filling the area from the waist to the shoulders. That was where the fun was. Unfortunately, it was also where my pain was at its worst.

The buzzer on the front door sounded as it opened. I looked up. It was too early for my first client.

"Hey, Kate."

I kept my face expressionless. "Good morning, Clay. I don't see you on the schedule." So much for the good day I hoped for. The gods were screwing with me.

Clay Duncan, the stereotype of a hedge fund bro, was dressed in his usual uniform. Armani shirt, no tie, pressed khaki pants that cost more than my entire wardrobe, and Italian leather loafers. He strode to the front counter and gently dropped his messenger bag, which also cost more than my wardrobe. I heard a clink.

"I need you to work on something for me." Clay opened the leather bag and pulled out a bottle of champagne. Without hesitating, he walked past me to sit uninvited on the adjustable tattoo chair.

I'd warned Clay again and again that alcohol was a bad fit with getting a tattoo. It thinned the blood, causing more bleeding and slower healing. He didn't care. He brought an expensive bottle of champagne with him each time to celebrate his bravery, I guess, or overcome his fear. Maybe a combination of both.

He never asked me to join him. Of course, I wouldn't have anyway. A tattooist under the influence would be all right for a *Saturday Night Live* skit. Not so much in real life. Although I would've been happy to share the bubbly after the work was done, he always took the half-full bottle with him when he left. Cheapskate.

In the past couple of years, I'd created elaborate tattoos on Clay's back and arms, always charging top-tier prices. He'd bragged about them to his friends, which meant more business for me. Money was the only reason I kept him as a client. His sense of entitlement grated on my nerves, not to mention the way he treated me like the not-very-bright hired help. I was able to tolerate him by slipping in an occasional dig that his ego managed to construe as a compliment. But at this moment, I just didn't have it in me to deal with him.

"I'm booked solid for the next month. I'm afraid you'll have to wait."

He looked like a child whose favorite toy had been snatched by his best friend.

"You don't understand. Kate, this is urgent."

He looked sincere but, seriously, a tattoo emergency?

"Should I call 911?"

My attempt at humor missed its target.

"I can't explain, but it's important to me. Very important. See?" He held up the bottle. "I brought the Dom. I'll even leave some of it for you."

I wasn't surprised he'd assume that if the tattoo was important to him, it would be important to me as well. I shook my head. "Sorry. It wouldn't be fair to everyone who's been waiting their turn."

I watched him close his eyes and take three deep breaths, letting each one out slowly. His therapist—of course he had a therapist—must have taught him that self-calming trick.

He opened his eyes and stared at me. I watched him weigh the pros and cons of confiding his secret. I thought about telling him tattoo artist confidentiality would protect our conversation, but I was afraid he might believe me. Finally, he decided.

"Okay. I'll tell you. But you can't tell anyone."

It was an easy promise to make. Who would I tell?

"I won't tell anyone. What's going on?"

He began by explaining bitcoin to me. I let him ramble on as he assumed I wasn't the kind of person who would know about bitcoin. He happened to be wrong. I was aware of it but found it inexplicable. As far as I could tell, it was make-believe money that somehow made a lot of people rich. My mind wandered until I realized he was saying something interesting.

"The key is the password. You make one up for your bitcoin account. No one, I mean no one, can get access to the password. Anyone who tries to get into the account gets ten tries before the account is locked and gone forever."

"What if the owner forgets the password?"

His leg began to jiggle. "He's out of luck. Millions, maybe billions of bitcoin dollars are lost by idiots who can't remember their password."

I needed to chew on it for a minute. Who wouldn't put the password in a safe place? It seemed bizarre to me.

He kept talking. "See, when bitcoin first started up, no one was sure it would work. People bought it mostly for fun. For bragging rights."

He would know about that.

"They had no idea that years later, it would be so valuable.

When it happened, they started trying to get into their accounts and couldn't. Huge fortunes have been lost."

I tried to muster sympathy for the wannabe millionaires but came up short. "Is that what happened to you? What's it got to do with getting a tattoo?"

Before he could answer, I got it. "You want your password tattooed so you can never lose it."

I understood his frown. How could someone like me figure out his plan? Maybe he wasn't so smart after all.

"I'll pay you double if you do it today."

I shook my head.

"Triple," he said.

"It's not the money. I have to make the design first. And I have people coming in for their appointments all day." He looked as if he was going to cry. I was almost starting to feel sorry for him. "I'll tell you what. Come back tonight, and let's see how far we can get." I held up my hand to stop his objections. "It's the best I can do. Tell me, what's the big hurry?"

I watched him trying to decide how much to say. "I can't risk anyone getting hold of the password."

"How about a safe deposit box?" Seemed to me to be the ideal answer.

"Not if they get a search warrant."

They? What had hedge fund dude gotten himself into? Before I could go down this intriguing path, he jumped up. "That's all I'm going to say. I'll see you after closing?"

"See you at seven."

As the door shut behind him, I noticed the bottle of champagne he had left behind. I picked up my cellphone and began to call the clients on my schedule. I told them I wasn't feeling well and would have to rebook. When they were nice about it, I felt a twinge of guilt, but the devil on my shoulder insisted on whispering the details of a plan in my left ear. His competition, the angel on the right, didn't stand a chance.

It surprised me I found it so easy to figure out a way to steal Clay's bitcoin account. I hardly recognized the desperate person I'd become. I told myself I wouldn't go through with it. It was just a game I'd play for the day.

I lied.

When Clay returned on the dot of seven, I was ready. As he walked through the door, I could see he was even more jittery than he had been that morning. He held out a piece of paper. "Here it is."

I tried to take it but he wouldn't let go.

"If you don't give it to me, we're not going to be able to do this. How about if I open the bubbly and you have a drink before I start drawing?"

He pulled his hand back with the paper in it. "I hope you kept it on ice."

I nodded. "I'll open it and get the glass."

Since it was the way we usually started our sessions, he seemed more comfortable. He sat on the tattoo chair. I had lowered the back and raised the foot section. I could adjust the chair after he told me where he wanted the tattoo.

I went into the bathroom where I had left the bottle and removed the wire cage over the cork. As I wrapped a towel over the top of the bottle, I held tightly to the cork and slowly twisted with my other hand. The cork came off with a satisfying pop that I was sure Clay could hear. I took the glass I had prepared and stared at it. I could still turn back.

"What's taking so long?"

His voice was whiny. I took it as a sign and filled the glass. I had to hope the taste of the drink would mask the crushed oxycodone I'd put in it.

When I brought the drink to him, Clay swapped it for the piece of paper. "Nothing fancy. Make sure you copy it exactly the way it looks except it needs to be a mirror image."

"A mirror image?" I wanted to be sure I understood what he said.

His tone suggested I was too dumb to understand. "So if anyone did figure out what it meant, it still wouldn't do them any good. Get it? If anyone asks, I can say it's based on an old hieroglyphic."

The champagne was definitely relaxing him. He actually winked at me.

"Where do you want it?"

"I figure it can go on the top of my thigh." I tried to block the mental image of some poor woman who would find herself in a position to see the tattoo.

I sat at my desk and pulled out a sheet of stencil paper. I held the password up to a mirror and began to draw. There were 20 characters, a mixture of letters, numbers, and symbols. I enjoyed the challenge of drawing each of them backwards. I took my time, and when the glass fell out of his hand, I went to check on him. He was out.

Moving quickly, I pulled his cellphone out of the case attached to his belt. When I woke it up, it asked for a fingertip ID. Raising his limp hand, I used his forefinger. I searched for the bitcoin app on the home screen. When the password request appeared, I carefully typed in the password and then held my breath. It worked. I had access to his account. Current value: $2,543,069.23. I looked for the withdrawal option. Should I take it all? Was that too greedy? Who could he complain to? If he was worried about search warrants, it meant this money was illegal in one way or another.

With shaking hands, I transferred $1,500,000 into the bitcoin account I had set up during my busy afternoon. It seemed reasonable. I could live on it for the rest of my life in the small town in Mexico I had discovered on the internet. I hoped leaving a substantial balance in Clay's bitcoin account would make it less likely that he'd come after me.

With that done, I turned to wake Clay. I planned to go ahead with the tattoo so he wouldn't be suspicious. I shook him but he didn't respond. Pinching, slapping, nothing worked. I checked to see if he was breathing. Barely. His arms dangled off the sides of the chair. I started to panic.

A tapping on the door made my own heart stop for a moment. I looked over and saw Anna Harper, the neighborhood beat cop, knocking on the glass. I ran to the door. Fumbling with the locks, I managed to open it.

"You're not usually here so late," she said. "I thought I'd better check on you."

"You're just in time. I was about to call 911." I knew I sounded hysterical. No acting was required.

"What's wrong?" She stepped toward me. "Are you hurt?"

The debate in my head was playing out at hyper-speed. If I told her my client had overdosed, she'd pull out Narcan and possibly revive him. If I didn't, he could die. If he lived to figure out what had happened, I was toast. Was I willing to spend my remaining years in a cell?

"I'm okay. It's my client. He had a heart attack." I waited to see if I'd be struck by lightning for my sins, but the gods must have taken the day off.

I led Anna to the client chair where Clay was sprawled. The champagne glass he had dropped was partially under the chair. I nudged it with my shoe, and it rolled out of sight.

"He grabbed his chest and fell back," I said. "We hadn't even started on the tattoo."

Anna checked him for a pulse and then spoke into the radio on her shoulder.

"I need an ambulance STAT at The Tattoo Shop. White male, suspected heart attack. Thready pulse."

She turned to me. "Do you know if he has a history of heart problems?"

I pretended to think about the question. "He did mention something about a family history of bad hearts when I tattooed him before. He bragged about how he worked out a lot so he could beat the odds."

I realized my hands were shaking and started to sway. Anna grabbed me and led me to my desk chair. "Here, sit. There's nothing we can do until the EMTs get here."

"This is terrible. Can't you do CPR? Anything?" That's what I said out loud, silently hoping the answer would be no.

Anna shook her head. "Not if he's still breathing. I'm sure they'll be here soon."

We waited in silence, both of us watching his chest barely rising and falling. There was still time for me to tell her the truth, but I couldn't bring myself to do it.

The door opened, and two EMTs came through with a stretcher. Anna explained what happened. I watched as they checked Clay's vitals, moved him smoothly onto the stretcher, and headed out.

"Nothing you could've done," Anna said. "Maybe he'll make it."

I nodded. If he did, my own life might be over, but I couldn't tell her that. "I hope so."

When Anna left, I gathered Clay's belongings. His phone, his messenger bag, the bottle of champagne, and the glass. I decided to take it all and decide what to do with it later. I couldn't trust myself to make decisions at the moment. The one I had already made terrified me.

I looked around the space I had created and nurtured. My only regret was leaving it all behind, but I knew that if I hadn't taken this chance, I would've lost it all anyway. It was time to move on.

Back at my apartment, I began to pack the two large suitcases I had bought earlier in the day. I didn't have a problem fitting everything in. My wardrobe had always been small, and I wasn't one for accumulating anything that didn't relate to my work. I tried to push away the memory of Clay's arm, hanging lifelessly over the side of the tattoo chair.

I had arranged to have a car pick me up to take me to the airport at 8 a.m the next day. It was no more than a half-hour ride, and it would give me plenty of time to go through TSA before my 11 o'clock flight to Mexico. I was looking forward to flying first class for the only time in my life, then felt consumed with guilt at the reason I had the opportunity.

I awoke to the alarm I had set for 6 a.m. It took a moment for me to remember that what happened with Clay wasn't a nightmare, but real. I knew that given the chance, I wouldn't change the desperate choices I had made.

I stumbled into the bathroom and finished my usual morning

routine. Brush my teeth, shower, finger comb my short graying hair. I was buttoning my shirt when I heard a knocking at the door. I knew at once what would come next.

"Police!"

In that moment, I thought my life had ended. "THE END" would make an appropriate final tattoo. But here's what did happen.

When I opened the door, Anna was there with a tall, heavyset man in a cheap suit.

"Hi, Kate. This is Detective Graziano. He has some questions for you about Clay Duncan."

"Is he all right?" I wasn't sure what answer I wanted to hear.

"Can we come in?" The detective moved past me without waiting. I hoped it was his personality and not a sign he was already hostile.

Anna shrugged and winked at me. "We won't be long."

They sat on the living room couch, while I took the recliner. Thankfully, the suitcases were safely behind the closed bedroom door. I didn't want to have to explain them.

The detective paid close attention as I described what happened. Clay was a repeat client. As a favor, I stayed late to do a new tattoo but, before I could start, he had a heart attack.

"Did he seem to be under the influence?"

I thought about the bottle of champagne and glass in my trash can under the sink.

"Not that I could tell. He was always nervous about being tattooed, so he might've taken something for the jitters. If he had been drunk, I wouldn't have gone ahead with a tattoo."

The detective didn't say anything.

"How is he?" I asked again.

Anna answered, ignoring the look the detective gave her to put her in her beat cop place. "He's doing okay. It turned out it wasn't a heart attack. They did a tox screen, and it came up positive for alcohol and oxycontin."

I tried not to overdo a look of shock. "No kidding. I had no idea."

"He says he doesn't remember a thing. Not surprising, considering what he had in his system. He also didn't have any new tattoos."

"I didn't get a chance. He passed out before we started. At first, I thought the nerves got to him. But I couldn't get him to wake up. Lucky Anna came along when she did."

We sat in silence until the detective stood, followed by Anna. He looked bored. "If you think of anything else, give me a call." He pulled a business card out of his jacket pocket.

"Of course. I hope he's okay."

Every inch of me was shaking as I shut the door behind them. What would Clay do when he realized half his Bitcoin account was missing? If I stayed and his memory came back, he'd figure it out and come after me for the money. If I told him I didn't know what he was talking about, what could he do? Call the cops? Not if the money was dirty, as I suspected. I thought for a second of the shop and everything I would be leaving behind.

Should I flip a coin to decide? Not a Bitcoin, of course. They weren't real.

My phone rang. "Kate Gordon? I'm your airport car service. I'm waiting in front of the building. Do you need help with your bags?"

I didn't hesitate. "I'm good. I'll be down shortly."

I doublechecked my large purse to be sure I had my ticket, boarding pass, passport, and the small slip of paper that held my shiny new Bitcoin account password. I would find a safe place for it, even though I didn't need one. The last thing I had done before leaving the shop was to tattoo it, mirror image, on my upper right thigh. I was good to go.

KEVIN R. TIPPLE

Kevin R. Tipple reviews books, watches way too much television, and offers unsolicited opinions on anything. His short fiction has appeared in magazines and ezines, including *Lynx Eye*, *Starblade*, *Show and Tell*, *The Writer's Post Journal*, and *Mystery Magazine*. Anthology appearances include *The Carpathian Shadows: Vol. 2*, *Back Road Bobby and His Friends*, *Crimeucopia: Strictly Off The Record*, and *Crimeucopia: Say It Again*. He is a member of the Mystery Writers of America and the Short Mystery Fiction Society. Find Kevin at https://kevintipplescorner.blogspot.com/.

THE HOSPITAL BOOMERANG

KEVIN R. TIPPLE

It was the damn beeping that woke me up. I opened my eyes, only to see the same crappy tile overhead that I had seen once before. A heart monitor and an IV drip machine beeped. I looked down my bed. Neither wrist was handcuffed to the rail of the bed. An improvement over my last visit.

The pain in my stomach was not an improvement. Neither was the pain that ripped through me when I moved my legs.

"Damn."

The door swung open and a man in nursing scrubs bustled in and checked the IVs. That done, he swung his attention to me.

"How are we feeling?"

"Like total crap."

"Yep. Gunshot wounds will do that to you. The real world ain't TV where somebody is just fine and can do whatever for hours on end."

I tried to shift in the bed as my back was not helping anything. A new wave of pain made me grunt.

"You have a pain pump for the next day or two."

He fiddled underneath the sheet with something and pressed the plunger into my hand. I could hardly think, I hurt so bad.

"Go ahead and give it a squeeze if you need some medication. It's all set up and won't give you too much."

I squeezed it. Hard.

He smiled. "You can hold that thing down all you want, but it won't give you any more."

"Damn."

"I hear you. Just relax and it will kick in pretty soon. I'll have Tina come around and get your vitals in a few minutes. Hang tight."

As if I could do anything else.

I glanced around for a minute. Pretty sure it was the same room as the last time, but the male nurse was new.

The first time I'd been here was about a decade ago. I'd gotten the bright idea to swipe the charity donation jar at Mike's Convenience Store. Mike's place was legendary in our small Texas town and the only place to get gas, bread, booze, and a few other things for at least fifty miles. Mike had passed away quite a few years ago and now his son, Phil, ran the place. He was pretty much a one-man band and was fairly lousy at it. I was pretty sure he only kept the convenience store open to smoke, talk to his redneck buddies, drink beer, and look at girlie mags.

Walking into the place meant you got a lungful of smoke. Often you got an unwanted earful of politics as well. If you were not the right skin color, you were quickly encouraged to take your business elsewhere. That would be a long drive. Phil didn't care, any more than his dad had before him.

The grimy counter held donation jars for every cause known to mankind. That night when I got stupid, I had counted ten donation jars of various sizes, each having its own urgent plea for help. Couple of locals dealing with cancer. The Baptist Church needed a new roof as God had done nothing to protect it from the hailstorm that roared through a few months earlier. The local scout troops, both genders, needed new gear for something or other and wanted money as they could not sell candy now without the mandatory county and state permits. Several more donation jars were scattered behind the front runners.

Off to the side was one that claimed to be raising funds to save the Texas Iguanas. I was pretty sure we did not have any such thing. Florida had them. You hear about them every winter when they got cold down there and fell out of trees. Never hear about that crap happening here. So, I was pretty sure there was no such thing.

I had a few before going into the store as Darlene and I had been fighting earlier. Again. She'd taken the kids to her mother's place in Tyler. Again. Which meant I was on my own, and probably destined to be that way permanently in the foreseeable future with Darlene threatening divorce. Again.

I was also broke, part of the reason for the latest fight, though not the only reason. Living at my mom's was not the future Darlene had expected, but that was our future after I got her pregnant in the backseat of my Chevy Nova a dozen years earlier.

Back then, at least the plant had been open, and I had a steady job. That went away, then did the Dairy Queen, and a few other things, including the Bowling Alley where I had been working part-time cleaning up puke and sweeping floors. So yeah, jobs were scarce. Plus, Mom was going downhill and losing all her marbles. There was no way I could leave and start over somewhere else. Darlene should have understood that.

I'd been standing there, eyeballing the fairly full Texas Iguana jar, when the team bus from nearby Jackson High came rolling in and parked out by the pumps. A bunch of kids in their uniforms came off the bus and began milling around the store. Seemed the basketball team had pulled off the upset and the kids were very pumped.

Phil was soon yelling at them to behave because two of the boys started flinging Pringles cans like they were footballs. Several more were clustered back by the beer coolers, no doubt trying to swipe a few, as their coach wandered back there. I looked around and saw confusion everywhere. Then Phil slipped off his stool, pushed by me, and headed to the back and the beer coolers.

I saw my chance and stupidly took it. I knew I needed that Texas Iguana money a lot more than the damn lizards, *if* they even existed.

I needed that and the case of beer under my arm more than anything. I grabbed the jar and lit out for the door.

Getting outside was no problem. I never was any good at running and weighed down by the case of beer and the donation jar, I was even slower. I'd made it just past the pumps where some woman, might have been Mrs. Douglas, stood and filmed me with her cellphone as I crashed to the concrete pad in the drive.

I struggled to get up and then Phil was on me. Took two punches to my face as he cursed me and then he slammed my head to the concrete. I don't remember anything after that.

I learned later that several cellphone cameras caught Phil bouncing my head off the driveway before he stood up and started drop kicking me in the ribs until one of the high school kids stopped him. The man probably would have killed me.

I spent a couple of weeks in the hospital with a concussion and broken ribs and other issues. When I got out, I went straight to jail. Spent quite some time there awaiting trial. Got tried and convicted by a jury of my alleged peers.

Sentenced for ten months, being a first offense and all, I soon wound up doing three years plus because of incidents in the jail. I took everything personally and had the scars to show for it. Those many months in solitary meant I was somewhat safer.

I was still thinking about Darlene, the divorce, and all the rest of it when I drifted off to sleep.

When I next woke up, Deputy Rick Wilson was in the visitor chair. He was also sound asleep. Just like he always was back in high school.

We'd been in the same fifth period English class that was boring as all get out. Rick worked his parent's farm every day starting around four in the morning, then went straight back there after school, working until things were done, sometime past dark. No choice, even if he'd wanted one. His dad had a useless right arm, courtesy of Uncle Sam, and his mom was not physically up to doing much. Rick and his younger brother, Todd, did the work of three men, maybe more.

All this to say that Rick and I never were friends, but we got along okay. After I got out of my forced incarceration, he had come by the house a few times to check in on me. He claimed it was because we went back, but he always did it in full uniform, driving a county cruiser. To me, it felt like a probation check, and I had enough of those as it was.

A nurse came in pushing a blood pressure deal on wheels. The previously mentioned Tina, I expected. She bumped Rick's chair and woke him up. He swung his long legs out of her way as she checked my stats. She wasn't particularly friendly, but the clock indicated just after three in the morning, so it was probably the hour more than anything.

Eventually, she finished up and left, leaving me and Rick staring at each other.

"How are you feeling?"

"Like crap."

"Willing to talk a little while?" He saw something in my face and added, "Don't worry, you are in the clear. We will do a formal statement later with your attorney. I'm just looking to have a conversation."

I wasn't interested in having one. After a minute or two of silence on my part, Rick tried again. "Why were you in The Tavern?"

"I was hungry."

"You aren't supposed to be there. It is a bar. They sell booze."

"So what?"

"It's a probation violation."

"Come on, man. You know it's the only place around that sells food. I can't go back to Mike's. I just wanted a burger and rings. I was gonna eat and go home. I just wanted a little time in the real world, like things were normal, and that was all I was going to do. I wasn't drinking."

"Not for nothing, but you apparently weren't there long enough to get a drink on."

"I know."

"Besides, just being in a bar could get you locked up."

It had been stupid and we both knew it. But, I'd just checked in with probation and really had just wanted to feel normal again. Being out this past month had been tough with the sideways looks and all. Darlene and the kids long gone. My mom dying while I was inside sure didn't help my mental state at all, the old house full of memories, good and bad.

"So, what happened?" Rick asked.

I shifted in the bed and felt my stomach twist and burn. I gasped, and that made me start coughing. Rick got up and grabbed the tumbler of water, pivoted and held it in front of me, making sure to put the straw in my mouth. I lay there and let him hold it while I took several swallows. Eventually he pulled it away, set it back on the rolling tray, and went back to the chair.

"Thanks." I coughed, then, "I walked in, and the place was almost deserted. Old man Leroy was at one end of the bar—"

"His stool by the bathrooms?"

"Yeah. He was just sitting there staring into his drink like he always does."

"Long way from running us ragged when he was our high school principal."

"Yep. Boinking Mary was a career ender. Gotta admit though, when she was in her cheerleader outfit, she rocked my world."

Rick laughed and said, "You ain't lying. She was something."

He shook his head and sobered up.

"Okay, so you walked in there, the place was pretty empty, and you saw Leroy at the end in his usual spot. What else did you see?"

"You know how slick that floor is, so I had my head down and was watching my step. I was almost at the bar when I realized Jessica had a problem."

I took a minute to think about everything.

Rick waited.

"Some guy had Jessica by her hair, half pulled over the bar counter. He had his gun upside her head. He kept screaming at her to give him the money. She had her hands up against the bar and there was no way she could get to the register even if she wanted to and she didn't."

"How do you know?"

"She kept telling him to eff off."

"Really?"

"Yep. You know how she is."

"When your parents are bikers and rode with the Angels and the Demons back in the day, it sticks with you."

I shifted in the bed feeling everything hurt. It took me a minute to get myself back together and focus on Rick.

Rick focused on me right back. "So…"

"So, she wasn't going to give him the money. They were yelling, she was trying to push herself off the bar, and he kept damn near pulling her over the bar. He finally noticed me, cussed me out a bit as he pointed the gun at me, and then swung it back at her."

"That when you jumped him?"

I shook my head. "Jessica had managed to get free. He slipped on the floor, fired and missed her head, and took out the mirror behind the bar. I jumped forward, slammed him into the bar, tried to get the gun."

"That was stupid."

The alarm on the IV started screaming and we both stopped talking. Eventually, a nurse walked in, looked at both of us, hit a couple of buttons, and stopped the alarm. She went out as silently as she had walked into the room.

"Maybe. Probably. But I thought he was going to kill her."

Rick sighed and said, "There is that."

I nodded and went on with the version he was going to get. "We wrestled for the gun and he shot me. Jessica leaned over the bar and smashed him in the head with a bottle. He let go of the gun. I grabbed it and emptied it into him. The end."

Rick looked at me for a long moment. I wasn't sure he fully believed me, but that was my story and I was sticking with it.

"You know you killed him."

"I figured."

I had managed to shoot him twice before he hit the floor. By that point, I was done and had gone down. I had a hazy memory of Leroy leaning over me and taking the gun out of my hand. There was a bang and then I felt the gun back in my hand before the world went dark.

"That all of it?"

"Pretty much. I don't remember anything else until I woke up here."

"Yep, getting gut shot will take it out of you." Rick stood up, put his Stetson back on his head, and looked down at me. "Hell of a thing."

"Jessica okay?"

"She's fine. She had the bar open the next day. Leroy was glad to see that, I tell you."

I started to laugh, and the pain stopped that quick. I gasped and coughed and waved off his offer of more water. The stuff had tasted like a swimming pool.

"When you are feeling better and out of here, come down to the station and give a statement. Bring your attorney and we'll make it all official. I think that new hotshot DA is going to want to have it reviewed by the grand jury, but the town sentiment is that you are some kind of hero."

"Who was the guy?"

"Some drifter. The U.S. Marshals were chasing him and not telling anyone he was raping and robbing across the southern states. They figure he was escalating and would have killed you and Leroy and then done what he wanted with Jessica. Probably dumped what was left of her somewhere to never be found."

"Damn."

"The Marshals told her to be quiet, but she told everyone in town and got folks stirred up. There have been news crews here all week. We even got the national talking heads here. Been something."

"Huh."

"Yep. Get some rest."

He started toward the door and then turned back. Tipped his hat in my direction. "You won't believe it, but Phil started a donation jar for you. He took all the other jars off the counter and set you up front and center. He has been strongly encouraging folks to donate when he isn't going off on the godless criminals running roughshod over our God-given way of life. He says it already has over a grand in it."

As he walked out, it hurt way too much to laugh.

But I did manage to snort.

KATE FELLOWES

Kate Fellowes is the author of six mysteries, including *A Menacing Brew*, which was a featured title in *First for Women* magazine. Her short works have appeared in many anthologies, and periodicals including *Victoria*, *Woman's World*, *Brides*, and *Romantic Homes*. Winner of the San Diego Public Library's Matchbook Short Story contest, she met the challenge to craft a mystery just 50 words long. Her working life has revolved around words: student newspaper editor, local reporter, hometown library cataloger. She is a founding member of the Wisconsin Chapter of Sisters in Crime. Find Kate at http://katefellowes.wordpress.com.

NO GOOD DEED

KATE FELLOWES

I'LL JUST SAY, that Bible should have been mine in the first place. Out of all the cousins, and there are just three of us, I'm the only one who cares about family history. They even tease me about it, "Halle, the historian," because I remember the details of our family tree. I should, after all the hours I've spent researching it.

Melanie only cares about how much things are worth, so she can sell them. More than one of Aunt Penelope's brooches had gone missing over the years, always after Melanie had made a visit. If Aunt P had willed the book to her, it would have been up on eBay in about two seconds flat. You could never trust Melanie with a treasure. I know I wouldn't.

Sophie, the perfect one, is too busy being perfect in the present to think about the past. She's the one who married well, and works tirelessly for good causes, because she can. She's kind and thoughtful and sweet, but she doesn't have a sentimental bone in her body. Why on earth she got the old family Bible, annotated with dates for births, marriages and deaths going back nearly two hundred years, is just beyond me.

Aunt P was pretty old and doddery by the end. That's the only logical explanation. It probably had nothing to do with the fact that

Sophie was the only one of us who still lived in town, near Aunt P. Or the fact that Sophie was therefore the one who ran the errands, drove to the doctor appointments, and managed the banking details, acting like the daughter Aunt P never had. I didn't care that Sophie inherited pretty much everything. I didn't want any of the jewelry or the art or the trinkets and things. I just wanted the Bible.

And now, here I was, presented with the opportunity I'd been waiting for. All three of us were spending the weekend together at Sophie's lovely home. Her only child was getting married, so Melanie and I had come from our respective states to rendezvous here, for a "Wonderful Wedding Weekend," as Sophie put it. The schedule was pretty jam-packed, with a bridal party luncheon on Friday, a spa morning on Saturday, the rehearsal dinner Saturday night and, at last, the wedding Sunday afternoon at the country club. I bought new clothes for every event, even the spa day. This weekend was costing me a fortune, but it would be worth it for the prize.

You see, I was going to steal that Bible. Well, technically, I planned to swap it out with another I'd purchased online. After Aunt P passed away several years ago, I'd asked Sophie if I could borrow the book to work on my genealogy project. She handed it over as if glad to get the grubby old thing out of her bookcase. While it was in my possession, I'd done my research, yes, but I'd also taken photos of those pages at the back, covered in a dozen different handwritings. And I'd taken lots more of the book from every angle, to note its condition. The title page gave me the publisher, and the verso—that's the back of the title page—gave me the edition and the year. I knew what I had to look for at the antiquarian bookseller, and I knew I needed to be patient, waiting for just the right imposter to show up.

Patience is rewarded, all right. When I'd almost forgotten about my plan, a Bible of the very same edition, similarly worn from the ages, eventually became available. It waited in my suitcase for me today. Sometime over the next three days, when this house was full of hustle and bustle and excitement and joy, I'd sneak into the study where our family Bible did nothing but take up a space and make the switch. It probably hadn't been opened since I returned it long ago and Sophie would never notice. Melanie's taste ran more toward jewelry and silver. I'd be home and dry.

Now, on Thursday afternoon, and feeling jazzed with anticipation, I joined Melanie and Sophie in the kitchen, a spacious affair remodeled in creamy vanilla with accents of red. The last time I'd been here, the room had been stark white and dreary gray.

"I love what you've done here," I gushed, giving Sophie a little hug.

"Oh, thanks, Halle." She gazed around the room, assessing. "It was just time for a change."

"Yeah, it's gorgeous," Melanie said. She held a homemade chocolate chip cookie, taken from the giant pile of them on a Wedgewood platter at her elbow. "And these are delish," she added, taking a bite.

Sophie dimpled. "New recipe," she said.

"What else have you done around the place?" I asked, giving my cousin a chance to show off the improvements to her already fabulous house.

"Not too much in here," she said, sounding disappointed, "but since Jack retired last year he's done amazing things with the garden. Let's take a tour."

Her husband and the other menfolk were golfing, which was on their own slate of endless activities for the weekend.

The garden consisted of nearly an acre, I knew. Dedicated flowerbeds dotted a weathered brick path that zigged and zagged in an artful way. This tour might take an hour…

"Sounds great," I said. "I have to make a stop, then I'll join you." I gestured at the powder room off the kitchen.

"Of course." Sophie led Melanie out the patio door, already talking.

I ambled in the direction of the powder room, then once in the hallway, took the stairs two at a time to the room that was mine for the weekend. In a matter of moments, the imposter Bible was in my arms and I was heading back down the stairs to the study.

My heart pounded with an unnatural intensity, at my shear

bravado. I'd never done anything like this before. I don't even speed when I drive. But the stakes were high. I might not find another chance this weekend. This was my moment to make my dream come true.

In the study, I spotted our family Bible—a huge book, taking up five or six inches on the bottom shelf. *Out of sight, out of mind*, I thought, disgusted, seeing it relegated to this lowly spot.

Setting my equally old and precious—but not to me—Bible on Jack's desk, I turned to the bookshelf.

Bending down, I slid our Bible from its nest.

"Come with me, you beauty," I whispered, lifting it with both hands to protect the ancient binding, and holding it up against my chest, breathing in the scent, the age, the history of it. I may have even teared up a little, before I came to my senses and realized I needed to get moving.

Quickly, I slid the imposter into the vacant space, where, of course, it fit perfectly. Then, checking the hallway to be sure the coast was clear, I bolted back up the steps, sliding my treasure into my suitcase before stowing the suitcase under my bed.

Then, I stopped in the powder room to wash my hands with Sophie's heavily scented soap, giving verisimilitude to my story of a bathroom break. The overpowering floral scent would rival the many blossoms in the garden and probably attract a few bees.

Melanie and Sophie hadn't gotten very far, I saw, as a rush of relief and adrenaline warred within me. A giddy smile threatened to burst onto my face, but I kept it in check.

"Oh, dinner plate dahlias," I enthused as I joined them, looking at vibrant yellow and orange blooms big enough to wear as a hat.

Beaming at me, impressed by my display of botanical knowledge, Sophie said, "Aren't they something?"

"Yes," I wanted to say, "something my neighbor grows against our fence." But I didn't, just falling into place instead, able to relax and enjoy our stroll, which did take nearly an hour.

Back on the patio, Sophie led the way inside.

"I thought we could have tea outside," she told us and I knew she meant tea as a light meal, not just a cup of Darjeeling. "But first, there's something I'd like to share with you."

She smiled over her shoulder at us. Melanie and I exchanged a look. Something was up. What could it be? I hoped Sophie wasn't suddenly going to ask us to do readings at the church, or make a toast or anything like that. Was it news she had to share? Maybe another grandchild on the way. No, she already had several of those. She seemed too excited for that.

We followed her like ducklings after mama, through the kitchen, down the hallway, and around to—I gulped—the study.

The imposter Bible seemed to call to me as we took the seats Sophie indicated. I struggled to tear my gaze away from it, keeping my eyes set on Sophie, now leaning against Jack's desk.

She clasped her hands together. "Jack and I have decided to move to a retirement community," she announced, her face wreathed in smiles. "It wasn't an easy decision, but we think it's the right one, since our nest will be empty now. My baby's flown!"

"Congratulations," I said on a whoosh of relief and surprise. "Which one? Near here?"

She spent a few minutes giving us the details and it sounded like it would be suitably upscale and active for the two of them.

"I'm happy for you," Melanie said. "That means you'll be selling this place."

Leave it to her to think of that, first thing.

"That's right. And, while our new place is big enough for us," Sophie said, "it isn't big enough for all this." She gestured at the room around us, indicating the house, the yard, everything. "So, it's time for us to downsize and I thought this weekend would be the perfect time to start."

Sophie got up, moving to a closed cabinet against one wall. When she opened it, I saw a heavy wooden chest with button feet on one shelf and knew immediately it was Aunt P's silverware. Service for twenty, it actually saw service only once a year at Thanksgiving before going back in the cabinet. Real sterling, not silver plate, the pieces were heavy and stunning, with an elaborate swirling pattern on the handles. What was my cousin up to?

Imagine my surprise when she carried the chest over to Melanie, who sat with her mouth open with reverence. Setting it onto my astonished cousin's lap, Sophie said, "I'm sure Aunt Penelope would want you to have this, Melanie. You appreciate fine things, just as she did."

"I...I...oh." Melanie stammered out a few sounds, her palms running over the scarred and battered surface of the wooden chest. "I don't know what to say."

"Don't say anything," Sophie said. "Just enjoy it."

Melanie lifted the lid and the gleam of the silver, struck by the sunlight coming in the window, was blinding. I think we all gasped.

I figured Melanie was already doing math in her head, wondering what this precious commodity would fetch on the open market. I looked to Sophie, who also knew Melanie's tendencies and raised my eyebrows as if to ask, "What the what?"

Sophie's shoulders came up in a shrug of dismissal and I realized she really had made a major decision. She was moving on in life, away from the past, her own past. I felt a lump of unease form in my throat.

Uh, oh, I thought.

Sophie looked from Melanie, still rubbing her hands over the precious chest, to me, meeting my anxious gaze with her own benevolent one.

"And for you, my dear," she began, moving to the bookcase, "I think you can already guess."

She bent down, easing the bulky imposter from the shelf and hefting it up. Then she carried it across the room, as carefully as if it were a holy relic, showing it a respect she never had before.

My brain was scrambling with thoughts as I watched her cross that small space. *Stay calm. Act surprised. Just go with it. You've got this. Take a breath. Stay calm.*

Sophie set the heavy book on my lap, and I wrapped both hands around it. They were shaking.

"This always should have been yours, Halle. I don't know why Aunt P left it to me and I only wish I'd made you take it with you right after her funeral. Or just told you to keep it that time you borrowed it. You're the historian, not me."

Melanie clapped her hands. "Hear, hear," she said. "Makes perfect sense."

I managed a weak, wavery smile. "I can't tell you what this means to me," I said, which was true enough. My voice sounded nearly normal and I thought it was going to be okay. But, then—

"I was thinking," Sophie said, "that we really should take the chance to add this weekend's wedding date to the list at the back."

My heart skipped a beat, maybe two.

"After I got the book from Aunt P, I never looked inside. I just stuck it in the bookcase. I never knew there was all that writing in the back of this until you sent us that genealogy and those copies of the handwritten notes," Sophie said.

It had seemed only right to pass on what I'd pieced together from my probe into the past. I'd typed up the facts and figures, written about who arrived on what boat, where they purchased farm land, and how we came to be where we were. I also added copies of the pages at the back of the Bible, the handwritten ones listing dates.

"That's a great idea," I said, faking enthusiasm. I knew the imposter Bible had similar pages, full of some other family's names and dates. I could just put today's entry at the bottom of the list and no one would be the wiser. "Do you have a pen?"

Sophie had one in her hand, ready for action. She smiled.

"As mother of the groom," she said, devastatingly, "I claim the privilege of writing it in."

I watched, helpless and frozen, as she carried the book over to her husband's desk, setting it face down with a thump. Lifting the back cover, she clicked on the pen.

Hastily, I got to my feet, joining her at the desk.

"You know, it really is fascinating," I prattled at speed, launching into some random family lore as a distraction. I placed one hand over a page, as if indicating the totality of the written record through history, but actually just trying to cover up as much as I could.

I looked down at Sophie's bent head, her perfect dye job disguising nearly every silver hair. My wonderful cousin, seemingly so selfless, actually was. Kind, thoughtful, dear. And I'd betrayed her, that very day. It isn't possible to feel lower than I felt, watching her enter her son's name at the bottom of the list of meaningless names. If she read even one or two of them, the jig was up. I did not feel especially lucky.

"There," she pronounced, adding a little heart shape next to the date. She straightened up, closing the book. "That was fun. Our own record for the great-great-greats to come."

"A real treasure," I agreed.

"Let me see." Melanie spoke from across the room. She set the silverware on her chair and joined us. A frisson of anxiety skipped through my veins at her approach.

Sophie flipped open the back cover of the Bible and this time I placed my hand with my finger pointing at the new addition, to keep my cousin focused.

"That's cool," she said.

"Let's have that tea," I suggested. "Breakfast seems a long time ago."

Melanie's hand was still in the book as I attempted to close the cover.

"Wait a sec. I'm reading," she said, pushing my hand away.

And I knew it was all over for me. Melanie would spot the names and realize they were wrong. She'd know what I had done and would announce my crime to Sophie. Life would never be the same. There'd be a permanent black blot next to my name, and I'd deserve it.

Melanie's finger trailed down the list of names as Sophie told us the menu for our afternoon tea, the Bible already forgotten.

"I'll put the kettle on," Sophie said, sailing out of the room.

Alone with Melanie in the study, I could hear the grandfather clock in the corner ticking away mournfully, like the voice of doom.

Eventually, Melanie looked up from the book.

"These aren't our people," she said simply.

I nodded.

"And Sophie didn't notice?"

I shook my head.

"Well, then, no harm, hey?" Melanie closed the book and gave it a shove toward me. "I'd go hide that away if I were you," she said.

Wordlessly, I lugged the imposter upstairs, cramming it in next to the genuine one. I'd be sure to carry my own suitcase when I left because it now weighed an unexplainable ton.

On the patio, Sophie was filling delicate china cups with a fragrant brew. A three-tiered tray filled with tiny sandwiches sat beside another filled with tiny pastries.

I straightened my shoulders and took in a big breath.

The Bible was mine. A gift from Sophie. That was all that mattered in the end.

As I took my seat across from Melanie, she caught my eye and gave me a wink, making me cringe inside.

For better or worse, she and I were in cahoots now, with my secret between us. My prize beyond price was going to cost me dearly, its heavy weight dragging me down forever.

In an instant, I knew I couldn't live like that. There was only one possible solution.

Lifting my teacup, I cleared my throat.

"Sophie, I need to tell you something."

WIL A. EMERSON

Wil A. Emerson is a registered nurse turned fulltime writer and artist. Her stories reveal people and situations encountered in the various states where she has lived. A three-year stint in Europe added another level of insight for her characters. Mystery, suspense, dead or the deadly, you'll find humor thrown in the blender, too. Her short stories have appeared in national and international anthologies. Wil is a member of the Short Mystery Fiction Society, Sisters in Crime, and Mystery Writers of America. Find Wil at www.wilemerson.com

INCIDENTS AND INTENTIONS
WIL A. EMERSON

LILY UNLOCKED the back door of the thrift shop using a key that didn't belong to her. The warm key, hidden in her shirt on a red and blue braid, soothed her nerves. With a steady hand and one quick twist, the door opened. To her surprise, no squeaks or groans came with it. An added benefit to the silent entry was the darkness of the room. No lights except the soft glow from the streetlamps at both corners. No shadows; safer that way.

Inside the air was musty. The building too old for central air conditioning. The thought that everything in it would smell old and musty, too, made Lily sad.

Mathews' Thrift Shop was smack dab in the middle of a short block on Main Street. If anyone happened to be looking for a good place to break into a shop, this was it. Seven small storefronts, late fifties vintage. A used bookstore, candy shop, and a liquor store to the left. Mobile phone store, a boot and shoe repair shop, and Daisy's Deli to the right. All were struggling to hang on to customers. The phone store doing the most business. Who didn't need a cell phone or updates? While the phone store didn't draw large crowds like the one at the mall, business was good enough for two phone gurus to keep showing up for work six days a week. They closed up shop around seven, however. Long gone and in no hurry to return.

The better stores, a chain pharmacy, a popular pizza and pasta restaurant, a gas station, and a car dealer were on MacEnroe Drive, the heart of Waynesville County. Beyond the county park, a quick turn and there you'd be on a well-lit street. The Sheriff's office and county jail in the middle of MacEnroe Drive. Which left Mathews' Thrift shop, a frequent stop for locals, far from the watchful eye of the Sheriff's deputies.

The shop served a useful purpose in the community, though. The owner, Walter Mathews, had a steady stream of customers who sold their used clothes and other whatnots on consignment. The better-heeled citizens of Waynesville felt it was a worthy cause to offer nice used goods to the less-than-prosperous folks that lived on the outskirts of town. No Waynesville resident was considered rich, however. Some just did better than others and were thought of as well off. And Walter Mathews happened to be one of those on the better end. So, a break-in, a grab-and-go gig, wouldn't set anyone back too much.

Near midnight, Lily had slipped out of her bed, dressed in dark clothes, and tiptoed off the front stoop of her home without being detected by her watchdog father.

It hadn't always been this way—the need to sneak out or to have Clancy Owens' heavy eyes watching every move Lily made. There was a time, and it wasn't all that long ago, when Clancy, for the most part, trusted his only daughter.

Being a month from sixteen, Lily felt she could make a lot of decisions on her own. She certainly didn't like to ask permission to go anywhere and definitely didn't want to tell her father every move she made.

There were still a few friends who didn't pity her, asked her to go out with them. A few others who shied away. Neither mattered. Tonight, she was going solo to do exactly what she needed to do. Lily was positive Walter Mathews would not miss a meal if she took a few items that he intended to sell. And as far as the donor, well, what harm could there be with the taking? Unwanted items, donations on the if-come. Money gained only if the items sold. All Lily wanted to do was make sure a few items would never sell.

Once safely inside and assured she was alone, she crept along the back wall and then gingerly stepped through a row of items. Men's wear on one side, children's on the other. The ladies and teen items were displayed close to the front. The best items in view from the sidewalk windows.

Eye-catching, outer garments in good condition sold like ice cream on a hot day. At least that's what old man Walter had told her earlier. She glanced out the front window and saw the street was as still as it had been when she'd slinked along the sidewalk, hiding in the shadows. She'd only had to step into a doorway one time when the Deputy Sheriff's patrol car drove down Main. Nothing unusual about that. A nightly routine; not a big crime watch needed in Waynesville.

Even so, she *was* in a store, closed for the night, without the permission of the owner. Her action warranted caution. Not that she considered it breaking and entering. Still, there would be more than enough damage done if she was caught. That certainly wouldn't go over well. Not well at all with her father.

Lily figured it would only take a few minutes to rummage through the stacks of folded garments to find exactly what she wanted. Then a few more minutes spent at the glass cases over by the register. If it took more than five minutes she was stalling, setting herself up for trouble. That was not her intention.

Walter kept a few items under lock, but she didn't think that would be a problem. She wasn't after expensive jewelry or numbered knickknacks like those porcelain keepsakes of little girls with the big eyes or Currier & Ives Christmas scenes some of the older women collected. If what she wanted happened to be under glass, though, she'd have find a way to get it.

Lily had given the matter deep thought. Considered how it might be viewed. If Lily's mother knew what she was up to, she'd be embarrassed at first. The daughter of a couple on the better side of Waynesville's demographics stealing from the thrift shop? Her mother's anger would have singed the air for a while. She'd pout, simmer most of the day. And like clockwork, dinnertime—back to her usual self. Most things that troubled Sarah Owens in the past, when revisited, made her sigh. Hours after, that is. She'd say, "what a foolish thing to do" and then say with a soft smile "think twice." Sarah just didn't have it in her to be angry or sullen very long.

Strange as it was, it often made her husband, Clancy, heat up again, all red-faced, that his wife didn't take Lily's impulsive whims as worrisome conduct. Incidents, in Sarah's view that involved her daughter, were just part of the growing process. Well, Clancy knew bad habits and impulsive behavior, too often, led to an outcome that neither one of them would have control over.

Lily, their only child, was a handful, they'd told her on far too many occasions. Toddler stage on, she had a mind of her own. Didn't like to share except when it suited her. Had a knack for misunderstanding "no" and "yes." Could make "no" sound like a command when given to her parents. By seven or eight, she settled into being a reasonable child, but the wily, adventurous girl came back again when she turned thirteen. Strong-willed, Sarah said. Bullheaded, said Clancy. So, they kept their daughter busy as an attempt to harness her energy and blossoming free spirit.

Clancy, always on the lookout for trouble, did his best to alter his attitude and accept the fact he had a daughter that mimicked his own impulsive boyhood days.

Now Lily stood in front of a pile of women's blouses and t-shirts and reflected on how often she'd been labeled impulsive. But this was different. She knew full well why she'd sneaked Walter Mathews' key when he hadn't been looking. Why she'd come tonight. Knew stealing items from his thrift shop wasn't something to laugh about. If her plan didn't work out the way she intended, she and her father would be more distant than ever.

Thing was, Lily and her father had been getting along better in the last couple weeks. Oh, they still cried occasionally. Went through the motions of denial, then acceptance, and, in many ways, it felt like they were moving on. Clancy back to work, doing his best. Lily focusing on her studies, training with the track team again. Bones healed. Five months.

Granted, the underlying heartache hadn't faded. It wasn't something either one would ever get over.

That was the reason she'd been in Mathews' earlier in the day, after practice. Sweaty, disheveled, Lily went in right before Walter Mathew put up the 'closed sign' on the door. Five p.m., he had dinner on his mind.

Lily knew her father had been there that afternoon, too. Clancy Owens had told his daughter what he planned to do, and she wasn't the least bit pleased about his reason for stopping by Mathews. He hadn't been there to shop; he had two bags to drop off. Didn't care about consignment. Just wanted the items out of the house. In her view, it wasn't necessary at all.

When Lily opened the door of the shop, heard the twinkle of the door's bell, she hadn't intended on taking Walter Mathews' key. It just so happened he was stacking a bundle of items on the women's table, they started to slip and slide, then the pile tumbled toward the floor. He darted to catch them, stumbled, Lily grabbed his arm and helped him stand upright. A mishap avoided. During his thank you hug, her head near his shoulder, she saw the key had fallen out of his pocket.

Like a pearl waiting to be plucked from the sea. She helped Walter Mathew pick up the items and put them on the table. He placed a pale blue satin blouse on top. Her plan was set in motion.

"This will be gone tomorrow morning. Isn't it lovely?" he said.

"More than lovely," Lily had replied.

She'd gone to the shop after practice to plead with Matthews not to sell the clothes, to give them to her and not tell her father. That would be the hardest part. Getting Walter Mathews to consent to a secret. With a key, there'd be no pleading. She could come back at night and take what belonged to her. Her mother's favorite satin blouse, the t-shirts she wore when out for a run, the slip-on camisoles she wore under her dressy jackets. Those awful Christmas pajamas that made Lily giggle when her mom suggested she buy a pair, too. Now the green and red flannel set were treasures in Lily's eyes. Something to cling to when vivid memories kept her awake at night.

Lily had the items tucked under her arm as she crossed to the glass enclosure to study its contents. A bracelet, two sets of earrings, and a silver necklace Lily gave her mother on her last birthday. And there was that one crystal vase her mother used when Clancy brought home flowers on special occasions. Birthday, anniversary, or what Clancy called an "I love you" day. The vase wasn't expensive by any means. But it was important.

Lily tried to slide the glass door open, but it wouldn't budge. A long hard gaze and her mind was made up. No matter the consequences, she'd break the glass, grab the items, and run. Definitely robbery, but it couldn't be helped.

She rummaged through a closet in the back of the shop and found a toolbox. A ball-peen hammer inside. Back at the counter, she made a swift plunge at the glass. It took a second, harder swing before the glass shattered. And in what seemed like less than an afterthought, a siren wailed.

Shrill, intense, loud.

Lily rocked back. Security alarm? In old Mathews' thrift shop? Why would the old man have a security alarm? No one would steal from him. Everything in his shop was used and inexpensive. Some of the locals called it a junk store.

Lily scrambled to secure the items in her arms. Why hadn't she thought to bring a tote bag with her? Tears streamed down her cheeks. The siren continued as she backed out the door. If she got to the corner, past the used bookstore, the candy shop, and the liquor store, she'd be safe. Lots of darkened doorways to hide in.

But luck had seldom been on Lily's side when she acted on impulse. The time she took her neighbor's new ten-speed without permission and couldn't work the brakes. A tree stopped the downhill ride and destroyed the frame of the costly bike. Lily had a goose egg on her forehead for a week. No concussion, though.

The time she didn't want to walk to school in the rain and decided to bunk out on the back porch until the storm blew over. It lasted far too long. By eleven o'clock, hungry and cold, she ran to school and the principal called her mother. Tardy, not lost.

The time she went into the candy store and didn't have enough money to buy the chocolate bar she wanted. Caught walking out the door. Of course, she'd pay for it, she told the owner. She was on her way home to get her change purse. Debt paid, and two weeks of home confinement, strictly enforced by her father.

Her father called her impulsive. Her mother called them a long list of awkward moments. Moments that had occurred long before what Lily could only call "the incident."

She turned the corner and at the same moment, the Deputy Sheriff's car pulled to a stop. Bright lights in her eyes, Lily couldn't see the driver's face but knew she couldn't outrun the tall, broad man who stepped out of the black and white sedan. He could run fast and at great lengths. They trained together. They shared the same genes.

"Lily?"

"Dad." Lily sank to the ground, sobbing hard now. "Why did you throw away her clothes? Why couldn't I keep them?"

Deputy Sheriff Clancy Owen leaned forward, hands on his knees. "I just wanted you to get better. All those reminders around you weren't helping. Every day the memories. It wasn't your fault, Lily. An accident. Remember. Everyone agreed it was an accident."

"I shouldn't have asked mom to let me drive. My fault. All my fault." Lily sobbed. "I want her back."

"I do, too, honey. But we can't always have what we want." Clancy sat down on the cement walkway, wrapped his arms around his fragile daughter and held her tight, felt her body warming, the tension in her muscles giving way to his touch. She hadn't let him hold her that long since the eventful night. The night they lost a mother and a wife. The night they both tried so hard to forget.

"Come sit in the cruiser. I've got a blanket in the back." He eased his daughter off the ground, opened the door, helped Lily inside. Then, with an eye on her, went back and gathered up the various items off the ground.

"Are you taking me in, Dad?"

"I'm keeping you safe."

He turned in the opposite direction, not toward what he called his second home. Not to the Sheriff's office. Clancy Owens had earned leeway on the job. Oh, he wasn't about to cover up, make excuses for Lily. He had to report the incident and, indeed, he'd talk to Walter Mathews.

Yes, he'd write a full report, just like he had done all those months ago when he was called to an accident on Route 77. He didn't race to it, safety on his mind. Blue lights on but no need for top speed. EMS on the scene and he was only a few minutes away from his office. He'd covered many auto accidents but wasn't prepared for what he came upon. The carnage was the most disheartening, unfathomable kind of accident a man could ever imagine. Sideswiped by an impaired driver. His daughter and wife in the tangled frame of their sedan. The chrome hubcaps, the black rubber tires still spinning like a Ferris wheel. Lily in the driver's seat. Jaws of Life needed to extract her. Sarah, bloody and broken. No rush to get her to the hospital.

A sight that haunted him every day, every night. The sight that kept Lily in the hospital for two weeks, her ongoing nightmares. Months of physical therapy, months of counseling.

He and Lily had been gaining ground. At least, he thought they were on the verge of it. Running together three times a week again, a burger night out now and then. Lily had a couple of evenings with her old girlfriends; an event that didn't leave her shaking. Baby steps, one day at a time. Then another outing and he hadn't stood at the window all night waiting for her to return. A major breakthrough for both of them. Slow, but sure, they'd mend.

A good life awaited Lily.

It led him to consider the future. Lily's future. Prepare her to welcome what lay ahead.

Clancy reconsidered. He no longer needed to touch the clothes of his late wife to know she had existed. But time and healing may be counted differently when a teenager is lost in sorrow. A daughter's needs are different than those of a grieving husband. Death of a loved one was something you got through, not over. Lily, not much more than a child, still needed to cling to her mother.

Clancy Owens brushed tears from his face. Admitted to himself that his actions had been a big mistake. Even with the best of intentions, a father can be impulsive.

LARRY M. KEETON

Larry M. Keeton's 43-year career as a U.S. Army Officer and senior executive in two Washington State counties provides him with plenty of characters for his short stories; his 52-year marriage to his high school sweetheart supplies him numerous combat boot-in-the-mouth dialogue best suited on the page. His stories have appeared in *The First Line, Mystery Magazine*, and Season 7 of *Mysteries to Die For* podcast/website, and its anthology *Games People Play: Opening Gambit.* Now retired, Larry lives in the Pacific Northwest and belongs to the Mystery Writers of America, Sisters in Crime, and the Short Mystery Fiction Society. Find him at www.larrykeetonwriter.com.

A TIGHT SQUEEZE

LARRY M. KEETON

My wife, Denise, was dead. Her tiny chest crushed by a twenty-four-foot python.

Blood thundered through my ears, drowning out the Monday night football game on my den's sixty-five-inch flatscreen television. A game on which I had placed a fifty grand wager.

This was a Zoom call, and my laptop screen showed a dazed Linda Wilson, our company's Chief Financial Officer. Mascara-stained tears streaked down her high cheekbones.

"Jack." Linda's sobs broke my trance. "They made me…" Sniff. "Identify…" Another sniff. She wiped her nose with a well-used tissue.

I muted the television and shifted my bulk in the sagging recliner. "Calm down, Linda."

"Her shoulder…her … head." Another sob. "In that damn beast's mouth." She shuddered.

I glanced over to the game. *Sonofabitch.* I hurled my glass at the fireplace. The explosion sent scotch and crystal chards flying.

"What was that?" Linda asked, startled.

"All hell breaking loose," I snapped. My team's defeat meant I lacked the weekly loan payment. My skin prickled at the thought of another jacked-up interest rate. Or the extracted pound of flesh for inability to pay. Though I could stand to lose a few inches around my gut, that wasn't my preferred option.

"Jack Robinson, are you listening?" Linda's scream brought me back to the present.

"Yeah…yeah." I rubbed the gnawing ache in the thickness of my neck. "It's a shock, that's all. What happened, exactly?"

"The resort held a private beach party." She raised a crimson red arm.

"Ouch," I said. "You need aloe cream?"

She lifted a tumbler. Gulped half of it. "Gin and tonic works better." Then related how the resort had thrown a party. In typical fashion, a bored Denise decided to take a stroll on the property. "She ignored the warning signs. The ones about dangerous animals prowling the area."

Typical. Once an idea cemented itself in her head, there was no blasting it out. A lesson I painfully learned early on in our five-year marriage and business partnership.

"Linda, I know this is hard, but you have to keep a clear head."

Thud. Clear liquid splashed as she slammed her glass onto a teak table. "Dammit, Jack, get your bloody ass over here and handle it." A visibly violent tremor quaked her body.

There was a loud knock at her door before I could respond.

"You expecting someone?" I asked.

"The police." She rose and disappeared from the screen.

Though it was late September, the Seattle weather was warmer than normal. Like most houses in the area, we didn't have air conditioning. Nor was it the den's overhead fan that caused me to shiver uncontrollably. *Get a grip, Jack.* I wasn't prepared to face any interrogation. I was about to log off when Linda reappeared and said, "Inspector Guret's here."

A swarthy, thin-faced man with a white eye patch filled the screen. He sat down at the teak table, withdrew a small notebook and pen, offered his condolences, then got down to business.

"Your wife was here with your permission. Is that correct?" I detected a hint of an Australian accent.

I grunted. *Denise did not seek my approval for anything.* "She was scouting for a sugar source for our company." I explained that we owned a candy cane company. To cut down on costs, she decided we needed a direct source to provide the sugar. The purpose of her trip to Indonesia.

Guret scribbled something in his notebook, looked up. "Why are you not here, managing this business?"

I leaned back in my chair and crossed my arms over my chest. "Denise grew up on a farm. Me, I'm a city guy."

Guret bent his head down, revealing a bald spot in his black hair. He tapped his pen on the paper.

"When can I bring her body home?"

Guret looked up, brought the tip of his pen to his thin lips, and cocked his head skyward. I swallowed, trying to lubricate my dry throat. Rose to retrieve a new glass. Filled it to the brim with scotch.

"It is apparent the python killed her," Guret said. "These matters require time." He shrugged. "The bureaucracy, you understand."

I sank into my chair and felt my shoulders droop. "How much?"

His stoic expression changed as his one eye narrowed. "Are you implying…"

My palms shot up. "No. No. No. It's not that. I'm trying to expedite my wife's return. I merely assumed that…that extra hours would be required. Naturally, at my expense. That's all I was offering."

Guret stared at me with one x-ray eye. A minute passed, then another. I locked my gaze on his, clenched my jaws, and pressed my fingernails into my palms. "Officer Guret…"

"Inspector."

"Sorry. *Inspector* Guret, would it at least be possible for Denise's body to be released for cremation?" Thinking now. An urn is easier to transport and less expensive. She could even fly first class as carry on.

"My superiors will decide." Guret glanced at his notebook. "Did your wife make it a habit to ignore dangerous animal warning signs?"

What came to mind was *Denise's many habits. Tormenting me. Emasculating me. Possibly an affair or three. Sex was merely an obligation to get what she wanted.* "I never saw her do it. That's not to say she didn't."

More writing, then, "Was your marriage stable?"

Most definitely. Partly because we co-owned the candy company. Partly because we were committed to its success. Mostly because we slept in separate bedrooms. Dinners were board meeting rehearsals, where I was the silent partner.

An ache formed between my shoulder blades, and I rolled my shoulders. It didn't help. I sighed and said, "I watch TV. The husband is always a suspect, right?"

Guret responded with a disarming smile. "Should you be?"

I shook my head, frustrated. "Do you seriously think I *hired* a python to lurk in a cane field and wait for my wife to stroll by? Isn't that a bit farfetched?"

"Is it?" He paused, studied me. "Especially if associates are involved."

Get a grip, Jack. Be polite. Cooperative. Win him over.

I rubbed my eyes, took a deep breath, exhaled. "Inspector Guret, I'm sorry. It's late and as you can imagine, I'm shocked and upset. I won't say Denise and I didn't travel a rocky path this past year. The stress of our business put quite a strain on her and our marriage. One purpose of this trip was to put some space between us, to clear our heads." *Evaluate our marriage.*

More writing in his notebook. I swear I could hear the pen scratch the paper. Finally, he looked up.

"Is your business profitable?"

"We cleared half-a-million in profits this past season. Like any good owner, Denise always looked for ways to further reduce costs. An opportunity arose in Indonesia, and we both agreed she should investigate."

Guret flipped several pages in his notebook. Tapped the pen's point on the paper. "Ah, yes. I must have forgot."

Unlikely. "Look Inspector, it's been a long day. Right now, with the shock of Denise's death," *not to mention losing fifty grand,* "I'm not sure I can answer any more questions. Can we continue this tomorrow?"

Guret pursed his lips and looked down at his notebook, flipped back a couple of pages, closed it. "I shall report what I've learned to my superiors. How to pursue the matter is solely their decision."

"And the offer of overtime?" I asked. "The cremation request?"

He rose and slipped the notebook into his coat pocket. "Again, on behalf of our department and our country, our condolences."

At last. I leaned forward to ease the pressure at the base of my back.

Guret made to leave, then turned to face the screen again. A frown crossed his face as if something had just occurred to him.

What now? "Something else?" I asked.

"I understand you gave a sizable donation to our local wildlife refuge."

"We donate to several charities. As part of our business model."

He sighed. "A business model that cost the python its natural habitat. Good day."

Linda's face reappeared on the screen. Now that Guret had come and gone, she seemed more composed. Mind you, it might have been the G & T.

"You need to get over here," she said.

"I'll book the next flight." I left the call, booked an evening flight, and texted Linda the details. Though tired, I reached for my scotch bottle and took a long pull. The liquid burned my dry throat. Losing Denise was horrible, but manageable.

The loss of fifty grand convulsed my body like a fast-food milkshake machine. Though the prevention of bodily harm was possible. Key was closing the deal with Mr. Bakshi.

Normally an early morning snail race, the Interstate-5 traffic gods cleared the way. I used the time to formulate the day's plan.

Seal the deal with Bakshi. Collect the check. Deposit it electronically. Near-term money woes evaporated. Hop my flight to Jakarta.

I pulled into the parking lot that serviced our facility, a combination of corporate offices, production plant, and distribution center.

Though several trucks stood at loading bays, all the doors were closed. *Now what?*

I pushed through the front door. A former Seattle stevedore, the plant's union steward stood in my path.

"What now, Alice?"

"Is Denise dead?" she asked.

"Yes."

She wiped her eye. "The crew wants grieving time."

"Not right now." I stepped passed her, then jerked to a halt. Mr. Bakshi didn't need to see the company's strained relationship between management and the union. I turned to Alice. "I'm sorry. I've got a lot on my mind. Of course, we'll have a meeting about Denise's death. Right now, though, it's imperative people are seen working."

"How did she die?"

"Not well," I said and hustled into the office.

A red-eyed Chuck, Denise's bruiser of an administrative assistant, blocked my office door. "Is it true?"

"Yes."

"The internet story said it was a boa constrictor that escaped a local wildlife refuge."

"Python." I checked my watch. The investor was due any minute.

"When's the service?"

"I don't know."

"There *is* going to be a memorial service. Right?"

"Go plan it," I said. "In the meantime, I have a client to meet."

"Bakshi canceled," Chuck said.

I cocked my head. "Canceled?"

He nodded. "Out of respect for Denise's untimely death. He

said this is your time to grieve. Business could wait. He offered his condolences."

A sinkhole formed in my gut. Head pounding like a jackhammer, I collapsed into a nearby chair and rubbed my closed eyes with thumb and forefinger. What the hell was I going to do? I needed that contract signed and the release of his investment today. I stifled back the acid rising in my throat. "Get him on the phone."

Chuck's broad face contorted into a questioning frown. "Are you sure? At a time like this?"

"Do. It. Now."

He went to his desk to make the call. I entered my office and pulled the folder from my center drawer. Acid reflux kicked in and I wished I had antacids to help settle my queasiness.

Chuck stepped into the doorway. "His assistant said he'll inform him once he arrives in India."

India.

"You don't look good," Chuck said. "Would you like some water?"

I raised my palm. My gaze fell to the floor as I shook my head.

Chuck shifted his weight. "In that case, Mr. Taylor is waiting to see you in the conference room."

"Who?"

"Mr. Taylor. The auditor. Denise hired him a couple of weeks ago."

The lilt in his tone should have warned me. It didn't. Instead, I raced to the men's room down the hall, my stomach muscles quaking waves of dry heaves. I leaned my back against the toilet, pulled my legs up to my chin, and wrapped my arms around my knees.

"Everythin' all right?" The man had a distinctive drawl.

I tightened my arms around my legs and rested my head on my knees. My heart thumped a pulsating rush of blood through my eardrums. *Is no place sacred?*

A card slipped under the stall door. *William Taylor, Financial Services.*

I heard the restroom door open. Heavy footsteps entered. "Is there a problem?" the newcomer asked.

I gulped. The voice belonged to Jago, a broker I called when I needed help. When the banks refused to loan our company money, Jago delivered several alternative sources of investments.

A couple of taps to my door were followed by Taylor's drawl. "This fellar's sicker than a lovesick bull. Jist checking on 'im."

I managed to rise to my feet and flushed the toilet. "I'll be out in a minute. Mr. Taylor, I'll meet you in my office."

"Shore thing," he said.

I heard the door open and close. "Is he gone?"

"Yes," Jago said.

I slipped out of the stall.

Jago leaned against the sink closest to the door. His brawny arms crossed his powerfully built chest, a smartphone in one hand. "My contact satisfied the contract." He lifted the phone to reveal its screen. A python's muscular body was wrapped around a demure woman, only the back of her blond head visible. The next photo appeared. On the ground lay the victim, the reptile's mouth clamped down on the neck, strands of hair extruding from its lips.

I shuddered and grabbed a nearby sink for stability and swallowed the acidic bile that rose in my throat. I managed to turn on the cold water, splashed it on my face, and took in the haggard shell of myself in the mirror.

Jago handed me a paper towel. "The preman wishes his payment."

I recalled Jago explaining that a preman was the local shot caller armed with a variety of resources to handle delicate problems.

Hands clutched to the basin; my gaze stared at my reflection. "The money's not here."

He pocketed the phone. "Shall we go to your office?"

"I don't keep twenty thousand in cash here."

"Now thirty thousand dollars." A thin smile showed tea-stained teeth. "Ten for the python."

"I've got to move some funds around. I'll wire it to him."

Jago pulled a *keris* from his pants pocket. Extracting the knife's blade from its sheath, it resembled a grizzly's single claw. "Give me your wrist."

My heart skipped a beat, but I kept my composure. "Killing me won't pay the preman his money."

He lifted the blade to my eye level and gripped my wrist with his other hand. "*Orang Amerika yang bodoh.*"

I felt a slight slice and the warmth of blood ooze from the opening.

"What the hell?" I shouted.

He let go.

I yanked a paper towel from the dispenser and applied pressure to the wound. "I don't believe in curses."

"Nor does the spirit of my *keris*." He closed it and then put it in a pocket. "Only a stupid American fails to honor his word." He nodded to my wrist. "Twenty-four hours." He exited the room.

Still gripping my wrist, I stepped into the corridor. I glanced down it to my office. Taylor would have to wait. I headed for the exit and managed to pass another hallway when a firm hand grabbed and squeezed my shoulder.

"Mr. Robinson," Taylor said. "You surely ain't standing me up, are ya now?"

I broke free and whipped around. An older man in a wrinkled gray suit, with thick gray wavy hair and a brushy mustache, frowned at me. I raised my wrist. "Need a bandage. You're Taylor, right?"

His eyes twinkled as he grinned. "Took my daddy's name when I was born."

A comedian no less. "Look, Mr. Taylor, I appreciate you coming here to see me. Frankly, I'm not in the mood. I've just lost my wife. My stomach's killing me. Let's reschedule for next week."

"Tough day, eh," he said. His tone carried genuine sympathy. "Sorry 'bout the missus."

"Yeah. See Chuck about a new appointment."

Sadness filled his face. "No need. This will take as much time as a bronco rider being thrown."

"I don't understand," I said, though I was beginning to.

"Denise hired me a while back to examine the company's

financial's. Instructed me to deliver them to you once I finished. Done early. Figured I'd save you some expense money. Looks like you'll need it." He removed a crimson file from his thin briefcase. "I must say, I'm impressed with the number of charitable contributions ya'all dole out. Most of them are foreign to me, but what the hey. Also, there are quite a few management adjustments you should review."

Damn Denise. Even in death she's screwing me over. I took the folder. "Thanks. I'll be in touch soon." I stormed down the corridor toward the parking lot exit.

"Again," Taylor shouted behind me. "I'm sorry for your loss."

Not as much as I'm regretting it.

FIVE YEARS of marriage had drilled into me three hardcore lessons. One: Take nothing at face value. Two: The grass on the other side is either artificial turf or more likely dead. Three: If you've made a bad decision, cut your losses and run. Which is exactly what I did. I bolted out the company exit, dashed through pouring rain, jumped into my car, and charged off into an uncertain future.

Approaching the interstate's interchange, I debated which way to go. South to SeaTac and take the flight to Jakarta, where the preman's welcoming would be gracious *if* I brought the thirty grand I didn't have. East to Leavenworth, a Bavarian wannabe, where we owned a cabin in the back reaches of Lake Chelan. Though remote, I'd be constantly on high alert. That left north to the Bellingham marina where I moored *Ol' Lucky Lou.* Then northwest to British Columbia's rural islands and fjords. A place I'd previously explored.

Inherited from my grandfather, the forty-five-foot trawler had upgraded navigation and communication equipment that included internet, a powerful diesel engine with two long range fuel tanks, and a water desalination system. Other than recently departed Denise, no one was aware of its existence. Knowing a well-stocked liquor cabinet awaited, the decision was obvious.

Americans love Costco. Evidenced by the Bellingham parking

lot, so do the Canadians who cross the border and make the short trek south.

Once parked, I considered texting Linda. A pang of guilt quickly passed when I decided against it. Stuck with handling Denise's remains and the company's financial situation, I felt it better to keep her involvement with my disappearance to a minimum. Maybe later, much, much later, I'd reach out. I valued my self-preservation over any of her hard feelings.

After forty minutes of dodging slow shoppers with overflowing carts, I checked out and headed for the marina and *Ol' Lucky Lou.* Enroute, I listened to the weather forecast. A major storm had swept down from Alaska and was barreling its way toward Bellingham. Smooth sailing wasn't in my immediate future.

Housed beneath a covered marina slip, I managed to load the trawler without getting soaked in the process. Next, I drove the car to a central Western Washington State University parking lot, removed the license plates, and used a burner phone to call for an Uber. Fifteen minutes later, I reboarded *Ol' Lucky Lou.*

The trawler's pilot house sat forward toward the bow. Entrance from the deck was through a door on the portside. Windows provided a 360-degree view. An array of navigational aids lined the counter behind the steering wheel. Below the windows on the starboard side sat a storage cabinet on which the radios, satellite phone, and computer were secured. The laptop could stream music, videos, and Zoom calls.

Grandpa taught me the necessity of prechecks. I ran through his handprinted card. The equipment passed. The engine fired up flawlessly. And the gun drawer had my flare gun and a Glock subcompact semiautomatic pistol with two six-round magazines.

Despite the gale force wind and wildly flapping warning flags, I unmoored the boat and pulled out of the covered housing, rain pelting the windshield. Wipers kept a steady beat as I headed for the Salish Sea.

And freedom.

A mile out, I chucked the license plates, my smartphone, and the burner phone. I had more phones in storage when needed. Back inside, I settled into the pilot's seat. Relief washed over me like a jacuzzi spa treatment as I steered through the choppy waters toward a dark horizon.

The satellite phone buzzed, and the computer screen showed an incoming video call, followed by a voice.

"You bastard."

My chest tightened as my gaze snapped toward the screen.

Denise's contorted face glared back at me. "Did you really think you could kill me and get away with it?"

Linda appeared next to my wife. "As you can see, she's quite alive."

Clamminess raked my skin. "Th...th...the photos."

Denise shook her head. "Photoshopped, you moron."

I stood. A wave slammed the starboard side of the trawler. I lost my balance and stumbled back to the door. It flew open. A wet wind blasted into the wheelhouse. I regained my balance, shut the door, and gripped the wheel.

Denise's strident voice filled the cabin. "You shouldn't have screwed with me."

"I...I..."

Lightning bolts stabbed the sky on the horizon. The choppy water churned my stomach.

"When did you become such a philanthropist, Jack?" Denise asked. "Hell, I never knew the company was so giving until Mr. Taylor sent me his audit last week." She turned to Linda. "Have you ever heard of the Big Bill Peckerhead Rescue Foundation?"

Linda pointed to me. "*He's* the only peckerhead I know."

Denise chuckled. "From experience, his couldn't..."

"That's enough," I shouted.

"Hardly," Denise said. "You need to know, Jack, that I've found a new, more reliable partner. Jago introduced me before I left the States."

I stared at my bandaged wrist. A wall of water slammed the trawler's port side. My grip broke free from the wheel. I stumbled and hit my thigh on the cabinet. Pain erupted as I struggled to stand upright and grab the spinning wheel.

The boat's bow plunged into an oncoming wave. It rose, momentarily blocking the horizon, then slapped the ocean's surface once more. Like a roller coaster ride with no end, a second wave followed. A third. A fourth.

The queasiness in my stomach roiled and rose in my throat, erupting over the window and navigation equipment. Slimy warmth covered my fingers.

"Oh Jack," Denise said. "You really need to clean that mess up."

"Screw you," I screamed as I flipped her the bird.

"Wouldn't you like that," Denise said, her tone taunting. "As I said, I've got a new partner. One who appreciates what I'm trying to do with this company."

"I'm the co-owner. You can't do a thing without my approval."

Denise sat back and clasped her hands on the teak table. Her eyes had a gleeful glint. "About that, the time has come to turn the tables."

I locked my gaze on her angry eyes. "What are you…"

The door leading down to the cabin slid shut, followed by audible clicks. I went over to open it, but it wouldn't budge. I tried the wheelhouse door. Locked. I turned and faced the computer screen. "You bitch."

Denise smirked. "Like I said, it's time to dissolve our partnership. And from the look of things right about now, I'm doing the humane thing by putting you out of your misery."

Denise's true character surfaced once again, as it had in all five years of our marriage. I struggled to get out. "You're…you're going to kill me?"

"Ouch," she said. "I abhor violence. How you die is your choice."

"I'm not committing suicide."

"Then I hope you can swim because the dinghy is useless." The video screen flickered, then died.

My mind raced. What did she mean, it would be my choice? Sweat beaded on my forehead and upper lip. Despite the cold outside, the wheelhouse felt like a sauna.

The starboard cabinet door swung open. A massive, triangular-shaped head emerged, its forked tongue flicking the air.

"Holy shit." I reached into the gun drawer. Grabbed the Glock. Aimed. Fired. Gunfire reverberated in the cabin, deafening me as the scent of gunpowder filled the room.

The python uncoiled and slithered toward me.

I pulled the trigger again and again until the pistol's hammer clicked.

Undeterred, the snake continued to advance.

I inserted the second magazine. Emptied it.

The python stopped, lifted its head, its tongue still sensing for my body heat.

It was then that I realized Denise had switched out the bullets and reloaded the magazines with blanks.

I threw the pistol at the humongous body, watched its polymer frame bounce off and thud on the floor. Grabbed the flare gun as Denise's words echoed in my ears. *"How you die is your choice."*

Countless videos of python attacks rolled through my memory. First, they strike and grab their victim with their mouth. Next, they wrap their body around the prey. And then, they begin to squeeze.

The python in the wheelhouse was well within striking distance. Squeezing distance.

I stepped back to the cabin door.

The python lifted its head. Reared it back like a batter ready to swing at a baseball.

I jiggled the door handle. Locked.

The snake's head was poised.

I fired the flare gun.

Heat and smoke and the smell of burning flesh filled the cabin. I kicked at the door's window and handle. It didn't budge. Pain volcanoed up my spine as the python wound itself around my left leg.

I slammed my shoulder into the door. Nothing gave. Slammed into it again.

The tightness around my leg increased.

A rush of adrenaline charged through me as I made another

assault on the door. Heard the merciful crack as it flew open, felt the sharp needles of freezing rain pelting my face. Dragged myself over to the rail, the python's grasp, harder, firmer.

I plunged overboard, headlong into the icy water.

DENISE WAS RIGHT. Jack Robinson did die that day. So did the python in case you were wondering. But Dick Wheeler is alive, runs a candy store in Dawson Creek, and plays poker every Friday night to supplement his sweet income.

MOLLY WILLS FRASER

Molly Wills Fraser once prowled the halls of academia but now she teaches high school drama in suburban Ontario. When she isn't standing up for students or challenging bureaucracies, she's nurturing her works in progress — three children, a garden, and more than a few fictional characters. Find her at www. mollywillsfraser.com.

NOT THIS TIME

MOLLY WILLS FRASER

I'm hiding in my ex-husband's closet when my phone rings. I have it on silent— no matter what he says, I'm not a maniac— but I'm pretty sure the vibrations are moving all the way down the studs of the hundred-year-old house. If I can hear when the radiator clicks on in the kitchen, anyone can hear my phone.

Lucky for me, I've got cover. Meredith, the new girlfriend, is downstairs, blasting music. It doesn't sound like proper music—no drums, no guitar, no vocals, no discernible proper sounds, really. It's one of those bassy, expansive meditation tracks. I can't tell what she's doing, but the music started twenty minutes ago, right after she walked in the door. I can't say hello and pretend it's an honest mistake, she's too dangerous for that. The reverberating tones also mask wherever she is in the house, making escape impossible.

I fumble for the phone and send the call to voicemail, but Miller never leaves voicemails unless he needs to create a trail of evidence. In this case, the attempt of a call will be enough.

Besides, I know what he's calling for anyway. I'm late for the custody hearing of our son, Jack. My lawyer has already texted twice.

Lizzie. Any delay I need to know about?

And then, minutes later.

This doesn't help our case.

Now Miller is calling, not out of genuine concern for my whereabouts, but so that he can claim this is yet another time where he's given me a chance and I've blown it. And no, I can't have joint custody of Jack, let alone get out of this lousy campus town. He wants me to shrivel up and die here, with no chance of winning back my kid or my future. Limiting my time with my son to supervised visits only is the next step towards erasing me from Jack's life entirely. It's the logical progression of the path Miller set out on at the first custody hearing.

"Your Honor," he said at the time, "it is my professional opinion as a psychologist that Ms. MacCallum needs a considerable amount of therapeutic growth before she can sustain fifty-fifty custody. Her mania still remains mostly untreated, and when she's in one of her high states, she has often neglected to care for Jack."

"Ms. MacCallum, what is your current treatment plan?" The stern-faced judge had peered at me overtop jowls that billowed out of his robes like a white lace collar.

"I don't need a treatment plan—I need my kid," I'd said, adjusting the cuffs on my discount black suit.

"See, Your Honor, she's in complete denial of her mental state. When she's manic, she spends more time on her ridiculous photography hobby than she does caring for Jack. And when she's in a depressive episode, she neglects his basic hygiene."

"One time I didn't change his diaper before pickup."

"He was sitting in his own feces, Your Honor. That's a significant psychological regression, given that Jack is fully toilet trained when staying with me. And then there is the matter of stability. The fact is, Ms. MacCallum has been unable to hold down employment since she was dismissed from her doctorate program."

"You're the one who dismissed me! You and —"

"I wasn't your supervisor — that would have been unethical."

"As unethical as knocking up your own student and then stealing her findings while she was on maternity leave? And then moving on to bury your head in between some sophomore's legs and —"

The judge had banged his gavel. "This is a court of law, Ms. MacCallum. Have some dignity and use appropriate language."

My lawyer had tugged at my sleeve. I shook my hand free and itched a spot on the back of my neck.

The judge saw the itch. "Any sign of drug use, Dr. Miller?"

"He was the first person to buy me weed!" I hollered, pointing at Miller. "He introduced me to his dealer when I was still in undergrad."

"That's absurd, I'm a respected… Look, I've seen the studies on marijuana use. I've written studies on marijuana use and rapid descent into schizophrenia, and I'm afraid that can't be ruled out in Ms. MacCallum's case."

The judge's jowls jiggled as he turned from Miller to me.

I should have said, "Test me, I'm clean." I should have asked for an independent psychiatric evaluation, a review of my transcripts before I got caught in Miller's web, a home visit, a new lawyer, anything.

But I was unprepared. I didn't know that Miller had been working towards this for months—years, really. The entire duration of our relationship. He had isolated me, kept me at home with Jack while all my friends graduated on time, and left me behind in a city I didn't know. He convinced me that my family was toxic and diagnosed them all with an encyclopedia's worth of psychiatric and personality disorders, then ordered me to cut them off under the guise of "establishing healthy boundaries."

Most damaging to my current predicament, he had kept me from using social media. He forbade me from sharing anything about my personal life online, citing a paper he had authored on the narcissistic panopticon surveillance state of Instagram.

Without testimony from family or friends, or even a history of Facebook posts, I had no evidence to prove that I was a good parent. No Instagrams of me cooing at Jack when he took his first steps while Miller was away at a conference. No posts of me asking a moms' group what to do to occupy my toddler while we waited in the ER while Jack struggled with another round of croup. Without evidence, I had lost that day in court, and now Jack was with me only a few days a month.

This time, Miller is going for full custody. He's going to say that I'm a narcissist with untreated bipolar and suspected schizophrenia and, in order to protect Jack, they have to cut me off entirely. Jack is only three, so he can't say otherwise. And I can't go up against Dr. Jonathan Miller, Department Head of Psychology at Limestone University, without evidence. So that's what I'm here to steal.

Evidence.

Namely, the baby pictures.

It turns out my "ridiculous" photography hobby may be Miller's downfall. Somewhere in this closet are stacks and stacks of photos of my son. Jack's cheeks covered in icing, the month he took the toy baby stroller everywhere, the T-rex phase he went through where he tucked his elbows into his round belly to walk. If I'm lucky, I will also find the camera I bought myself with my first paycheck as a Teaching Assistant. And, if I find the camera, there's a good chance I will find the stack of SD cards that have the videos. Not just the ones of Jack, or of Jack and me together, but the ones of Miller. The ones I took when I was getting ready to leave him.

If I find those videos, I can show the judge, his department, the world, who he really is—a gaslighting, manipulative, emotionally abusive fraud who preyed on his young female protégé in a way that makes MeToo look quaint. This is my last chance.

The closet smells like him. Wet wool from his Aran sweaters and tweed jackets that he wears when playing professor, dry cleaning chemicals from the shirts and ties he wears under his white lab coat when playing doctor. Before the girlfriend had arrived, I'd checked Jack's closet. The photos weren't there. I heard her coming up the front steps and dove in here just as she was opening the door. Jack himself is at the campus day care, so at least there's no chance of him toddling in and catching me.

The yoga music downstairs doesn't fool me. Meredith is lethal.

She worked hard to destroy my life. And if anyone is going to end up in corpse pose today, it'll be me.

I first met her when I was TA-ing Miller's Cognitive Development course. She had found out that Miller and I were secretly together and threatened to expose us if I didn't give her an A+. I don't know why she bothered with the blackmail. She would have gotten an A+ thanks to her own genius anyway. By the time she hit first year of her own graduate studies, she was already working with Miller to ruin my life.

I remember sitting across from her, me in a pencil skirt I had thrifted because none of my old clothes fit me postpartum. A blouse too big, smelling of sour milk because that's what I always smelled like after Jack. My hair was a mess, my face tired. Her pale skin shone against her sleek, black hair. She wore tailored trousers and a black shirt so impossibly lint-free I wondered if she just stepped out of shrink wrap.

The Dean was there too, of course, and the heads of academic integrity and human resources.

"The record of harassment that Ms. Harkness has detailed is not insubstantial," the Dean had said. "And is particularly troublesome given the…intimate nature of your relationship with Dr. Miller."

"Former relationship," I said. "We aren't together anymore."

"Exactly, which is what makes your stalking of Ms. Harkness all the more concerning."

"I'm not allowed to know who is spending time with my kid?" I rolled my eyes and looked at Meredith. She stared me down like a jaguar considering her prey. "If you're so concerned, call the police. There's no way this meets the threshold for criminal harassment. The cops won't buy it, which is why you've brought it to the Dean instead. Because they will never admit that their golden boy professor has a schoolgirl fetish."

I had leaned back, thinking I had played my trump card. Less than three months before, I had opened the single stall office bathroom to both of them, well…let's just say she was adjusting her kilt.

I thought Meredith might flush. Show embarrassment,

weakness, anything. But she leaned in. "That's a disgusting insinuation."

She tapped two file folders in front of her and slid them across to me. "It's almost as disgusting as this."

I opened the first file.

It was bad but not impossible. Plagiarism charges that I could have beaten in time. Photocopies of her notes and my papers, her rough copies becoming my good copies. I knew that her notes were actually transcriptions of hypotheses I had floated in my TA seminar class, but it looked the other way around—that I had stolen her ideas, not that she had transcribed mine.

I opened the second file. It took me a while to see what was there. But as I did, my world fell away. Some of it I didn't recognize. Some of it was in Miller's handwriting. How long had they been working on this?

"You conducted an unethical study, traumatized your subjects, and then when it didn't go your way, you falsified data to prove your hypothesis," Meredith said. "You're a fraud."

"None of this is true," I had said, looking up at the Dean, pleading.

He shook his head. "The combination of harassment, plagiarism and considerable ethical breaches gives us no choice but to dismiss you from the doctoral program and rescind your Master's degree."

Then, Meredith had smiled.

And now, the music downstairs stops.

I have two choices: freeze or keep going. If Meredith finds me, I'm as good as dead. But if I don't steal my stuff back, I'll lose Jack, which feels almost the same.

I dig myself deeper into the closet. There, under an old leather jacket, are stacks of shoe boxes, large ones that I know contain Miller's skates, his dress shoes, his combat boots from his grunge phase. Nestled in between them is a cardboard box the size of a toaster, unlabeled.

I ease it out of the stack, cradle it in my arms and flip it open. Jack's toothless six-month-old smile beams up at me. They're all here—hundreds of photos I took of him, and then printed so I could always touch the memory of Jack from a month ago, while I marveled at Jack today. Tucked in beside them is the mint tin that I know contains the SD cards. The one with the videos of Miller.

I listen, but don't hear anything from downstairs. Even my breathing feels too loud.

I flick the tin open. There are only seven cards. The last one, the worst one, must still be in my camera. I slip the tin into my coat pocket, close the cardboard box, and tuck it under my arm.

I need that camera.

I hear a sound. It must be Meredith, coming up the stairs. The squeak of the fourth step is unmistakable. But now all is quiet. Where is she?

If it was any other day, I would wait her out. My pocket buzzes with another text, presumably from my lawyer. I have to get across campus and to the courthouse, or I will screw up this chance so badly that no amount of evidence will grant me another.

I ease the closet door open, just a bit.

Meredith is sitting on the bed, smiling her jaguar smile, kitchen knife in hand.

"It's you," she says, standing up slowly, moving between me and the door. "Now we can finish this. It will make it all so much easier, don't you think?"

I raise the box of baby photos like a shield and shove her down.

She exhales sharply when she hits the floor.

I run out of the bedroom, past my son's bedroom, down the stairs.

She screams.

I'm out the front door before I realize the back of my left hand is sliced open. Blood drips down over the box, down my arms and onto my jeans.

I clutch the box to my chest with my bloody hand and run down the street. I go past the houses abandoned by wealthy frat boys who are all off skiing or sunning on winter reading week. There's nobody shoveling their sidewalks, so I slip on a patch of ice and go down hard.

I look back. Meredith is a hundred paces behind me, a massive black parka hanging over her frame. She's seen me fall and knows she only has to walk. She shouts my name. She's coming for me.

I try to push myself up, but my right wrist can't bear the weight. One wrist broken, one hand bloody. I struggle to stand. Still gripping the box, I flee down the walkway between the student centre and the gym, my feet crunching on the salted cobblestones. Past the pub where the engineers drink themselves stupid, between centuries old limestone lecture halls, across the field in front of the old theological building. I pause before crossing the fresh blanket of snow. Where's Meredith?

The blood on my hand is chill against my skin. I'm soaked with it. I have to keep going. I may have lost Meredith, but that doesn't mean I can lose time. The hospital can wait. I have to get to the courthouse. My lawyer will clean me up when I get there.

I just need to make it past the MedSci building and then across Miner's Park and up Quarry Street. That will take fifteen minutes.

I need to call a ride. I need a bandage. I need my son. I need to stop losing so much blood.

I'll just sit down for a moment. Call a ride. Call for help.

I turn the corner of the MedSci building.

Meredith is in my path. She will kill me here. And she and Miller will raise Jack to forget me. Her hands are in front of her, holding something black. I can't see—it blends it with her coat. She's all jaguar. My knees are melting and…

"The SD card you want is in this camera," she says.

My legs give out. The box crashes open beside me, scattering Jack's face all around me. His beautiful face, bloody and covered in snow.

"You're hurt," she says, running to me.

"You stabbed me."

"You ran into my knife."

"Why did you have a knife?"

"I thought you were him, hiding," she says. "He's been so crazy lately."

I look at her, suddenly understanding.

She is still talking. "But I thought it was my fault. I thought I was… I've been getting ready to leave, but I didn't know what would happen to Jack. I didn't want to leave them alone together. And then I saw your videos and —"

I nod. "I've got to get to the courthouse."

"He stole my work, too. When he made me…he promised he wouldn't do that to me. I thought I was smarter than you, that I wouldn't let it happen to me but —"

"He's unstoppable," I say, feeling the cold of the snow swim into my legs, my arms, my heart.

"Not this time," Meredith says, taking off her parka and wrapping it around me. "We're going to stop him."

She calls someone—a ride, an ambulance? I'm not sure. Things get fuzzy after that.

The only thing I'm sure about? Tonight, I'll get to hold Jack.

JOHN BUKOWSKI

Dr. John Bukowski was previously a researcher and medical writer with professional publications ranging from journal articles to website content to radio scripts. In fiction, he has two novels and numerous short stories in publication. He's a native of the Midwest, but currently lives in eastern Tennessee. Dr. Bukowski teaches fiction writing at the Imaginarium Conference in Louisville Kentucky and is a member of the Knoxville Writer's Guild. Find him at www. thrillerjohnb.net.

WHEEL OF FORTUNE
JOHN BUKOWSKI

Karl slid his last token into the slot and pushed the glowing button. The Wheel of Fortune spun.

The brightly lit slot machine paused, the fourth wheel quivering before changing from a bell to a cherry. Three tokens clunked into the payout tray. Karl scooped them into his brightly festooned Golden Eagle cup and scanned the room. Then he glanced at his watch.

Mo was supposed to meet him here at ten thirty. It was already quarter of eleven. Karl was antsy about this score to start with. His partner being late didn't help his piece of mind.

He deposited another coin and pressed the button.

Karl had told himself that he was finished with heists. Seven years in two different state prisons was enough. That was almost twenty-five percent of his life. Once more and it'd be three strikes and one hundred percent. The risk was considerable, but Mo had promised this time was the big one.

Karl looked at his watch again, then deposited another coin.

How often had he heard that? The big one. The one big score, the sure thing, the road to easy street. Such promises never seemed to pan out for Karl Shoemaker. For Karl, the road to easy street had only led to gray walls filled with skinheads, rape gangs, and bad food. Not that his time outside the joint had been all unicorns and rainbows. His other twenty-two years had been poverty, low-life jobs, and one ball-busting marriage that earned him an anchor of debt and a restraining order.

So, what else could he do? Divorced ex-cons weren't exactly candidates for the brass ring. They didn't become CEOs or even shipping clerks. They mopped floors, bussed tables, and tended bar. They lived in shabby little rentals with hot and cold running cockroaches. They got rousted by the cops whenever there was a robbery in the neighborhood. They never got married to a good woman. They never had a family. Never had a decent home. That was his future until he died. With his luck, he'd live to be a hundred.

Karl reached for the last coin in the bucket when his bargain-basement cell phone rang. The number was familiar. He punched the green handset symbol and said, "Where the hell are you?"

The voice of Mo Kane filled his ear. "Hold your water, bro. I was deelayed, okay. You get that piece from Leo?" Leo being Leonidas Watts, an elevator repairman who could get past the casino metal detectors to tape a handgun behind a men's room toilet.

Karl felt the hard edge of the revolver snugged into the waistband of his pants, then tugged his jacket lower. "Yeah," he whispered, "and that alone is enough to send me back."

The voice in his ear chuckled. "What you worried about? We gonna make enough today so you ain't never going back."

"I've heard that before."

"Yeah?" Mo said. "Well, this time you hearin' it from me."

"Fine." Karl said. "Just get your ass over here and let's do this thing."

"Little change of plans. I ain't gonna get there until we ready to move."

Karl almost dropped the phone. "But you were supposed to be helping me." He lowered his voice and smiled at the startled old lady feeding a machine at the end of the row. "You're supposed to be with me, grab the guard's guns when I get the drop on them."

"And I will be. But instead of now, I come in a little before twelve. Stewie bust in with the AK when the lights go out. You get the drop on the guards while they worried about Stew. I take their guns and put the twist ties on 'em. We grab the moneybags and split. Only change is, you gotta wait without me holding your hand."

Karl felt the knot in his gut tighten. He mechanically dropped his last coin into the slot. The wheels spun, a few more coins tinkled into the tray.

"What you worried about?" Mo asked. "You got the gun, and them guards gonna be freaked when the lights go out and that AK start blasting. They won't have time to do more than shit their pants."

Karl took a deep breath, trying to ease the steel bands that bound his chest.

"Awrigth?" Mo asked.

"Yeah," Karl answered, words whooshing from him like air from a balloon. "I guess so."

"There you go. See you in an hour. Hang loose."

The cell went dead. "Yeah," Karl whispered. "Loose." He dropped a coin into the slot.

Karl didn't feel loose. He'd been living with a knot in his gut ever since he'd agreed to travel to Green Valley Arizona to meet his old cellmate. Waiting on Mo hadn't helped. Now he had to wait another hour.

The spinning wheels matched the spinning in Karl's head. Mo was always smart, a real hustler. He could get you anything you wanted in Quentin: drugs, stroke books, booze…anything. On the outside, he'd hustled his way to dealing blackjack at the Golden Eagle, the smallest casino run by the Pima Indians. He'd been fired for passing signals to a guy who won big. Nothing was proven and no charges were brought, but Mo was escorted off the premises just the same. Mo was not a man who liked to be escorted off of anywhere. And now he wanted payback.

The setup sounded good to Karl. Mo knew the place, the layout, the guard changes. There was beefed up security on the weekend, but just three guards on Monday morning, one of those in the poker room. The new guards came on at noon while the old crew took the weekend take from the counting room to the vault. The old crew was supposed to wait for the noon shift to arrive first, but usually started to collect the cash a few minutes early, no doubt anxious to get breakfast, then home to bed. So, it'd just be two guards in the main area, their heads occupied with thoughts of food and home, their arms occupied with moneybags. That's when it would all go down.

Karl didn't know all the details, that was Mo and Leo's department. Apparently, all the electric cables ran together through the elevator shaft. Besides being an elevator repairman, Leo had been an engineer in the army. He'd placed a little surprise package in the shaft, timed to explode at noon. When the bomb blew, the casino would lose power, alarms, cameras, door locks, everything. Then it would be three guys with one automatic rifle against three guards too surprised and worried about their families to put up much of a fight. Easy peasy. They'd be on the road in five minutes, a straight shot to Mexico and a little village that their driver, Enrique, knew about. Sit in the sun, drink Mexican beer, and relax with a senorita for a long time. Piece of cake.

So why was Karl's heart racing? Why couldn't he breathe?

Karl dropped a coin into the slot. Heard the wheels spin. The Wheel of Fortune, he thought. Like the wheel of life. You never knew what number would come up. Never knew when *your* number would come up. Karl suddenly had a startling image of one of the guards, his face grim, his pistol popping to life. Karl could almost feel the bullets punching his flesh, hot knives slicing his gut. Maybe that wasn't such a bad thing. At least it'd be quick.

Karl looked at his watch, then looked toward the elevator. What if Leo had screwed up? What if there was no explosion, no loss of power? What if Stew was late? A lot of what ifs. Karl tried not to think about them.

He glanced at the slot machine ready to deposit his last coin. That's when he noticed that the display window on the Wheel of Fortune looked different than before. Before he could figure out exactly what that difference was, the last wheel quivered and dropped. The slot machine erupted in a blaze of flashing lights. A siren sounded.

Karl jumped back, hand on the pistol in his waistband. Someone tapped his shoulder, and Karl almost pulled the gun as he spun around. A man in a green and gold jacket grabbed Karl's hand. The man's nametag read Lyle Rosenthal.

"Congratulations, sir. You hit the jackpot!"

Karl's eyes flared wide. He turned slowly, as if swimming in syrup or moving in a dream. He looked at the slot machine display window, which now depicted four golden eagles instead of lemons, cherries, or bells.

The old lady at the end of his row started clapping. Other players clapped as well. A few cheered. Karl just stared, mouth open, eyes glued on the flashing eagles.

Karl swallowed hard. "How much?"

"Normally," Rosenthal said, still pumping Karl's hand, "four eagles is one-hundred-and-twenty-thousand dollars. But this is a progressive machine." He pointed to the red strobe atop the bank of eight, one-armed bandits. Beneath the flashing light, a digital display read $335,460.

Karl blinked in rhythm with the strobe. "Over three-hundred grand?"

"That's right." Rosenthal placed a hand on Karl's shoulder and turned him toward a pretty lady, also dressed in green and gold. She held up a digital camera and said, "Smile."

Karl stared at her blankly. A light popped from her camera, sending a blue dot dancing across his eyes. The red strobe and blue dot made it feel like the Fourth of July.

"What's your name, sir?" Rosenthal asked.

"My, my name?"

"Yes. For the check."

"Check?"

Rosenthal laughed as if astonishment was to be expected. "The cashier's check for the money. Less taxes, of course." He smiled. "Can't forget Uncle Sam. Oh, and I'll need your driver's license."

Karl moved mechanically, mouth still agape. He passed his almost empty bucket to Rosenthal, who laughed as he shook it for the gathering crowd. Then Karl dug out his wallet. He almost handed over his parole card before remembering his driver's license. A cocktail waitress brought out a flute of champagne. Rosenthal took the driver's license, handed the champagne glass to Karl, and said, "I'll be right back."

Karl turned to the crowd of well-wishers pushing in to look at the machine and pat him on the back. He gulped half the flute. The wine was cold and slightly sweet. A guy in blue shorts and red t-shirt yelled, "Wanna give me some of your luck?" People laughed. Karl smiled.

Rosenthal handed him the check. Karl felt the embossed surface, red and black letters spelling out more money than he had ever seen. Even after the government took its cut, it was more than Karl had earned in all the pissant jobs he'd ever worked plus all the robberies he'd ever pulled. What the newspapers called a "life-changing" amount of money.

"The management is quite impressed with your play, Mr. Shoemaker. We'd like to comp you one of our executive suites." Rosenthal pointed to an attractive brunette. "Just see Candi at the desk and she'll have someone take you to your room." He shook Karl's hand again. "And if you haven't had lunch, please be our guest at the Eagle's Nest restaurant." He released Karl's hand, smiled, then walked away.

Karl stared at the check, still not quite sure that it was real. Not quite sure that any of this was real. This was usually the time when the alarm went off in whatever fleabag he was staying. Time to put the dream aside and head for another eight hours of dishwashing or day labor. But this was no dream. He folded the check carefully, almost afraid to crease it, then started to tuck it inside his jacket.

"Hey bro. We all set to do this?"

Karl almost dropped the check. Mo snatched it from his hand.

"What you got there?"

Before Mo could unfold the paper, Karl snatched it back and shoved it into his jacket pocket. "None of your business. It's mine."

Mo smiled a Cheshire grin, palms raised. "Cool it, bro. I ain't taking nuthin' from you." He scanned the room and got serious. "Stewie gonna hit the front door just as soon as the lights go out. You ready?"

Now the dream collapsed. Karl's hopes fell, his spirit emptier than after a wet dream about a supermodel. But this time, he couldn't just change his shorts and soldier on. This time there was something he was supposed to do. His gut tightened.

"You okay?" Mo asked. "You ain't gone pussy on me, have you?"

Karl just stared at his former cellmate, his face numb as a drilled tooth.

Mo looked worried. "You scarin' me now," he said, smiling at one of the guards coming out of the backroom, a canvas bag in each hand. "Tell you what, maybe you better give me the gun." He scanned the room and held out his hand.

Karl was moving mechanically again, his body on autopilot as his brain sought a solution to his present dilemma. A thousand scenarios flashed through his head, so many he couldn't understand them all. He saw himself running for the door. He saw himself shooting a guard. He saw himself being shot, the guard's face set and determined. He saw himself in a fancy hotel room having dinner with a woman in a slinky red dress. He heard Mo talk as if from a fog.

"I said, hand it over."

Karl unzipped his jacket and felt the rubber grip of the revolver. Then there was a muffled rumble, and the lights went out.

Mo looked toward the elevator. "That's the signal. Give me the gun."

He reached to take the pistol. Karl grabbed his hand. Mo said, "What the…"

And then all hell broke loose.

A blast of fully automatic fire rang through Karl's ears. People screamed. The revolver fell. Mo snatched it from the floor and shoved Karl back, Mo's face a mask of contempt. The security guard from the poker room ran in, pistol drawn. Mo rose and turned toward the onrushing guard, dropping him with two quick pops. Karl watched as the guard fell, red splotches on his green shirt, astonishment on his face.

The whole scene became disjointed, kaleidoscopic images flashing by in the dim glow of emergency lighting. The pistol flashes. The look of hatred on Mo's face. The look of surprise on the guard's face. That surprised look was fixed in Karl's mind as his body reflexively grabbed for Mo's pistol.

Karl and Mo struggled for the gun. A battle for survival. A battle for a new future. Mo delivered a backhand to Karl's face, busting his lip in a spurt of blood. Karl held on, grappling for the gun. Mo turned toward him, eyes flaring from anger to shock as Karl bent the short barrel into his ex-cellmate's chest and pulled the trigger. Mo backed away, his body haloed in red mist, his eyes as astonished as the security guard's. He staggered and fell.

Stew Beauchamp rushed in with the AK-47 chattering. One of the guards was hit. Another dropped his moneybags and ducked under the roulette wheel. Lyle Rosenthal stood in the middle of it all, eyes wide, jaw slack. Stewie turned the gun toward Rosenthal and snugged it to his cheek.

Karl pointed the snubbed-nose revolver and pulled the trigger.

EX-CONVICT HITS JACKPOT IN MORE WAYS THAN ONE

By Maddie Patterson

(*Tucson Gazette*)

Green Valley, September 27— On Monday, Karl Shoemaker was associating with a bandit. Normally this could earn an ex-convict a visit from his parole officer. Only this time, the bandit was the one-armed variety at the Golden Eagle Casino. A lucky silver dollar won Shoemaker over $300,000. That's when two gunmen broke in to rob the place, one of them packing an AK-47 assault rifle. Most people would have taken their newfound wealth and run for it. But Shoemaker wrestled the pistol from one of the criminals and shot them both dead.

When asked about the incident, assistant manager Lyle Rosenthal said, "I heard the commotion and found myself looking down the barrel of an assault rifle. Mr. Shoemaker saved my life and probably other lives as well, not to mention the Casino's money. I'd comped him a room after his big win. Now, he has a home with us for as long as he lives."

Mr. Shoemaker could not be reached for comment. Rumor has it that he has traveled south, where the days are lazy and life is long. Good luck, Karl. God bless.

CATE MOYLE

Cate Moyle writes mystery stories; she's won numerous recognitions, including the latest as a Silver Falchion Award finalist. She is also an award-winning poet, having been published in literary journals from *The Southeast Review* to *Wicked Alice*. Moyle's stories appear in *Mystery Tribune*, *Bowery Gothic*, *Crimeucopia*, and *ParABnormal Magazine*. Cate is a member of Sisters in Crime and the Short Mystery Fiction Society. Find her at https://catemoylepens. weebly.com/.

ROBBERY AT THE BIRDCAGE
CATE MOYLE

Deputy Michelle Simmons received the dispatch call at 05:49 and steered her cruiser toward the village of Dunecrest. The sun promised a bright day along the Florida 30A coastal highway. A promise for most of today's beach dwellers at least, except for the shooting victim in the 10-71 call. These days trouble found its way even into the sleepy coastal communities they rarely patrolled. Simmons sighed.

At the given address, she pulled her squad car into The Birdcage's gravel parking lot. A charming clapboard house converted to a breakfast-lunch cafe, the restaurant's front door and tiny porch were dominated by a metal Welcome sign featuring a human-sized painted parrot. "How original," she muttered.

Several people loitered in the lot. A twenty-something man in gym shorts and flip-flops approached her parked vehicle as she stepped out. Simmons instinctively touched the belt near her holster, then noticed a lanyard around his neck displaying his badge. A local village officer. A young Barney Fife with a boogieboard.

"Taylor Hulse," he said, then yawned. His tousled hair indicated he may have rolled out of bed to respond. "I live close." He pointed to the cinderblock former-motel-now-efficiency apartments across the street.

"What can you tell me, Hulse?"

"The restaurant owner, Charlie Spiers, appears to have been shot dead before the rest of the crew arrived this morning."

"Appears?"

"I heard nothing until the police scanner went off, sorry."

"Ah, you slept through it?"

He grinned sheepishly. "But we do have witnesses." Hulse nodded to a stout, sullen-looking man hovering by the restaurant dumpster, his mouth agape. Then he gave a follow-up nod to a spiky, white-haired woman with tanned legs—too thin for her torso—clad in bright yellow sneakers. She reminded Simmons of a snowy egret.

"Haven't interviewed them yet," Hulse said. "Thought it best to keep them separated from the crime scene and each other."

Simmons nodded and turned her attention to the spry old woman, who stood closest.

"May I have your name, ma'am?"

"Layle. Nutley."

"Okay, tell me what happened, Ms. Nutley."

"Just Layle, please." She ground her toe along the gravel as if crushing an invisible cigarette butt. "I arrived to work early like I always do—Charlie says I don't need to be in until seven, but who would entertain the boys if I stayed home? And I'm up at first light anyway, even on Sundays when we're closed."

Simmons made a note to ask about "boys" but allowed the woman to talk uninterrupted. She knew Layle's type. In other parts of the country, women her age wilted in retirement. Down here, they bloomed like greenhouse flowers.

"I left my condo at 5:20 and arrived here about half-past. Went in through the kitchen door like always, except there was no sight of Charlie. He's usually prepping the front stations since Trout doesn't arrive until a quarter to, well, maybe six o'clock if we're lucky…"

"Trout's the cook," Hulse said in a low voice.

Simmons rapped her pen against the notepad. "Trout has a full name?"

"Jimmy. Jimmy Rodrigue." Layle pointed to the large man now crying near the garbage dumpster. "Everyone calls him Trout."

"So, Jimmy and Charlie are the boys you referred to?"

Layle nodded and began tearing herself. "Yup."

"Did you see anyone else? Hear anything?"

"No, it was eerily quiet. Not even the coffee pots brewing." Layle flicked her gaze to the restaurant entrance. "But I didn't see Red. And that's odd he wasn't with Charlie…"

"Red?"

"Redbeard," Hulse said. "The parrot."

Simmons smirked at such a clichéd Florida pet. It would be fun to pass along this amusing tidbit to the arriving deputies when her shift ended.

"Charlie brought Redbeard in every morning and took him home each afternoon. That parrot was a crowd favorite." Layle rolled her eyes. "Not necessarily mine."

"Oh?" Hulse sounded genuinely surprised, as if everyone loved parrots.

"I like my pets quieter and a little less beady-eyed."

"So, there was no sight of Charlie or his bird…" Simmons prompted the witness.

"Correct, and no answers to my calls as I made my way through the kitchen to the dining…well, into the room, I saw Charlie laying on the floor in front of the hostess station… and the blood—so I telephoned immediately."

"Did you touch anything before you stepped outside?" Simmons asked.

Layle shook her head. "Do you think he was shot?"

"Looked like a gunshot wound," Hulse said. "Fatal."

The older woman's lips puckered, and she blinked back tears. "We really should find Red."

Simmons frowned. "I thought you didn't like that parrot."

Layle shrugged and swept the gravel again. "Might be the only eyewitness."

Simmons closed her notepad. The radio piece strapped to her shoulder crackled in broadcast. She stepped away to listen.

"Deputy Simmons, what's your 20?"

"10-97. Interviewing a witness. Looks like the shooting was fatal. Dunecrest police officer—a Taylor Hulse—is also present."

"Copy. Work with the local and keep the scene secure for the forensic team. Dunecrest P.D. may need guidance on working a homicide. All other units responding to an Armed Robbery. 211 at Sunshine Gas & Go."

Simmons tried to brighten her tired voice. Not the end of her shift after all. "Yes, Sergeant. 10-4."

When the deputy rejoined the group, she noted Trout posed, arms folded across his thick chest. "I barely saw Charlie's body because Layle stopped me from entering the dining room. Looked like he was near a pool of blood. On the floor." His voice cracked.

The Crime Scene Unit van pulled into the parking lot, the crew setting out safety cones and taping the perimeter. Hulse drew back to escort them inside and Simmons moved with him. Trout stopped her, distraught.

"Redbeard's gone?" he asked.

Again, with the bird? To his serious expression, she nodded. "An issue, maybe, but not the main concern."

"Man, we have to find him ASAP." Trout began scanning the overhead tree limbs. "I'm not saying the parrot is a wuss, but he's used to the finer life, ya know? Charlie drove into Pensacola for a special Brazil nut mix. He loved that bird. Even had insurance for Redbeard."

"You mean the parrot benefits from Charlie's estate?"

"No, unless it's been changed, I inherit The Birdcage." Trout grimaced and lifted a hand in a wave of surrender. "There *is* provision for Redbeard, but what I meant is there's a separate policy *on* the parrot. Those birds are pretty damn pricey."

Simmons flipped her notebook back open. "I assume this parrot is red."

"Green, mostly, except for a bluish sheen on his head. He's an amazon parrot, with a smudge of red plumage across the throat."

"Like a beard?" Simmons smiled despite herself.

"Exactly, sir, er, miss…deputy."

A crowd of bewildered regulars hovered on the sidewalk, speaking in hushed tones and trying to catch the attention of either Layle or Trout, who were still sequestered in the parking lot. When the forensic team finished, a silent ambulance carried the body of Charlie Spiers off the premises. Layle, hands entwined as in prayer, and Trout, hat over his heart, stood at respectful attention. After the removal of their friend, Simmons requested that they join her inside.

The restaurant was casually decorated in tropical colors and nautical items without a thematic pattern. Fish and mermaid bric-a-brac intermingled with parrots and shoreline birds. Atop the cashier's desk stood a carousel of postcards with the usual campy varieties, including a row of comical parrots. Trout picked out a postcard with a costumed parrot pirate touting, *Ho matey, tell them Redbeard sent ya!* and flashed it at the officers. "That's him."

Simmons took the postcard, placed it on the counter after a glance, then pointed to the open cash register drawer. "Who had a key to the register?"

"Any of us." Trout reached to the top ledge of the door frame leading into the office. "It's gone." He looked at Layle, who frowned.

Hulse and Simmons exchanged glances. "Seriously?" Simmons said. "How much money did Charlie keep in the cash drawer?"

Layle touched her throat. "We open in the morning with about two hundred in the till. Unless Charlie skipped going to the bank the day before, then he'd have a full deposit bag, but, yeah," she hesitated, "he'd have moved larger amounts to the safe overnight."

Simmons made a note then aimed her pen at the small safe—open and bare. "And if he had made a deposit, an empty bag would be inside?" To Layle's nod, she added, "How much could be in that bag?"

"A grand or more, easy. We have a large cash-only crowd."

"This was a robbery?" Trout asked.

"Likely," Hulse said. "Looks like a surprise shooting." He gave a nod to a pile of cups strewn across the floor near a blood stain.

Simmons shook her head, wishing Hulse would keep his thoughts to himself. Layle moved toward the overturned pile, halting when Michelle lifted her finger to motion "stop." Instead, she directed everyone's attention to the wall of photos behind the counter and, in particular, a photograph that hung askew, featuring five guys with fishing poles aboard a boat. The two in the foreground included Trout and a jovial fifty-something man with a wide grin.

"Is this Charlie?" Simmons asked, pointing to the grinning man.

Trout's face softened. "Sure is. About ten years ago. And yours truly." He studied the picture. "Shirtless guy at the wheel is Frank—always the designated driver. Those were good times. Miller times." He winked. "Before Robert left town and Gary had to sell the boat."

Layle coughed and said, "The *boys* were a larger crew back then."

"Are these guys still around?" Simmons asked, making notes while Hulse snapped a picture of the photo wall.

"Yeah, Frank comes in all the time," Trout said. "The others I don't see much."

Layle picked up the discarded postcard and replaced it on the carousel. "Gary's son got accepted to one of those fancy Ivy League colleges and he sold all his man toys to help pay tuition."

"I see him now and again," Trout said. "But Robert's hiding from his ex-wife and child support payments, so he keeps a low profile. Might have even left the Panhandle for 'Bama."

"He's always been a deadbeat," Layle said in a heated voice.

"What did Robert do to deserve your scorn?" Trout's voice, clipped.

"Outside of his serial sponging?" Layle's birdlike legs shuffled. "Just think that drugs change a person, that's all. He's no longer the life of the party."

Trout nodded slowly. "Parties end and people change. Officers, are we done?"

Simmons addressed Hulse. "We need official statements."

He brushed back the top of his surfer shag hair. "If you all walk with me to the station, I can write up statements now and let you get back to the day."

They exited The Birdcage while Layle sniffled back her tears and Trout implored everyone to help him find Redbeard.

Layle and Trout left the station after signing their statements, which Hulse dropped into a file folder. He took a long, tired breath. "How do you see this, Simmons, a burglary gone wrong?"

"Looks to be. That gunshot wound to the stomach wasn't particularly life-threatening. It was the lack of medical care that proved fatal." Michelle walked to the water cooler, took a long second drink before discarding the paper cup. "Canvass the surrounding area to find out what anyone might have seen or heard."

"Canvass? Well, there's only me here today, Deputy, but I'll be sure to stretch myself as far as I can." Hulse extended his arms upward, arching his back and yawning, as he watched her add notes to the office whiteboard. "You know, given the location of that cash register key, we may want to focus the suspect pool on restaurant regulars."

"Good point, Hulse. Anyone who was there at opening, or closing, could have seen Charlie place the key on that door frame." Simmons fiddled with a whiteboard eraser. "For now, let's look closer at Charlie's innermost circle."

"So, you want to interview all the *boys*?"

"If it's not a random burglar, obviously Trout and Layle are prime suspects, but the whole crew warrants our consideration. Frank still drops by and is definitely of interest." She tapped his name on the board. "And even if they're not around anymore, let's dot the i's and confirm the whereabouts of those other two—Robert and Gary."

"And there's a parrot to be found?"

Simmons waved her notepad. "A red-necked amazon parrot."

"Aptly named." Hulse grinned.

For the first time, Michelle noticed a midwestern tone in his accent. Because of his tanned skin and sea-kissed hair, she had pegged him as a resident beach beatnik.

"Not red-necks—crackers. That's what we call 'em around here. Where you originally from, Hulse?"

"Central Indiana. And you?"

"Defuniak Springs—born and reared."

"Native Floridian? Aren't you a rare bird."

Simmons gave him a singular smile. "C'mon, let's roll. I'll help you find the source of this *fowl* play." She winced. "Can't believe I just said that."

"Wait," Hulse scanned the computer screen before hopping up. "There's been an ambulance called to The Birdcage. We'd better start there."

AFTER LEAVING THE POLICE STATION, Layle remembered the hole in the access hatch to the attic and headed back to The Birdcage. On more than one occasion, Redbeard slid his way through the gap to hide in the rafters—usually when the groomers arrived to clip his wings.

She nimbly ducked under the police caution tape to access the kitchen. Then she hauled a tall aluminum ladder into the stock room, climbed to the ceiling, and shoved open the hatch.

From within the darkened space came the sound of wings flapping.

"Heya, Red?"

Squawk—that's enough boys.

At the familiar phrase, she smiled. "That's right. It's Layle and I say that's enough." She held out her gloved arm as a perch.

Squawk. Pipe down. Over easy.

"You pipe it, Red. And get down from there."

Redbeard pipe down. Squawk. That's enough boys. The parrot tucked his wings and squatted, collapsing into a lump of feathers on the ceiling joist.

"Don't try to play dead with me," Layle said, reaching for the parrot in a long stretch that took her to tiptoes. The ladder wobbled and she lost her footing, smashing an elbow on the ceiling hatch edge as she fell and smacked against the metal ladder on the way down.

Over easy. Pipe down. Squawk. That's enough. Redbeard's beak peeked through the opening, neck craned in concern. After a painful stretch into her pocket to call 9-1-1, Layle remained on the floor. The emergency responders found the parrot roosting on the ladder above her, as if on watch.

Hulse called Trout to come collect Redbeard. During it all, Layle and her protests that she was "just fine" became the more difficult challenge. She finally agreed to emergency care after Simmons convinced her the sheriff's office would reprimand the deputy if "standard protocol" was not followed.

A broken leg forced Layle to the hospital, and the concussion-making gash on her head kept her in overnight.

ON THE DAY after the murder, the Dunecrest Police Station experienced a parade of curious citizens, trying to be helpful. They provided all kinds of trivial details and conjectures, but not one person had heard or seen anything meaningful the previous dawn. Most interviews operated a little like grief counseling sessions, including one for the ruffled Redbeard who had been dropped off by Trout on his way to the funeral home.

Despite the waste of his morning, Hulse was grateful for a visit by Max Bliss, the local insurance agent, who'd brought copies of Charlie's current policies, and with a dour expression, silently laid the documents across the officer's desk.

Hulse pushed the papers back to the agent. "I need a warrant for this."

"Understood. I'll have official copies ready, but to aid the *direction* of inquiries…" Bliss left the policies and visited with Redbeard.

Hulse smiled at Bliss's cloak-and-dagger demeanor before glancing at the insurance policy documents and making a note.

"Hello, little fellow." Bliss poked a finger into the birdcage and was promptly nipped. "Ow!"

Squawk. Redbeard turned on his perch and dropped a small blob of green and white feces.

WHEN SIMMONS RETURNED Hulse's phone call, it took a fast minute for the update on the day's stream of "witnesses" because the only item of import was the addition of Layle on Charlie's insurance paperwork.

"Thanks again for pitching in with this investigation, Deputy." Hulse tapped a pen on his desk. There was a clicking sound as if in response.

"No problem, Hulse. Is that an echo or is the crazy bird there?"

"Until Trout returns for a follow-up, Redbeard is caged up with me."

"Well, while you've been parrot sitting, I've been scouting Main Street, and do you know the only business that has video surveillance is the Palmetto State Savings Bank?"

"What can I say—it's a friendly kind of town. The Surf-n-Swim Shop has a camera, but inside. I recommended it because people kept helping themselves to the cheap made-in-Taiwan towels. I mean, I get it, someone drove all the way to the beach and forgot a towel, but geez, plunk down the five dollars."

Simmons cleared her throat to bring him back on topic.

Redbeard seemed to do the same. *Tap, Tap. Click, Click.*

Hulse focused. "So, did the bank's footage reveal anything?"

"Looks like Charlie drove past there just before five in the morning on his moped—headed toward the restaurant. That's a bit earlier than his usual arrival time, which supports the idea of an interrupted robbery." Simmons paused. "Unless someone was lying in wait for him. What do we know of the boys?"

"When I contacted Frank's accounting firm, the office manager told me he's on the road back into town today. He's spent the last three days at a family reunion in Walt Disney World."

"Hmm, 400 miles away. Seems like a solid enough alibi," Simmons said. "And what about Gary?"

"I talked to him on the phone and, wow, he was ripped by the news. I could hardly understand a word he said between sobbing. He promised to come in later, see if he can help, but I doubt he'll add much. Umm, he's sort of a drinker. On the night in question, he was sleeping with the bartender from The Spinnaker, and she's already dropped by to alibi him."

"Convenient. She's believable?"

"She's…eager…to assist."

Based on Hulse's tone, Simmons could imagine the bombshell. A thought confirmed when Redbeard began catcalling in the background.

"Didn't get the feeling she was lying, though. She mentioned the reason Gary can't come by until after work is the lack of staff at his construction company. Sounds like money problems." Hulse drummed his pen, again. "And the last of the boys is a lost boy. I couldn't find any whereabouts on Robert. Appears he did skip town."

"Okay, keep at it. Let's also press on Trout and Layle about Charlie's insurance payment and their newly acquired assets. I'm heading to the hospital now to check on Layle."

"Follow the money. Copy that," Hulse said.

Trout entered the police station just as Hulse ended the call with Simmons. Redbeard perched, unmoving and wary, inside the cage until he spotted his friend. *WhazUp Trout.* The parrot bobbed his head, swaying side-to-side.

"Heya Redbeard. Who's the best parrot?" Trout pulled several almonds from his shirt pocket and dropped them into the seed bowl. He turned to Hulse, "Thanks for letting him stay here. I didn't want him to be alone."

"No prob. Gave me a chance to interrogate him." Hulse smiled.

"He given up anything?"

"Outside of the various oddball names, just loads of squawking."

The parrot ran through a repertoire of whistles and vocalizations, one suspiciously like Hulse's phone ring.

Hulse consulted his notes. "The names include Charlie-boss, Frank-O, Diver-Dave…and…" He turned so Trout could see his expression was serious, not kidding, "Is there someone named Over Easy?"

"That's Layle." Trout chuckled. "Charlie taught him to call her Over Easy. Like the breakfast egg order, sorta."

Hulse gave a slow smile. "Seems Over Easy is the only hen in his vocabulary."

"Redbeard's kind of a guy's guy—in a parrot way." Trout shrugged. "Not that being male is an instant *insider*. He's not keen on suits or pencil necks."

The bird in question elevated his volume as the men joked.

After a good chuckle, Trout helped himself to water from the cooler and glanced over the whiteboard. "Just so you know, none of these guys had anything against Charlie."

Hulse cringed, knowing he should have protected the material better. "We have to work the process, Trout. And right now, that means talking to everyone who knew Charlie. It also means confirming that you are a beneficiary in his death."

"Well, I already told you that. Now, I'm telling you it was a burglary gone wrong and you're letting that lady deputy take the investigation way off." He threw his spent cup in the trash can. "Don't shoot the messenger, man."

Hulse shrugged, adjusting his shoulder holster.

Robber!

"Wait, did Redbeard just say robber?" Hulse stood and approached the bird.

Robber—robber—robber. The parrot shuffled sideways along its perch and repeated, seeming to like the attention.

"Well, I'll be." Trout moved closer to the bird as Redbeard shifted his routine to include a loud noise like a gun blast.

Don't Shoot! CRAK—robber—robber. Redbeard's wings spread wide and his pupils dilated. *Charlie-boss. Don't Shoot! CRAK—robber—robber.*

"Whoa," the men said in unison.

Hulse picked up his phone and began recording the parrot.

When the bird went silent, Trout said, "Hey, if he was an eyewitness, maybe Redbeard can ID the robber. You can get a lineup." He rubbed his hands together.

With a wry face, Hulse began, "That's ri…," then finished, "We'd need a suspect first."

SUNLIGHT SPILLED into the hospital room where Layle rested under its rays. She edged up when she saw her visitor.

"Good afternoon, deputy, how's the investigation going?"

"In need of good leads and the only eyewitness we have to the crime can't testify in court. How are you feeling today, Layle?"

"For a fit chick confined to bed, I'm okay, but I can't believe Charlie is gone. Just gone…" Her gaze drifted for a moment, returning to a direct and determined look. "We have to find the killer. Tell me, do you think Redbeard witnessed the shooting?"

"There are indications, like dried blood on his claw."

Layle frowned. "Ah, poor little guy. Makes me wish Red wasn't there for that moment."

"Officer Hulse is having a difficult time keeping the parrot quiet. He appears agitated and keeps repeating the sound of a gunshot followed by 'robber, robber.'"

Layle pursed her lips and gazed for a moment out the hospital window. "Robber? That makes no sense. How would he know that word? There were occasions the boys talked about Buccaneers, or pirates, but not *robbers*." She turned her gaze to the deputy. "Parrots only repeat what they've heard—they can't actually talk, you know."

"You don't say," Simmons deadpanned.

"I need to see him for myself." Layle scrambled the covers off her legs to rise.

"No." Simmons held her in place with an extended arm. "You're not going anywhere. I have a few questions for you."

"If I answer, will you let me go talk to Red?"

"The doctors are the only ones who can release you."

"Can you put the bird on the phone?"

Simmons nodded. "Trout tells us that Charlie had a load of insurance policies and he thought himself the heir to the estate. Know of any of this?"

Layle shook her head. "Charlie didn't tell me all of his business. But that makes sense—naming Trout—he'd run the restaurant and see that the parrot had a long, happy life."

"Of course, you wouldn't harm the parrot either—you rescued it. We found the insurance paperwork and Trout was wrong. Or hiding something."

"What are you insinuating?"

Simmons raised her eyebrows and waited. She didn't have to wait long.

"Trout is often mistaken. He's a good listener but not skilled at remembering details."

Simmons lifted her phone. "Charlie Spiers' life insurance policy lists Jimmy Rodrigue and Layle Nutley as joint beneficiaries." She studied Layle's face. "That would be you and Trout. You're both named and gain from Charlie's death."

"What?" Layle's uninjured hand covered her mouth. "But if I didn't know…then there's no motive."

Despite her attempt to read something different, Michelle could only find sincerity in the woman's expression. She decided to let it go for now. Instead, she called Hulse via FaceTime.

After a single ring, she and Layle saw the inside of Dunecrest Police Station and Hulse's lopsided smile. "At your service," he said.

"Hey, I know you're busy, but Layle wanted to hear Redbeard's report."

"He's been quiet the last half hour." Hulse waved at someone off screen.

Trout came into camera view, walking to Redbeard's side. "What happened to Charlie-boss?" He asked the bird.

Silence.

Layle leaned into the phone. "Hey, Red. What happened to Black—two sugars?" She whispered to Simmons, "That's what he sometimes calls Charlie."

"Black—two sugars," Trout repeated.

Squawk. Redbeard made a low, guttural growl and his neck feathers rose.

They waited for more. Nothing.

Trout addressed Hulse. "Hold on, last time…could you touch your gun, officer?"

Hulse tapped the weapon in his shoulder holster.

The parrot flapped open his wings, flicking them top to bottom. *Black—two sugars. Don't Shoot! CRAK—robber—robber.*

"Deputy," Layle's voice hoarse with anxiety. "That's Robert. RobERT, not robber!"

Michelle moved the phone closer to herself. "Do you copy, Hulse? Redbeard is saying that *Robert* was the shooter."

"Copy that, deputy. I'll put out an APB for him."

Trout stepped behind the officer now furiously typing on the computer. "His last name is Brown. Robert Brown. I can't believe he did this, though. Must have been…desperate."

Redbeard shrieked.

 "Desperate or surprised or high." Layle grabbed Simmons' arm. "His ex-wife still lives on County Line Road. They're at odds, but if Robert made a grave mistake, she'd probably protect him."

"On it." Simmons stood.

"Watch out for her guard dogs," Layle added.

Trout crouched, looking into the phone screen. "They're large, but friendly."

Officer Hulse secured his gun into its holster. "See, deputy, even with the animals, it's that kinda town."

"Yeah Hulse, meet you there. Over," Simmons said, before aiming to disconnect.

"Wait," Layle called out. "Officer Hulse, tell Red that he's a very good bird."

"The best," Trout agreed.

"Hear that Redbeard?" Hulse said. "I'd say you're a hero."

Simmons smiled. "Hey, if we get the right guy, I'll personally keep that parrot in cashews."

Redbeard began singing.

TRACY FALENWOLFE

Tracy Falenwolfe's stories have appeared in more than twenty publications since winning the Bethlehem Writers Roundtable Short Story Award in 2014. Publications include *Heartbreaks & Half Truths*, *Moonlight & Misadventure*, *Black Cat Mystery Magazine*, *All Due Respect*, *Spinetingler Magazine*, *Crimson Streets*, and several *Chicken Soup for the Soul* volumes, as well as online at *Flash Bang Mysteries* and *The Lorelei Signal*. Tracy is a member of Sisters in Crime, Mystery Writers of America, and the Short Mystery Fiction Society. Find her at www.tracyfalenwolfe.com.

THE CRIMSON SALAMANDER

TRACY FALENWOLFE

Since her induction into The Modus Operandi Supper Club, Billie Burgess often said Mark Luxor was the devil. On Thursday, over Beef Wellington and prosciutto-wrapped asparagus, she decided it was true. Mark poured them each a coupe of champagne, then lifted his glass in a toast. "It's the fourth, Billie. You know what that means."

It meant that her dues were, well, due. And not the monetary kind of dues. Billie sipped. The champagne burned all the way down her throat. "It's a bad time."

Mark snorted. But elegantly. As if the breath he exhaled were somehow smoother, silkier than everyone else's. "When is it ever a good time?" He rubbed a thumb across the back of her hand.

Silverware clinked against fine china. The pianist played just loud enough to keep conversations private. In a few hours, the brass jazz band would take the stage and play into the night.

Billie pulled her hand away.

Mark snorted again, handed her an envelope, and left the table. Billie guzzled her champagne and tore open the heavy, gold-foiled paper. The names on the card inside were written in careful calligraphy: Cynthia Sablehaus and Lilliana Blankenship. As partners in crime went, Billie could have done worse. She could have done better, too.

Cynthia and Lilliana were mother and daughter, which put Billie at a disadvantage. While there was no honor among thieves, the mother/daughter bond between Cynthia and her daughter Lilliana appeared strong. That would make Billie the odd man out should things go south.

The three met the following day at Cynthia's country club after her bridge game. She ordered whiskey sours for all of them. Billie guessed she thought it was daring.

"So," Billie said, after she sipped her drink. "What'll it be?"

Cynthia and Lilliana shared a glance. They could have passed for sisters. Albeit old spinster sisters. Cynthia wore a pink tweed suit shot through with silver thread, a blouse buttoned up to her neck, and a string of pearls at her throat. Lilliana's suit was gray and lacked the silver thread. Both wore their hair scraped back into severe buns, applied their makeup with a trowel, and had perfected the art of looking down their noses at commoners like Billie.

Both, though heiresses in their own right, had married rich men. Lilliana's husband was even richer than her father, which, according to the gossip bandied about the supper club, annoyed Cynthia.

Lilliana leaned across the table. "We want to pull off an art heist."

"Like in *The Thomas Crown Affair*," Cynthia said.

"Or *Entrapment*," Lilliana countered.

"Or *Ocean's 8*," they said in unison.

"We're a team of three." Billie downed her drink. "You two need to reign in your expectations."

"You know you have to help us." Cynthia sipped her drink daintily.

Yes. She knew.

Mark Luxor, or Satan, as Billie usually referred to him, had lured her into the club under the guise of love. He knew all about her background as a thief, but believed in reform. Or so he said. He introduced her into his world. Made her feel like she could be one

of them. The elite. The upper crust. The wealthy. You know…
respectable folk.

Her membership in the supper club was his gift to her to
celebrate their engagement. Then he told her what she owed in dues
twice a year. By then, it was too late to get out.

Members had fantasies. They paid their dues in cash money and
got to play at being criminals. Billie paid by being a tour guide of
sorts—a facilitator. She helped the cash paying members plan and
execute their criminal fantasies. And if it went bad, she took the fall
while the wealthy members suddenly became victims and witnesses.

If she refused to do the job, she'd be implicated in another
member's crime. It had happened to someone last year. A guy
named Joshua. Safecracker. Former safecracker. He'd been inducted
by a romantic partner, just like Billie had, but he had refused to
facilitate a crime. He'd made a scene and stormed off. Less than
twenty-four hours later, Joshua was in jail, accused of an armored
car heist—a job that Billie had orchestrated.

Billie had no part in implicating Joshua, but she hadn't had to.
Mark Luxor's supper club had paying members whose fantasy it was
to witness a crime. To be the victim of a crime. Money. Those with
it had strange fantasies. Those without didn't give fantasy much
thought. Billie had done what she'd done in her old life in order to
survive. Her fantasy had been to have a roof over her head.

Now, she realized it wasn't the roof or the money she'd wanted.
It was the freedom. Thanks to Mark, she was as imprisoned now as
when she'd been incarcerated. Since she already had two felonies on
her record, one more could put her away for life. She had no choice
but to do as he demanded.

Cynthia and Lilliana wanted to steal The Crimson Salamander
—an upper arm cuff bracelet comprised of one-hundred and
sixteen rubies, fifty-six diamonds, and two emeralds set in platinum
—simply because they'd been told it wasn't for sale. The piece was
on display at The Monarch, a local museum with a top-notch
security system.

"Technically, this is a jewel theft, not an art heist," Billie said.

Since their third meeting, Cynthia and Lilliana had been

dressing in black cat suits. "It's not jewelry if you can't wear it." Cynthia's hand landed on her throat where her pearls usually were.

"And it's in a museum." Lilliana stretched, as if she were limbering up for a jog. "That makes it art."

"Either way," Billie said. "Do you both understand what you have to do?"

Cynthia put her foot on the ballet barre in the gym in her mansion and raised her hand up over her head. "I'm going to create the diversion."

Lilliana rolled her neck. "And I'm going to retrieve The Salamander."

"And you're going to be there, Billie." Cynthia switched legs and continued stretching. "In case anything goes wrong."

In case anything went wrong and they needed a fall guy, Billie thought. But she kept her mouth shut about that. "I think we should go in on Sunday. The museum will be closed. Less chance of being seen or distracted, for that matter."

"No." Cynthia put both feet on the floor and grabbed for a towel. "The owner of the piece will be there for the reception on Monday." She blotted her face. "That's when I want to do it."

"Mother," Lilliana grabbed a matching towel. "Maybe we should take Billie's advice on this."

"I want the satisfaction of snatching it right out from under him." Cynthia turned to Billie. "You *are* good enough to do this while the museum is open, aren't you?"

"I am," Billie said. "But the two of you are not."

Cynthia snorted. "You underestimate the power of having good character." She dropped her towel on the floor and went to the mini fridge for a bottle of Italian sparkling water. "No one would ever suspect either one of us of stealing anything."

"Fine," Billie said. "Monday it is."

"Where should we meet?" Lilliana asked. "The supper club is closed on Mondays."

"We can't meet," Billie said. "From this point on, we shouldn't be seen together. We shouldn't call or text, either. Now, let's go over the plan one more time."

BILLIE ARRIVED at the museum reception after Cynthia and Lilliana were already in place. They were both dressed to the nines, but Billie could see their nervousness. They couldn't stop looking at each other, or at Billie. Billie ignored both of them, mingling with strangers, appearing engrossed in the exhibits.

At two minutes after nine, Cynthia positioned herself in the northwest corner of the museum and fainted the way she'd been practicing for weeks. As soon as Lilliana heard the gasps from the crowd, she made a beeline for The Salamander.

"Is there a doctor in the house?" one of the museum patrons called.

Nosy people rushed to Cynthia's side. Those who didn't rush, gawked from afar. Lilliana was reaching for The Salamander when a well-meaning socialite called to her. "Come quickly, Lil. It's your mother."

Caught, Lilliana didn't have a choice. She glanced at Billie. Billie nodded discreetly.

Lilliana rushing to her mother's side gave the museum patrons yet another thing to focus on. While they were all occupied, Billie walked up to The Salamander, then slipped out the side door empty-handed. As the door closed, she glanced back and met Lilliana's icy gaze.

BILLIE IGNORED calls from both Cynthia and Lilliana on Monday night and Tuesday morning. When she got to the supper club on Tuesday evening, the women were seated at a table with Mark. He called Billie over.

"What the hell, Billie." He didn't offer her champagne this time. "What happened?"

"Too many moving parts." She shrugged. "Can't control everyone."

Dinner was over. Cocktails were flowing, and the brass band

took the stage.

Cynthia leaned closer. "You told us it would be easy."

"I told you there was a risk going in during the reception."

Lilliana swirled the drink in her glass. "I saw you."

"I saw you, too," Billie quipped.

"I looked back at you when that woman was dragging me over to mother." Lilliana leaned closer as the music swelled.

"And?"

She slammed her glass down on the table. "And you slipped out the side door. But you went to The Salamander first. You could have taken it, but you didn't. Why not?"

"Because you and your mother wanted to be the ones to take it. What fun would it have been for you if I had taken it?"

Mark frowned. Shrugged. Approval? Acceptance? Understanding?

Lilliana didn't look convinced. She and her mother both wore hoity-toity sneers.

"A friend on the museum board called this morning to check on me," Cynthia said. "She said the police are investigating a robbery at the museum. It's a big secret, but she told me someone took The Crimson Salamander last night after the event."

"It was you," Lilliana said. "You went back by yourself, didn't you?"

Billie didn't answer her.

"You'll go to jail," Mark said, shaking his head. "For a long time, Billie. Three strikes." Apparently his shrug hadn't indicated approval, acceptance, or understanding. It was him writing her off.

The club hostess approached the table with two detectives and one uniformed police officer trailing behind. "Mark Luxor," one of the detectives said, dropping a folded document on the table. "We have a warrant to search these premises."

Mark raised his arm and snapped his fingers. His lawyer, a club member, appeared at his side. He scanned the document. Frowned. "Gentlemen, couldn't this wait until after hours? People are in the middle of drinks."

"They can finish their drinks," the shorter detective said. "We'll start in Mr. Luxor's office."

"With the safe," the other detective said. He stretched out his arm. "If you would, please, Mr. Luxor."

Mark looked at his attorney.

His attorney nodded.

"This way." Mark looked smug as he led the police to his office.

Billie knew he didn't keep anything incriminating in his safe. At least nothing that he was aware of. She picked up his champagne and finished it. Cynthia and Lilliana both looked horrified, so she finished their drinks, too. "See you around, ladies."

She scanned the room and winked at Joshua. Dressed as a busboy, no one had recognized the former safecracker. No one had spared him more than a passing glance.

Billie left Cynthia and Lilliana at the table, mouths agape. She and Joshua snuck down the hall and listened outside of Mark's office. "Open the safe, please," one of the detectives said.

Billie met Joshua's eyes. He'd been granted early parole last week, and Billie had been at the jail to meet him, to apologize, and to begin plotting their revenge.

Step one had been to commission a copy of The Crimson Salamander, which she'd done the moment she'd drawn Cynthia and Lilliana as partners.

Step two had been to slip into the museum to take the real Crimson Salamander and replace it with the fake, which she'd done on Sunday the way she'd advised them to do.

In the office, the safe creaked as it swung open. "Wait." Mark sounded alarmed. "That's not mine. I don't know how that got in there." Billie couldn't hide her grin. Joshua gave her a fist bump.

Step three had been to meet up with Joshua after she'd acquired The Salamander. They'd slipped into the supper club where Joshua had cracked Mark's safe, and they'd placed it inside.

"Is this your pinky ring?" One of the detectives asked.

Mark was sputtering now. His attorney told him not to answer any more questions.

Billie risked peeking inside the office. The detective held Mark's ring up in a clear plastic baggie. Mark looked at his hand. "I misplaced it weeks ago. Where did you get that?"

Billie knew. They'd found it on the floor right next to The Crimson Salamander exhibit at the museum. She'd taken it off him the night he'd assigned her Cynthia and Lilliana, caressing her hand as if they were still lovers. Gloating over his control.

Who was in control now?

Last night, when she'd gone back to steal the fake salamander, she'd tripped the alarm on purpose, and had left that ring like a giant breadcrumb. It was what had led the police directly to where they stood.

"Mark Luxor, you are under arrest for grand larceny," the detective said.

"Grand larceny?" Billie heard the fear in his voice. "Are you crazy? I didn't put that there."

"Mark, please." His attorney raised his voice. "Don't say another word."

That was probably good advice. What could he say, anyway? If he sold Billie out, Cynthia and Lilliana would go down, too. After that, it wouldn't take long for the rich and powerful members of the club to turn on Mark. He'd be better off keeping his mouth shut and doing his time. The best part of the whole deal was that he knew it.

Joshua folded his arms. "You think he knows it was you?"

"I'm sure he does. But what can he do about it?"

Joshua grinned. "Wanna go get a drink?"

"Sure." Billie grinned back. "It just so happens I feel like celebrating."

GINA X. GRANT

Gina X. Grant writes witty fiction both super and natural. Storm Grant writes engaging gay fiction, more light than dark. Gina/Storm lives just north of Toronto, Canada, in a little house nestled among thirty-two trees, much to the delight of Canoli, a rescued Mexican street dog who might be a bit spoiled. Watch for Gina's new cozy mystery series, The Unlikely Murder Club, coming fall 2024. Gina/Storm is a member of Sisters in Crime and the Writer's Circle of York Region. Find her at www.ginaxgrant.com.

THE CASE OF THE PILFERED PARKA
GINA X. GRANT

Based on actual events.
Sort of.

Five minutes into the interview, Noah was ready to confess.

He'd arrived at 53 Division expecting to make a report. But Stefon—Officer Johnston — was treating him like a criminal, interviewing him with narrow-eyed suspicion. Noah feared a harsh light and rubber hose would make a dramatic entrance any minute now.

Oh, sure, he and Stefon barely knew each other, although they'd often exchanged the manly head jerks that passed for greeting at the gym. But apparently that counted for nothing now. Officer Johnston was a serious bodybuilder, and it turned out, a deadly serious cop.

While Noah was in it for the fitness. Mostly.

"I didn't steal my own coat," Noah insisted for the third time, running one hand through his sandy blond hair. "I don't have a receipt because I bought it off Facebook Marketplace."

"Tell me about that," Officer Johnston ordered. Sympathetically, patiently, but an order nonetheless.

Noah felt cold and sweaty as he described again how he'd bought his coat in a dark parking lot, handing three-hundred dollars cash to a woman he didn't know. Of course, he'd asked why she was selling a man's coat. She'd said her boyfriend had walked out owing her money, so she was selling his stuff to recoup some of what he owed her. The story had sounded reasonable to Noah at the time, but now… not so much.

There was something accusatory in the way Officer Johnston made a note. "Tell me again your movements on the night in question."

"You mean last night?" Noah asked, just to screw with the cop-script. "Okay, it started with me arriving at the gym an hour before closing…."

NOAH ARRIVED at the gym about an hour before closing. Temperatures had plummeted, and he'd almost skipped his workout, but it was leg day, so he'd forced himself. He drew his head further into his new—or at least new-to-him—parka, feeling like a turtle too stubborn to hibernate. A shiver raced down his spine, a reaction to both the icy temperatures and to his guilt over the waterfowl who had given their feathers so he could be warm.

Standing at his open trunk, he extracted his gym pass from his wallet, shoving it into his parka pocket before hiding the wallet behind a box bound for Goodwill. "Gotta donate this stuff," he mumbled, as he had each time he'd opened the trunk over the last few weeks. Grabbing his gym bag, he slammed the trunk closed, the freezing metal stinging his fingers.

He jogged across the parking lot, arriving at the double glass doors where he checked his look in the reflection. In his new puffy coat, he resembled a khaki-colored Michelin man, but he liked the way the hood's faux fur trim framed his face in a fuzzy halo. Natural goose down, but faux fur. Go figure.

He wrapped his fingers around the icy metal door handle. Would he be able to let go afterwards, or would his hand fuse to the door like the time he'd licked a hydrant as a kid? On the second try —the first didn't count because he was just testing—he yanked the big glass door open. Noah one, wind zero.

Gratefully, Noah stepped from the bitter night into the moist, near-tropical gym. It was like a sauna but with an aroma of *eau de swampy armpit* instead of cedar.

"Hey, there." Indira looked up from her phone and smiled as Noah struggled to close the door behind him. "Damn cold out there tonight, eh?"

Noah gazed at the attractive gym manager. She rarely worked on the reception desk, but no doubt someone had called in sick, which probably meant they were just too cozy to freeze their ass off for minimum wage. Unlike him, who, as a member of this fine-*ish* establishment, paid for the privilege of freezing his ass off to work out there.

Indira looked lovely tonight. She always looked lovely to Noah, whether fully made-up and clad in the latest spandex fashions or sweaty and makeup-free coming off a grueling workout.

She was around Noah's age of twenty-five. Tonight, she wore her dark shoulder-length hair down, minimal makeup, and, uncharacteristically, a bleach-stained hoodie. Probably a rescue from the lost and found. Somehow, the lobby felt simultaneously drafty and moist, so no doubt she needed the extra layer.

"Love your coat," she said. "Is it new?"

"Thanks, yeah," Noah turned his left shoulder toward her, showcasing the brand logo.

"*Oooh!* Canada Canard. Those coats are *tres* expensive, right? Like over a thousand bucks."

"Yeah." Noah straightened up to his just-a-smidge under six feet. "I got a deal, though. An *outstanding* deal."

Indira nodded. "Ouch," she said, a few strands of hair caught in the hoody's zipper teeth.

Should he offer to help? Was that a suspect move? He clutched the gym bag handle so tight his knuckles ached. He took a deep breath, relaxing his grip and his shoulders. In the meantime, Indira had freed her hair and was pulling it back into a ponytail, a black hair elastic caught in her teeth.

Desperate to break the silence before it became awkward, he said, "So, uh, how come I had to park so far away? The gym's usually empty this time of night." And then he mentally kicked himself for sounding whiny.

Before he could shove his foot further in his mouth, Indira said, "There's some big wedding at the event venue next door. A couple of people paid the day rate to use our showers to get ready."

"Are the locker rooms crowded?" he asked.

"I think there's one or two still here." She cupped her hand to her ear. "If we listen closely, we can hear the distant humming of blow dryers."

Noah laughed, cupping his own ear. "All I can hear is the grunting of feral muscle-heads."

He grinned, enjoying their banter because, in reality, all they could hear was the eighties techno-pop pounding throughout the gym. Their eyes met for a long, nervous-making moment before she dropped her gaze to her phone again. "The gym is practically empty. There's just a couple of regulars and one guest working out. You won't have to wait long for equipment. Leg day, right?"

His grin widened. If she'd memorized his workout routine, she must like him, right?

"Yeah. I'm going to hurt tomorrow. I guess I won't be going dancing in the next couple of days."

Her smile slid from her face. "Yeah. Me, either."

Noah didn't like to pry, but he had to ask. "Is everything okay?"

Indira bit her lower lip, almost as if she were trying not to cry. "Tomorrow's my last day here. I got a new job at the gym across town. I was supposed to have a going away party tonight, since it's Saturday, but one by one all my *friends* canceled." She gave the word *friends* an ironic twist. "Nobody wants to go out in this cold." She looked down at her phone's lock screen, making no effort to wake it.

"The wimps!" Noah cried, shaking his fist theatrically. "Who wouldn't brave a bit of bad weather to spend a night with you?"

A small smile toyed at the edges of Indira's lips. Slowly, she raised her gaze to meet his, looking, dare he dream, hopeful?

In many things, Noah was a brave man. Ask for a raise? No problem. Defend a friend? He's got your back. Support a cause? Just say when and where. Ask out a woman he liked? Well, okay. But what if she says no? *I'll just wait for a sign,* he'd say. Then, unless the sign was clear and direct, such as, "Hey, Noah. Wanna go out with me?" he never trusted his own ability to interpret these things.

He had wanted to ask Indira out from the day he met her. But he feared rejection, and worse, rejection followed by having to see her every time he came in for his workout. He knew some guys (and probably girls, too) hit on her all the time. He never wanted to be one of *those* guys. But now she was leaving, heading to another gym in another part of town.

This is my last chance, he told himself. *Don't wimp out on her the way her so-called friends have. It's now or never.*

"Are you okay?" Indira asked, her brow furrowing in concern.

Before he could overthink it, he blurted, "How about I take you out tonight?"

Indira blinked at him, then her gaze returned to her phone. "You don't have to take me on a pity date. Besides, most of the clubs have closed because of the bad weather."

"Then let's grab a coffee," Noah said, praying his tone didn't give away his desperation.

After another awkward moment, she smiled again, saying, "Yes. I'd like that."

But where should he take her? What was the nicest coffee shop that wasn't too expensive in case she ordered dessert? Would she follow him in her car or go with him in his? Was his car clean? Was he dressed nice enough for a date? Was it a date?

With these earth-shattering questions occupying his mind, he said, "Can't wait." He glanced at his watch. "See you in an hour. Those heavy pieces of metal won't lift themselves." He patted the laminate countertop before stepping into the entry turnstile. *"Ooof!"* he grunted as the metal arms locked into place.

"I'm okay," Noah said, hoping Indira would attribute his

reddening cheeks to windburn. He fished around in his coat pocket, glad he hadn't paid retail for the coat because *"gaping hole in the pocket"* wasn't one of the many features and benefits listed on the Canada Canard website.

His fingers nearly reached the coat's hem before wrapping around the little mag card. He brandished it triumphantly, then slapped it against the scanner. The turnstile unlocked with a click loud enough to be heard over the beat of the workout music. Eighties forever.

Indira had been right. The gym was almost empty. Noah nodded a greeting to a couple of regulars spotting each other at the bench press. They were serious bodybuilders, shiny with sweat. Stefon and… Noah couldn't recall the other guy's name, but it didn't matter. They weren't there to socialize. Not with him, anyway.

There was one other guy doing dumbbell curls in a corner. Noah smirked, knowing from experience you could watch yourself from several angles in the mirrored corners, not to mention viewing everything else going on.

This must be the guest Indira had mentioned. He was pretty fit, falling somewhere between the bodybuilders who were grunting and shouting encouragement to each other across the room and Noah's own lean and lanky body. Someone had once described him as "made entirely of elbows." Noah played hockey a couple of nights a week. He'd dreamed of playing in the NHL, just like every other Canadian kid, but couldn't hack the five a.m. practices.

The guest had blond hair several shades lighter than Noah's. He guessed it was probably bleach-kissed rather than sun-kissed, but it looked almost natural against his fair complexion. Like Noah, the guy wore dark sweatpants, his phone shoved in the pocket, and a faded tank top with some logo on the front.

Noah squinted at the other guy's shirt, trying to read the logo. Caught looking, the other guy gave Noah a "what-up" chin jerk.

Noah jerked his own chin back in acknowledgement before plopping into the leg press machine.

AN HOUR LATER, the lights flashed, indicating closing time. Noah glanced around, realizing he was the last person on the gym floor. Grabbing his frayed workout towel, he wiped down the machine he'd just used before heading to the locker room.

Eager to get to his date with Indira, Noah shoved the locker room door harder than he'd intended. As the door banged shut behind him, he heard swearing and a locker slamming. He stepped around the short cinder-block hallway. "What the…?"

Locker doors hung open. With another curse, the blond guest slammed the next locker door so hard it rattled and bounced open again.

Rounding on Noah, breathing hard, he said, "Dude. My wallet's been stolen." He held up a padlock, the shank sliced in two. "You better check yours."

For the two seconds it took Noah to locate his locker, he felt smug—after all, he'd been clever enough to lock his wallet in the car. Good thing, too, because his lock also lay in pieces on the floor.

Mouth hanging as open as his locker, Noah peered in. His gym bag lay squashed at the bottom—a noticeably different squash than the way he'd left it. He could see that clearly, because nothing blocked his view. Nothing, like, say, his new parka. He'd squeezed his parka in the locker with the rest of his stuff. Now it was gone.

His new, gloriously warm Canada Canard parka was gone.

Noah collapsed onto a nearby bench, face in hands. Behind him, the other guy continued his fruitless locker-to-locker search.

Eventually, the wallet-less guy gave up and sat across from Noah. By this point, Noah had gone through his gym bag, yanking out his street clothes and dumping them on the bench. Nothing else of value was missing because his parka had been the only thing of value he'd brought into the gym with him.

"I didn't notice my wallet missing until I'd already changed."

The guy gestured at himself. "Luckily, I had my phone upstairs with me, so I've locked my credit card. I'm going up to report the theft to the front desk. Come up and tell them about your coat when you're dressed. I'm Dylan, by the way."

"Noah," he whispered, staring forlornly at his jeans and wrinkled button-down lying on the bench beside him. He was going to freakin' freeze!

And what did all this mean for his date with Indira?

A few minutes later, Noah joined Dylan at the front desk. Indira was in the middle of an apology.

"Oh, Noah. Not you, too?" Her teeth dug into her lower lip. "Your new parka?"

Dylan gave her a sharp glance. "How come you know exactly what was stolen?"

"Relax, dude," Noah snapped. "We were talking about it when I got here."

"Oh, sorry." Dylan sort of deflated. "At least they left us our street clothes. It's pretty cold to be leaving in sweaty sweats."

Noah tried to smile. Dylan seemed like a nice guy, despite practically accusing Indira of being the thief. Now he held up a large duffle bag stuffed to the gills. "I got my work stuff in here. I'd be in big trouble if I lost it."

Mirroring his wan smile, Indira turned to Noah, saying, "I've called the police. They say they can't get here tonight. Too many accidents because of black ice on the roads. They'll send someone tomorrow. I guess this isn't a big deal to them." Flicking her gaze back to Dylan, she added. "But I'm sure it is to you. Again, on behalf of the gym, I'm so sorry."

"It's okay," Dylan said, laying one hand on the counter near her arm. "It's not like you stole our stuff." Glancing at his watch, he added. "Look, I gotta go. Night shift. I'll check in at the police station tomorrow and make a report." He patted her wrist where it peeked out from the old stained sweatshirt, his pale hand ghostly against her brown skin.

"Um, yeah. I guess that's all right," she said, gently extracting her hand. "I don't have any experience in this sort of thing. It's never happened before." Dylan turned to leave, but she called him back. "Wait." She grabbed a little card, then rooted through a drawer for a pen. "Here." She handed him the card. "Have a month's membership on us."

"Thanks." He accepted the little beige card. "That's nice of you." He adjusted his grip on the overstuffed equipment bag and, after a brief struggle against the wind, pushed the door open.

Both Indira and Noah shivered as the cold snaked in the open door. When she turned to Noah, he half expected tears, but instead, her eyes glinted like steel. "When I called the cops, I didn't give your name. But when they come by tomorrow, Noah, I'm going to have to."

"Do you think I stole my coat from me?" Then his stomach dropped. "Or do you think I'd already stolen it?"

She shook her head. "I don't believe that for a second. You're a nice, honest guy. But you bought the coat off Facebook Marketplace."

Relieved and impressed, he asked, "How did you figure that out, Sherlock?"

"Elementary, my dear Watson. The coat looks brand new, but you got an…" She made little air quotes. "'Outstanding deal,'" she finished, referencing his earlier statement.

At his nod, she added, "The thing is, when you buy something secondhand, you have no way of knowing if it's hot merchandise."

"Uh…" Noah saw her point.

"While you were working out, I did some googling. And even though possession of stolen goods could mean a fine or even imprisonment, you don't need to worry. I checked the Canada Canard website, and it says that while there are counterfeit coats out there, it's not like they have serial numbers sewn into the lining or anything. Anyway, tomorrow, the cops will check the records of who swiped in last night. They're going to want to speak to you."

Noah sighed. "I guess that means no coffee tonight."

Indira grinned. "On the contrary. We've got twelve hours to solve the case of the pilfered parka ourselves." She picked up the pen again, flipped a flyer over, beginning to write on the back.

"Okay, but I'm Sherlock," Noah protested.

"Sure you are." Indira reached under the counter, extracting a tape. "I don't suppose you own a VCR player?"

Noah wasn't surprised that the gym's security system, like the workout playlists, heralded from the eighties. Indira, however, seemed shocked and delighted when Noah said, "I do, in fact, own a VCR."

Two hours later, Noah and Indira were settled on his couch, a half-demolished pizza on the coffee table. Noah had finally stopped shaking from the chilly run to his car—the stained hoodie Indira had worn earlier doing little against the frigid wind. He'd retrieved his wallet from the trunk and rescued his old coat from the box of items intended for donation. "Procrastination is its own reward," he'd muttered, zipping up the ice-cold jacket.

Now they sat, shoulders almost touching, scarfing pizza and watching grainy security footage.

"So," Indira said, crossing out names. "We know the wedding guests never went near the men's locker rooms."

"And," Noah added, sinking deeper into the aging couch cushions. "We know that Stefon and…"

"Winston," Indira supplied.

"Right. Stefon and Winston wore their sweats into the gym, dumped their coats in one corner, and left directly without changing."

"And that I never left the front desk." She glanced at him sideways. Maybe she was embarrassed that they'd just fast-forward through her last hour at the gym. During that time, she'd scrolled through TikTok, touched up her makeup, and even done a little actual gym work. All at super-speed. "I usually work when I'm at work, but I'd been there since seven-thirty this morning."

"No explanation needed." He'd enjoyed watching her and wondered if she'd refreshed her makeup with him in mind. "So that leaves us back where we started." Noah sighed. He was thrilled she was there with him, but distressed about losing his coat. He could hardly afford to purchase a second one, even with another "outstanding deal." Plus, the situation didn't seem like an auspicious beginning to a relationship. He wanted to kiss her, but under the circumstances, he couldn't possibly—

"So, Noah," she said, pivoting on her left knee and swinging her right leg over his lap, straddling him in one smooth move. "Are you ready to confess to stealing your own parka?"

Before he could answer, she gently put her lips on his, and he forgot he'd ever owned a coat.

"I CERTAINLY WOULD HAVE STOLEN my coat ages ago if I'd known I'd wake up next you." Noah topped up Indira's coffee before refilling his own.

"Is that a confession?" she asked, smiling as she brought her mug to her lips. Her damp hair curled attractively around her face. When he realized he had that goofy grin, and she didn't, he quickly added. "Uh. No? Why would I do that? Why would anyone?"

"To throw us off the scent." She tapped the side of her nose. "At least the weather's better today."

He drew back the kitchen curtain, squinting in the bright sunshine. "Yup. Too bad it's still cold. It's not like I have a warm coat or anything."

Which didn't stop him from walking Indira to visitor parking, where they exchanged phone numbers while saying a kiss-filled goodbye for several freezing minutes before she climbed into her car. The gym opened later on a Sunday, but she still had to work. Since it was her last day, and she told Noah she had several things to finish before leaving.

JUST BEFORE NOON, Noah opened his laptop. Before he could start searching, his phone rang. Indira's name popped up on his screen. His stomach fluttered, and his lips curved into that stupid smile. Again.

"Good morning, Noah." In the background, music pounded an outdated soundtrack to the hubbub of a busy gym. Nothing like a bright Sunday morning to draw in hoards of people trying to atone for Saturday night's bad decisions.

"Good morning to you, too." Noah crooned. "I'm so glad you—"

"Look. Sorry, but I'm calling because the cops are here." Her voice sounded thin, clipped.

Noah shook off his fond thoughts of the previous night. "Oh, right. Have they cracked the case?"

He had to repeat himself as Indira spoke with someone at the gym. "Not yet. Hey, did you know Stefon was a cop? Me, neither."

"Stefon?" Noah pictured the bodybuilder who'd been lifting with his partner last night. "No, I didn't know that."

"Yeah," Indira plunged on, "And he's in charge of our case. He said there'd been a rash of thefts at gyms and yoga studios across the city. Anywhere where people put their stuff in lockers and then leave the room for a predictable length of time. They're finished here and want you to come down to the Station."

FIVE MINUTES INTO HIS INTERVIEW, Noah was ready to confess he'd stolen his own coat.

"Did you get the receipt?"

Noah barked a laugh, causing Officer Johnston to narrow his eyes even further.

"Haven't you ever bought anything off Craigslist or Facebook Marketplace?"

"I'll ask the questions here," he'd expected Officer Johnston to say, but instead, the cop said, "Yeah, actually. I just bought a set of snowshoes for my husband." Noah relaxed a fraction before Stefon added, "I don't mean did the seller give you a receipt for *your* purchase. I meant did you ask to see the receipt of the *original* purchase. You could be buying stolen goods." He squinted at Noah again.

Noah shifted uneasily on the hard wooden chair. You can't arrest someone for *not* possessing stolen goods. Can you? "But she told me she'd got the coat…" He repeated the story. "I'll know for next time," he added, trying to sound like he'd learned his lesson, although a note of sarcasm might have slipped in.

"We found the bolt cutters used to cut the locks shoved on top of the lockers," Stefon said, flipping through pages of notes.

Noah leaned forward. "Like the guy planned to come back?"

"Or like he was interrupted." Officer Johnston stared. "Anything you'd like to say, Noah?"

Noah almost said, "Hey, I'm the victim here," but figured that was a waste of breath.

THE INTERVIEW HAD BEEN UNCOMFORTABLE, but TV crime dramas had prepared him for worse. Nobody had left him alone in a room for hours, shined a light in his face, or made him stand in a lineup. The coffee had been wretched, but he'd had crappy coffee before and survived. The worst thing about the interview was that he'd frozen getting there and back. The station had no public parking and was only a couple of blocks from his apartment complex. So, it being a sunny day, he'd decided to walk. Five minutes later, his old nemesis, the wind, had returned, and once again, Noah found himself ducking his head into the collar like the damn turtle too stubborn to hibernate.

As soon as he got home, he checked his bank account. He could either afford a new coat or to take Indira to dinner a couple of times. Probably not both.

Well, it cost nothing to look, so he started with Craigslist. A half-hour of depressing scrolling later, he switched to Facebook Marketplace. No luck there either—all the coats were the wrong size, the wrong color, or mostly, the wrong price. As a last-ditch attempt, he adjusted the little slider to broaden the search area. New listings popped up. "No. No. Not pink. Not XXXL."

And then he saw it.

He was just about to click on the "Is it available?" button when his phone rang.

There was no, *"Hello."* And no, *"I've missed you terribly these six hours."* Indira just launched into, "Have you seen Facebook Marketplace?"

Ten minutes later, they had a date, er, plan: just Noah, Indira, and Officer Stefon Johnston.

At the cop's direction, Noah texted the seller to arrange a meetup. There was some back-and-forthing, but Noah told the seller he didn't own a car and wasn't prepared to hang out in a parking lot or on a street corner in this weather because he didn't own a warm coat. He restrained himself from sending the *facepalm* emoji or typing, "Duh!" Finally, the seller agreed to meet in a café that evening at seven. "I'll be the guy wearing a black leather jacket and carrying a big shopping bag," the seller had texted.

Noah was tempted to text back that he'd be the guy with a red rose in his lapel. "I'll be wearing a red beanie," he typed instead, as instructed by Officer Johnston.

Noah couldn't help but smile when the cop really did say, "We'll take it from here." At Indira's protest, he added, "We can't take civilians along on a bust."

"But they can't stop us from peering in the window," Indira whispered, squeezing Noah's hand when they arrived at the café a few minutes before seven.

At 7:01, a guy passed them and entered the café, a hoodie pulled forward, masking his face. He wore an expensive-looking black leather jacket over the sweatshirt, completing the ensemble with a giant shopping bag.

Stefon, in plainclothes, had snagged a table by the counter. Noah squinted through the condensation to see the cop catch the newcomer's eye and gesture at the red hat perched unflatteringly on his short afro. A female officer sat facing him, her back to the room.

Hunching low, Indira pulled Noah over to the middle of the window so they could see clearly…

And clearly be seen.

The leather-jacketed guy met Noah's gaze. His expression changed from wary to angry as he turned and rushed toward the door.

Stefon leaped up, ready to give chase, but at just that moment, a woman pushed a stroller in front of him. He tripped, knocking into the stroller and spilling her coffee. Even out on the street, Noah could hear the first of many infant wails.

No such obstacles impeded Noah's dash to the café door. As the seller burst outside, Noah yelled, "Hey, Dylan!" just before body-checking the thief. Years of hockey had trained him for this moment.

Both men crashed to the icy sidewalk.

Stefon appeared seconds later, glaring at Noah while simultaneously snapping handcuffs on the guy who had apparently stolen his own wallet. "I thought I told you to stay out of it," he snapped at Noah.

The second officer arrived, having calmed the young mother, if not the still-howling infant. Together, the two cops dragged Dylan— if that was his real name—to his feet.

Noah also rose, rubbing his bruised hip. "But if I hadn't been here…"

While the three men glared at each other, Indira shouted, "Chain of custody!" pointing the policewoman toward the fat shopping bag, khaki fabric spilling out of the top. The female officer swapped knitted mittens for latex gloves and retrieved the shopping bag.

People began to gather. Not a crowd, really, but a few people gawking and, of course, filming.

Noah spoke loud for the recordings, doing his best BBC Sherlock impression. "Well done, Officers. Now, if you would be so kind as to put your hand into the right pocket, you'll find there's a hole. If you reach further, almost to the hem, you'll find a mag card for the gym with my name and info." He stepped back with a flourish. "Then you can return my stolen property." He felt warmer just saying it.

"Sorry, Noah," Stefon said as he led Dylan to a waiting police vehicle. "The coat is evidence. We'll have to take it downtown."

"Well, that sucks." Noah shivered, despite his burning cheeks. His attempt at theatrics would be all over social media in minutes. "And I still don't have a warm coat."

Sweaty from his workout, Noah raced across the parking lot. Spring might be right around the corner, but that corner was still weeks away. He beeped the trunk open and quickly stripped off his old, not-very-warm coat, swapping it out for his beloved Canada Canard parka. Noah had only gotten his parka back yesterday, and there was no way he was bringing it into the gym. He stuffed his wallet into the pocket, the hole now repaired with a few awkward stitches.

Stefon had informed them the cops had found a ton of stolen items at Dylan's place. And shockingly, Dylan was also the "boyfriend" who'd "walked out owing money" to the woman in the dark parking lot. And guess what? She had the receipt. Dylan might have been a thief, but he preferred his own clothes bought retail. Since the girlfriend had purchased the coat and later sold it to Noah, the judge decided he could keep it.

Noah ducked his head further into his newly returned parka. *Thank you, waterfowl who gave your feathers so we could be warm.*

At his side, Indira zipped up her own Canada Canard coat, wrapping a long scarf around her neck.

Yeah, she was definitely more Sherlock, leaving him Watson.
And he couldn't have been happier.

Or warmer.

KAREN GROSE

Karen Grose is a writer from Toronto, Canada. Her debut novel, *The Dime Box*, was selected by Amnesty International for its 2021 Book Club. The Chinese language version, retitled as *The Lost Daughters*, was published by Sharp Point Press, Taiwan, in 2023. Karen's second novel, *Flat Out Lies*, was released June 2024. 'A Promise Kept' is her first published short story. Karen is a member of Crime Writers of Canada, Sisters in Crime, and the #thrillsandchills writing group. Find her at www.karengrose.ca.

A PROMISE KEPT

KAREN GROSE

THE ONLY REASON I'm working at Big Jim's is because no one else wanted the job, let alone applied. Why would they? The diner—and I use the term loosely—is a greasy hole-in-the-wall in what can best be described as a dodgy part of town. My job is to take orders at the till, which I relay to Jim. Each time I turn, I can feel the heat of the grill on my face, smell his breath, stale with coffee and cigarettes.

It's the last place I want to be on a Friday night.

But I need money.

Five teens arrive just as we're about to close, an arrogant group who relish their reputations as grade twelve assholes. Oversized square-shaped sunglasses, chunky sweaters, brand name kicks. Smartphones in hand, they snap selfies, take photos of the plastic menu, of their fully loaded burgers and gravy-drenched fries.

Of me, at the cash. My mustard-stained apron, the hairnet, nails bitten to the quick.

I clean up as soon as they leave, throw out the remnants of their half-eaten food, my stomach rumbling. Scrub tables, hose down the stainless steel servery. Replenish the condiments, think about taking a packet or two of ketchup, but don't. I got fired from my last job for stealing a single piece of cheese.

I lock up and say goodnight to Jim, who's outside having a smoke. The street is still, silent. Taking a deep breath, I swallow, dig out a can of mace from my purse, hold it tight in my hand. This is not a neighborhood to be out late and alone.

Three blocks over, the apartment building appears. Relieved, I scuttle through the scratched front door and pass through the graffitied walls to the elevator, grateful it's working today. On the tenth floor, I open the door to number 1017.

"Mom," I call out. "I'm home."

No answer. I'm not expecting one.

I go straight to my room. I'm tired. It's been a long night and a longer week. Homework can take a back seat.

Sleep doesn't come easy and when I awake, it's past eight a.m. I scruff a hand through my hair and head to the kitchen. It's freezing. There's not a stitch of food in the fridge.

I call Mom's name again, to no avail. Instead, my baby sister pokes her head out from around mom's bedroom doorframe. As soon as our eyes meet, Ruby crosses the living room on wobbly legs. Picking her up, I spin her around. A mop of unruly brown curls tug at my heartstrings as I drown in her love.

"More, Jane," she begs as I place her gently on the floor.

"Shhhhh." I press a finger to my lips. "You hungry?"

She holds up her fingers in a peace sign. "Me two, tomorrow."

I swear, inwardly. It's Ruby's birthday. I gapped it. My sister smiles, barely able to contain herself. Her sweet face breaks my heart.

Opening the cupboard, I retrieve a package of instant oatmeal and make it in her favorite green bowl. Between mouthfuls, Ruby insists all she wants is a stuffed rabbit like the girl down the hall.

"Soft," she describes earnestly, "the one with the ears."

"I know it," I say, and promise her it's coming. "Yellow, right?"

Ruby nods as I glance around. No cake. No wrapping paper. Nothing to eat. Has Mom remembered? I take stock of the situation.

We are drowning. Money is tight, eviction knocking on the door. Despite the paycheck from Big Jim's, ends will never meet. But I made a promise and I intend to keep it. That yellow rabbit will be in here tomorrow if it's the last thing I ever do.

After dressing Ruby in warm layers, I settle her on the couch in front of the Saturday cartoons, and retrieve my go-bag. I grab a jacket and head out.

I jump the turnstile at the Pape subway station down the street and wait on the platform. My bag hangs lose from my shoulder. Six months have passed since my last five-finger discount.

A line of carriages bursts through the tunnel, sending wrappers and empty paper cups into the air. I sway with motion of the train, bodies pressing up beside mine. Contemplate what I need to do next.

There are three ways to shoplift.

One item, a quick in and out. A chocolate bar. A loaf of bread. A Mother's Day gift. Desire or desperation.

Multiple small items. This approach takes longer, even when the location's been scouted beforehand. Plain-clothed security officers demand heightened vigilance. I roll it through. Troll the store. Locate what you want, filling your pockets. Walk to the front and choose one cheap item to buy. Door crashers or something on deep discount. A roll of lifesavers is usually my go-to.

"Is that all for today?" the cashier will ask.

"Yes, ma'am." Smile my biggest smile. Practice makes perfect.

The third way targets jackpots. Large expensive items that demand patience and strategy. They aren't easy to grab in shops preoccupied with the bottom line in a struggling economy. Nor are costly small products, which are often tucked behind the cashier or locked up in glass cases.

Bigger bag, bigger haul, bigger risk.

But I am not worried. I've had plenty of experience.

When the train pulls into the downtown station, I hop off and walk through the maze of tunnels leading to outside, check my phone to find a message from Ruby's childcare.

A lady with a singsong voice explains she cannot reach my mother and reminds me my sister needs pull-ups after having been moved from the toddler to the pre-school group. But I'm not listening. I'm thinking. Of what's in my purse, of my wallet, of the pointed nail scissors, of the ring of odd-shaped keys to get into places that are locked up for the purpose of keeping people out.

The mall appears a block ahead, an enormous green glass building. I make a mental note to add pull-ups to my list. People flood out onto the sidewalk, purses and heavy bags and children in tow. Matching jackets, blue jeans, squeaky new shoes.

Should I add clothes, too? The idea grows on me.

It wasn't always like this. It used to be easy. In elementary school, the lost and found was a treasure trove. Stained sweatshirts, crusty t-shirts and leggings discarded as garbage. But not anymore. The cupboard is adjacent to the high school guidance office, wide open to teachers and students strolling by. Making friends is impossible, as it is. The guidance counselor assured me it gets better after tenth grade, which in my opinion is a lie.

Besides, times have changed. What the cupboard holds no longer lures me in. This past year, I sprouted eight inches. I need soap. Deodorant. A razor for the tangled mat of hair spreading in my pits.

I twist my long brown locks into a bun before entering the mall and pull on a baseball cap. Fewer hairs for me to shed and for the police to find. I tug at the rim and push through the revolving door.

Inside, the scent of woody beans and cinnamon wafts up from the bottom floor. But I can't afford to think about sticky buns dripping with icing. I'm here for one reason. Thirty minutes, in and out. Fast and efficient. Get the job done.

Weaving through the throngs of shoppers, I take a quick look around. There are too many unknowns. To quell the uncertainty, I sweep the first floor. Eyes forward, alert. Focused.

There are only two rules to follow in any mall, in any part of the city. Never attempt a snatch-and-grab at the old fruit stand. Not the one at the corner. The corporate one. Apple is too well-lit, with products intentionally laid out. Eyes of staff. Eyes of security. Eyes of the courtroom. No one stands a chance.

Second, avoid doorways. In a rush, they're difficult to get

through and with their limited visibility there is no way of knowing who or what is lurking on the other side.

After conducting surveillance, I find a seat by the fountain. I like to review the details before solidifying a plan.

On the one hand, I could stick with what I came for. The rabbit. Ruby cannot be forgotten. I will not let that happen. I made a promise, one I fully intend to keep.

On the other, I could knock off multiple items from my burgeoning list should the opportunity arise. It's important to remain open to possibility, if and only if time permits.

Either way, my execution must be solid. After mulling both options, I choose the latter plan, leave my seat, then shoulder my go-bag.

First, I find the toy store. Halfway inside, I spot the rabbit. It is the identical yellow stuffie of the girl who lives in 1003 down the hall. Ruby's desire, a quick in and out. An easy win.

I approach the entry of the pharmacy next, which is halfway down the left side. Two people with their backs to me, a couple. Following them inside, I troll the aisles for small items. Pocket a stick of deodorant, toothpaste. The packages of pink razors and pulls-ups are too bulky. Abort. I put on my face of deception.

At the front of the store, I find the discounted items. Rummaging through the bin, I examine hair pins and scrunchies. Heat rises in my face. Even at half price, my toonie won't cover the cost.

When I glance up, a woman in a white shirt, gray pants, and black thick-soled shoes stands twenty feet away. I recognize the uniform. She could have been recruited for a police academy ad.

Slowly backing up, I slide behind the display of tooth-whitening products set out along the side of the store. Big blue boxes, stacked to the ceiling. I hold my breath. Nothing to do but wait, wait, wait.

The woman circles around, sniffing the air. Eagle eyes and red pursed lips as she focuses her attention on the customers. When she disappears to the back, I dart out from my hiding place. Grabbing a roll of mints, I walk straight to the cashier. Don't wait for change. High tail it out of the store.

I find a vacant bench to sit and catch my breath. My heart is beating hard and fast. I'm not sure what the uniformed woman was looking for, or if she even suspected me. It doesn't matter. Too close for comfort.

I check the time. Maybe it's best to go home. What I've achieved today is enough. Ruby's birthday gift is in my go-bag, my pockets filled with toiletries. While it's not a record haul, it's not a bad one.

Blending into the crowds, I head south. Pass Bath & Body Works, American Eagle, Banana Republic, an independent bookstore. Beside it, Sport Chek.

Then I spot them.

A pair of White Nike Air Force. Size Seven. Out on an open rack, beckoning me closer.

No. Forget it. This is not the time.

Head low, I walk by. A minute later, I pass the treat store in the food court. There is a lineup ten people deep. My stomach rumbles. I stop, breathe it all in.

Maybe I'm overthinking. What would it hurt? Thirty seconds are all it would take. A fast in. A fast retreat. Caution is overrated. I can't resist.

Retracing my steps, I return to the store. Look left, right. It's now or never. Grabbing the shoes, I stuff them in my bag. The entire maneuver took five seconds. No one saw a thing.

I head south toward the glass revolving doors, pleased with the operation. Until an unpleasant feeling rises from the tips of my toes. Something is off.

Turning slightly, I freeze. The hair on the back of my neck stands up. This time it's a man in a black uniform, blocking the exit. I can usually spot that police kit from a mile away. Not today.

What the hell is wrong with me?

What to do next? I could drop the bag and cut my losses. Go back to Sport Chek and return the shoes to the rack. Or run.

I run.

Spinning around, I bolt north. Back along the first floor, up the escalator, darting between shoppers. On the second floor I turn south, using my key to slip into an unoccupied utility room, just as it was during my last four visits.

It's dark inside, but not black. I slam the door shut. It's dank and stinks. Wiping the sweat from my face, I shed my jacket and ballcap, loosen my hair, let it flip over my shoulders. Put on glasses.

I step out. There is no camera to catch me. I know every vantage point in the mall, every nook and cranny. When forced to do things against the law, it's critical to be prepared, to plan ahead.

I move south, take long, smooth strides. Downstairs, a man shouts. A woman responds, a clear voice. Others appear from nowhere below, closing in around them. They run north, their voices buzzing like angry hornets.

The coast is clear.

Now. Go.

I take the escalator steps down, two by two. The woman is at the bottom. Hands on her hips, she regards me closely, doesn't give an inch.

Sweat trickles down my back. I look away, taking the sting out of her suspicion. Calm, cool, collected. Nothing to see here. She lets me pass.

I cross the food court to the public washroom. Locate an empty stall, dart into the space. Lock it. Stagger back from the door, focus hard to keep my footing. One step in front of the other. On the edge of the toilet, I catch my breath. I will not have a heart attack and drop to the floor.

I am not my father.

Moments later, the washroom door bursts open and bangs off a wall. I suck in a breath. Lift up my feet.

Footsteps pound nearby, moving faster, closer. A fist bangs on doors.

"Police."

Some occupants scream, others swear. I stay silent.

I retrieve my scissors. Cut tags and shove them in the sanitary napkin holder. Empty my go-bag, turning it inside out to reveal a black and white checked lining, and then refill it. My last resort. My last chance.

I shrink against the wall as the footsteps recede. My stomach clenches and saliva fills the back of my throat. Am I going to be sick?

I reach for the door. It squeaks as I edge it open. I flinch, then pause, blood pulsating through my temples. I cock my head, listening, straining to hear.

Nothing.

Finally, a break. With one hand on the wall to guide me, I inch forward. Jaw tense. Cautious, careful. Will they be outside? Waiting?

The door groans. Outside, the food court is packed. I walk the perimeter, slow and careful. Suppressing my panic, I brace myself to be tackled from behind. To be slammed on the floor, headfirst.

I shiver, eyes cast to the ground. No one yells or stops me. I return to the subway, pay my fare, and head east. The go-bag is on my lap, my arms wrapped tightly around its bulk. Closing my eyes, I thank the higher power who gave me a pass today.

I am safe, I am free.

Pitching, the train comes to a stop at Pape Station. My mood lightens. I approach the apartment and take the elevator upstairs. Ruby greets me at the door. Reaching into my bag, she pulls out the yellow rabbit and clutches it tight to her chest. Her face lights up the room. She winds her fingers around the soft fabric ear, rubbing it on the side of her cheek. Gently. Back and forth.

She smiles, and for a moment the world is right.

I am a good sister.

A sister who keeps her promises.

BRENDA CHAPMAN

Brenda Chapman is a crime writer who has published twenty-five books, including the lauded Stonechild and Rouleau series, the Anna Sweet mysteries for adult literacy, the Jennifer Bannon mysteries for middle grade readers, and the Hunter and Tate mysteries. Brenda's work has been shortlisted for several awards, including four Crime Writers of Canada Awards of Excellence. A former teacher and senior communications advisor in the federal government, she makes her home in Ottawa. Brenda belongs to Capital Crime Writers, Crime Writers of Canada, the Writers' Union of Canada, and Sisters in Crime. Find her at https://brendachapman.ca.

THE POOL

BRENDA CHAPMAN

Greg opened the gate to his neighbor's backyard and surveyed the wide expanse of fresh sod, his gaze coming to rest on the newly installed inground pool that sparkled like a box of gems in the June sunshine. The work crew had spent the spring digging and raising dust, annoying the hell out of everyone, but he had to admit that the final outcome might have been worth the noise and chaos. The heat and humidity had climbed steadily since the weekend, and a swim sure would feel good, maybe ease the cramping in his belly. He wiped the sheen of sweat from his brow and turned as Lila called his name from across the street.

"Hey Greg, did Charlotte get away okay?"

He waited for her to make her way up the driveway, worked at giving her a smile. "Taxi collected her highness before dawn to make a 7 a.m. flight. I'm scoping out the new pool."

Lila sidled up next to him and peered through the opening in the gate. She whistled. "Wow, that must have cost her a pretty penny. Too bad Charlotte hates anyone's company but her own. No way we'll ever get an invite. She'd freak if she knew we were staring into her backyard."

The decision to embrace her absence came surprisingly easily.

"Yeah, well, she's gone for the rest of the month and I'm in charge. Put the word out. Pool party in an hour and everyone bring their own drinks and snacks."

Lila choked before laughing. "I almost believe you said we're going to have a party in Charlotte's new pool. She'd turn you over her knee and beat you with the garden rake if she knew you'd joked about that."

"She'll never find out, and what she doesn't know…" He shrugged and grinned.

"Well then." Lila's face lit up in a wide smile as she realized he wasn't kidding. She pulled graying curls over her head with both hands and let the hair cascade down her back. "Let's get this party started." She turned to leave but stopped after a few steps and swung back to face him. "I can hardly believe she let you collect her mail and newspapers. Are you watering her indoor plants?"

"There doesn't appear to be anybody else she could ask."

"Good on you then. Everyone is going to be delighted to be rid of her for a few weeks if it means we can get some relief from her brooding malevolence and this heat."

Shannon was in the kitchen when Greg entered their house. He walked on bare feet across the tiled floor and wrapped his arms around her waist from behind. She stretched and tilted her head to the side so that he had space to kiss the nape of her neck. "Everything okay?" she asked.

"Get your suit and grab some wine and nibblies. The street will be showing up in an hour to christen the new pool."

"God, we're really doing this?"

"When the universe sees fit to give a golden opportunity, you gotta roll with it." He spun her around and kissed her lips. "The place next door is ours until it isn't."

She lifted her arms around his neck and wriggled her hips. "Free from the wicked witch at last."

A WEEK LATER, the heat wave continued to bathe the city as if it had no intention of ever leaving, and the street had settled into a happy, drunken routine. At two o'clock, Greg unlocked the back gate and filled a large bucket with ice, beer bottles, and vodka coolers. He turned on the Bluetooth and got the tunes blasting while he waited for Shannon to show up with bowls of chips and nuts. They took a leisurely swim before the neighbors began drifting in with their towels and snacks. By the second day most had made trips to the nearest Walmart and bought pool noodles and blow-up floating mats and toys in every vibrant color under the rainbow, now bobbing gaily in the water. They'd hauled over their fold-up chairs and loungers and staked out spots around the perimeter of the pool. Greg and Pete Sherman from two doors over had rolled in their gas barbecues and set up a cooking area at one end of the yard, and as supper hour drew closer, the hamburger patties, buns, corn, and barbecue ribs appeared along with bottles of white wine and rosé.

GREG STOOD at the edge of the lawn and surveyed the space. He used to lament that the people on the street had aged out of the child-rearing years, but now he celebrated the lack of kids who, let's face it, would have cramped the drinking and party vibe. He counted sixteen tanned and barely clad bodies in and around the pool on this particular afternoon, and not a one of them under fifty. It was a street of retirees for the most part. The couple of younger families with children at the far end near the intersection hadn't been invited by silent agreement. He waved at Shannon stretched out on a lounger talking to her best friend Rita, who dangled her feet in the water. Satisfied everyone was having a good time, he slipped out the gate and unlocked Charlotte's back door.

He was familiar now with the layout of her house and crossed to the liquor trolley in the far corner of the dining room. Charlotte had expensive tastes when it came to booze, and he poured a shot of single malt into the crystal tumbler he kept for a daily pick-me-up. The bottle had one more shot for tomorrow and then he'd crack open the bourbon. As the liquid burned smoothly down his throat, he set the empty glass on the cart and reached for a bottle of pinot noir in the wine cooler. On his way past the kitchen, he detoured to pick up the two T-bone steaks he'd left defrosting on the counter. Happily, as it turned out, Charlotte also had expensive tastes when it came to meat.

A clatter of footsteps up the back stairs and Shannon arrived in the kitchen doorway. "Those the last of the steaks?" she asked.

"Yeah, but she's got pork and lamb chops that will go good on the barbie."

Shannon walked over and traced a finger over the new coffeemaker on the counter. "This is one of those fancy machines that makes cappuccino and whips the milk."

He made a mental note to return after the party broke up to bring the coffee machine home. He already pictured Shannon's face in the morning when he brought her a frothy brew in bed.

CANADA DAY, after the last kernel of corn and slice of steak had been swallowed, Greg thought it time to make the announcement, which was certain to be a crowd pleaser. There was still a couple of hours of daylight left and the ice bucket had been restocked with beer.

"I received an email from Charlotte when I checked a little while ago. Turns out she's broken her leg and won't be able to travel back to Ottawa for another month at least. She has a blood condition that prohibits flying with the injury. Clots are a worry, apparently." He raised his glass of wine. "To Charlotte's good health and to our great fortune that she won't be returning to spoil our summer in the pool."

A round of cheers and clinking bottles and glasses followed his words.

"Good thing Charlotte likes one person on the street," Travis

Beatty said. He thumped Greg on the back. "She seemed sweet on you, which none of us could believe since she couldn't tolerate the rest of us. Say, was she ever married?"

"Once, but they divorced before she moved in here. From the way she talks about her ex, I'd say he's on her hate list too."

"You might be the only one she hasn't called bylaw on," Lila said.

"Greg wore her down with his kindness." Shannon beamed a smile in his direction. "She knew the right one to ask when she needed a hand."

A DAY of gray skies and rain shut down the pool party two weeks later. Greg had moved Charlotte's laptop to his kitchen and finished paying off her credit card before logging off. Online banking made his life so easy and Charlotte had been thoughtful enough to save her password on the site. The living room furniture he ordered through her account had arrived that morning and Shannon lay stretched out on the new leather couch reading.

He checked the weather report on his phone and made the decision he'd been putting off. "Shannon, it's time," he called, and she appeared at his shoulder a moment later.

"You're sure about this?" she asked, resting an arm across his shoulder. "I was on my way upstairs to bed."

"We're in too deep now."

"And lord knows, I don't want to return that delicious sofa. It's like lying on a buttery cloud."

"Then let's get this over with."

They put on their rain gear and boots before stepping outside, using the back entrance. Greg had gotten the shovels out of the shed earlier in the day and he carried both with him through the side entrance into Charlotte's yard. The rain pattered on the hoods of their raincoats and dampened their faces as they dug up the recently planted bushes along the back end of the fence. They set them carefully to one side and continued digging. When all was ready, they entered her house and clumped down the basement steps, using flashlights to guide their way. Greg needed Shannon's help to pull Charlotte's body out of the freezer, but between the two of them, they wrestled her onto the floor and carried her upstairs.

"This is the diciest bit," Greg said. He opened the door and checked up and down the street for dog walkers or anyone crazy enough to be out jogging on such a night. Luckily, a misty fog obscured his sightline and made the darkness even murkier. Golden light glowed in the bedroom window of the house next door, but the curtain was drawn and he didn't detect any movement. Satisfied that nobody had eyes on him, he opened the gate to Charlotte's backyard and propped it ajar with a rock before returning to lift her body. "Out we go, then," he said.

Filling in the hole and replanting the bushes turned out to be easier than digging up the root bulbs and carving out the grave, and they were back in their own house with a bottle of Charlotte's finest port before midnight. Unlike Hitchcock's *Rear Window*, nobody had peered outside at the worst possible moment, and they slept like babies, helped along by a couple of glasses and all that physical exertion.

Before Charlotte's death, Greg had been at a loss as to how to spend his retirement. All this changed that June morning when he went over to drive her to the airport at 5 a.m. with dawn still an hour away. After he entered the house, she'd given him the key to her back door and the code for the lock on the gate so that he could test the new pool's PH levels daily. However, he was not invited to have a dip or permitted to let anybody else into the back yard. She was very clear on the last point. "Not one of our no-good neighbors gets near my pool, you hear?"

He'd lugged her suitcases down from the second floor and set them by the back door while he caught his breath and bent to tie his running shoes. Greg had learned the first time he entered her hallway to fix a light fixture that Charlotte wouldn't abide outdoor shoes worn in her house. Even now he could recall her shriek as he'd started up the steps in his sneakers.

That June morning, Charlotte had come up behind him, carrying the loafers she intended to wear on the flight, while he was putting on his second shoe. He'd lost his balance and lurched backwards as he grabbed at something to steady himself. He heard, rather than saw, the heavy suitcase fall like a domino into Charlotte, who tumbled down the basement stairs with thumps and bangs as she hit each step before landing with a sickening crack on the concrete floor.

The horror of her scream echoed in his ears long afterward in the silent aftermath. He'd rushed downstairs to help her get to her feet, but her glassy eyes had stared up at him as blood pooled around her head. He'd needed fresh air to keep from puking his guts out and hurried outside, gulping in mouthfuls as the nausea abated. Opening her back gate and seeing the pool for the first time had given him breathing space before calling in the cavalry. A swim would erase the horror and give him time to make sense of the accident, or so he believed then. The longer he put off calling the paramedics, the easier it became to ignore what had happened and to let the day unfold as if Charlotte wasn't lying dead at the bottom of the stairs. By the time he revealed the story of Charlotte's demise to Shannon the evening after that first pool party, the dye had been cast.

HE SPENT the morning writing an email from Charlotte to his own email account in which she thanked him for agreeing to open the pool for the upcoming season. She planned to remain in Florida for the month of June at least and hoped he would continue to mind the house as he had the past four years when she was away.

Greg raised his head and looked out Charlotte's window into her backyard bathed in sunlight. Robins, chickadees, and cardinals dove at the birdfeeders he'd hung in the branches of the maple trees, which had grown to the height of the eaves. The spirea bushes had filled in and were now as tall as Shannon. Charlotte's private and government pensions, deposited monthly into her bank account, had paid for several vacations, a new car, and many nights out. For the past four years, he'd laid breadcrumbs from her account to various stores, the bank, his email. He'd even sent letters to the editor of the local paper with her name as the signatory. She'd become something of a cause célèbre in the op-ed community. Nobody in the neighborhood missed their cranky neighbor's presence or questioned her extended absences to warmer climes. Not one person had come forward to express concern for her welfare. Becoming Charlotte had become his fulltime hobby, and he'd grown to embrace the challenges.

He shut off Charlotte's laptop and made a final check of the house before standing on the landing in front of the back door. The usual twinge of anxiety coursed through him as he relived that moment when he'd lost his balance and fallen backward. He remembered the feel of the leather suitcase on the calf of his leg, and then the knee and foot of his other leg rising. It was here that he stopped the memory from fleshing out into a truth he could never reconcile. Had he in fact kicked the suitcase with all of his might like a donkey? Or was this a fabrication arising from the dreams that woke him twisting in the sheets in the middle of the night?

He stared down the dark staircase, recoiling from old terrors before opening the screen door with a shaking hand and stepping outside into the late spring sunshine. Fresh mouthfuls of air kept him upright as he crossed the distance to the back fence. Wiping sweat from his forehead, he pushed the gate open and stared at the clean blue water in the pool, until a calmness stole through him yet again.

Pool party season was about to begin, and Charlotte's absence would be heartily toasted many times over before her anticipated autumn return. Lucky for him, nobody had expressed concern when she hadn't come home the past four autumns as expected. In pre-emptive strikes, he'd written and shown her lengthy emails to whoever was interested. They outlined the great time she was having in Cancun, or whatever locale he'd picked for her that year, including her decision to stay on. It was a communal joke now that Charlotte might never make it back. Little did his neighbors know he was considering putting her in assisted living somewhere in Arizona this winter, because he was tired of making excuses for her extended holidays.

Charlotte was loved in death as she'd never been in life. *A fitting epitaph*, he thought as he picked up the paper from her front stoop on his way home to Shannon, where they'd enjoy a second cup of frothy coffee on the leather couch as they read up on the day's news. Then, he'd get started taking down a panel in the fence separating his yard from Charlotte's. Her latest email suggested easier access would make all their lives better, and he was only too happy to comply. After all, she'd offered to sell him her house in several recent messages, and once he figured out the intricacies of the paperwork, her legacy on the street would fade to those perfect, stolen, summer afternoons spent partying around her pool. He could only imagine how many times she'd rolled over in her final resting place as they danced the night away to Fleetwood Mac and popped open one last cold one before staggering home to their beds.

JUDY PENZ SHELUK

Judy Penz Sheluk (author/editor) is a former journalist and magazine editor and the bestselling author of *Finding Your Path to Publication* and S*elf-publishing: The Ins & Outs of Going Indie*, as well as two mystery series: the Glass Dolphin Mysteries and Marketville Mysteries. In addition to the Superior Shores Anthologies, which she also edited, her short crime fiction appears in several collections. Judy is a member of Sisters in Crime, International Thriller Writers, the Short Mystery Fiction Society, and Crime Writers of Canada, where she served on the Board of Directors for five years, the final two as Chair. Find Judy at www.judypenzsheluk.com.

THE LAST CHANCE COALITION
JUDY PENZ SHELUK

I watch Jake McFadden strut into O'Leary's Bar & Grill with the swagger of a man who's dabbled with the big time and likes to flaunt it. His hair, now gunmetal gray shot with strands of silver, is still thick, wavy, and carefully tousled. He's also grown a beard, presumably to hide the sagging jowls of a man in his mid-sixties, though that presumption may be somewhat unkind.

The authors seated at the long, banquet-style table rise, their greetings effusive, and he accepts their adoration as his due. McFadden's last "critically acclaimed" novel may have been a decade ago (in the publishing world, critically acclaimed is invariably a euphemism for poor sales), but he's made a serious name for himself as an editor. Anthologies mostly, multi-author collections of mystery and suspense. He's even been nominated for a Cleopatra Award for his work on *Border Crossing*, which is what rankles the most.

More than rankles, if I'm being honest. I mean, what sort of narcissistic egomaniac writes about nothing but his own publishing career and caps it off by including his own short story in the introduction—and not even a very good story, at that? What sort of pompous ass forgets to acknowledge the volunteer who spent countless unpaid hours vetting, formatting, and logging submissions?

Jake McFadden, that's who.

I can still remember anxiously awaiting my pre-ordered copy, picking it up at the writers' conference, and scanning the introduction for my name, my first "publication credit" as an aspiring author. Okay, maybe not technically a publication credit, but it still had to count for something with an agent, right?

Except my name wasn't there. I scanned the intro again, as if searching for the missing piece in a jigsaw puzzle, sure that it was hiding in plain sight.

It wasn't.

It was cold comfort that McFadden had neglected to acknowledge anyone else. No nod to the organizers who'd spent the last three years of their lives to make the conference—and the associated anthology—a reality. No mention of the publisher, who was doing this pro bono for a local, literary-based charity (also not mentioned). Nary a word about the three judges—also volunteers with full-time jobs—who had waded through 117 submissions in as many days. There wasn't even so much as a snippet about the twenty-two selected stories and their authors.

Had this man never read the introduction to an anthology before?

Apparently not. Unless, of course, he'd chosen to ignore convention for the sake of shameless self-promotion.

Too harsh? Hang tight. I haven't even gotten to the humiliating part of the experience yet.

You see, one of the perks of being included in the conference anthology is taking part in the multi-author book signing event. Not being one of the authors, I hadn't expected to be signing anything, but after all the work I'd put in I did want autographs from the attending authors, a lasting memento of my labors. I located the room, the lineup already long and almost out the door, and took my place, my copy of *Border Crossing* in hand.

The authors had been seated alphabetically in a u-shaped configuration, the last chair vacant. I realized it belonged to Jake

McFadden, standing in the middle of the room. He cleared his throat to address the crowd.

"Thank you so much for coming here to celebrate with us today," he began. "It's my pleasure to introduce you to each of the authors who were able to attend the conference." He rattled off name after name as each author stood up in turn, then said, "It's also my pleasure to thank the individuals who made this anthology possible. Without their hard work and Herculean efforts, we would not be standing here today."

I relaxed, channeling my inner adult. True, McFadden hadn't acknowledged anyone in the book's intro, but he was going to correct that oversight now.

Except that's not what happened. Oh, he thanked a bunch of people. The publisher. The conference organizers. The judges. The hotel's conference liaison. Even the caterer. *The caterer!*

The one person he didn't thank was me.

I could have stayed silent. Should have, really. There was nothing to gain by speaking out beyond fueling my own anger and embarrassment at being omitted yet again.

Of being unworthy of a single, simple, accolade.

And yet…

"What about me?" I asked, my voice barely a whisper, and all eyes turned in my direction. I thought I saw a hint of sympathy in a few. Most just looked surprised. The conference organizers, both of whom had gotten to know me well, couldn't—or wouldn't—look in my direction. McFadden may have broken protocol, but they weren't about to dwell on it. After all, they'd been thanked.

"What about me?" I repeated, louder this time.

McFadden frowned, as if trying to place me, even though we'd been introduced earlier that day. After a moment, his frown faded, and he gave a relieved smile, as if the memory of the morning had come back to him. "Right, I'm sorry Melanie. You, umm, you…" his voice trailed off.

"It's Melody," I said. "Mel-o-dy. Not Melanie. Melody Pulford? I was the volunteer intake coordinator on the project."

He nodded, fingered his chin thoughtfully, as if trying to

remember what a volunteer intake coordinator did, then, "Of course, of course. Please, come up and say a few words."

Except there was nothing to say now that I'd made a complete ass of myself, was there? And Jake McFadden, standing there, a smug look on his arrogant face, knew it.

"It's okay," I said, fighting back tears. "I'm just here for the signing, like everyone else."

McFadden stared at me for a brief second and gave a dismissive shrug of his shoulders. "Maybe next time."

I managed to make my way from author to author, deliberately avoiding eye contact and conversation. Finally made it to the last seat and Jake McFadden. He scrawled his signature on the front page of my book—no "best wishes," or any other such sentiment—and slid it back across the table. I swear I saw a glint of amusement in his pale blue eyes.

I walked out of the room, shoulders erect, head held high, and never spoke of the incident again.

Until now.

McFADDEN SIPS ON A MARTINI, chitchatting with the authors as they regale him with updates on their latest publications. He feigns interest, though I can't help but notice the way his eyes don't quite focus on the individual speaking, the way he continues to scan the door, as if waiting for the cool kids to arrive.

I've stayed silent, watching and listening from my spot at the end of the table. Maybe it's my silence that triggers some instinct in him to turn his attention my way, or maybe he's just tired of pretending to be engaged.

"Hey," I say. His blank stare assures me that he has no idea of who I am or why I'm here, and furthermore, doesn't care.

Perfect. The last thing I want is McFadden messing up my plans with an apology after all these years. Seven, to be exact, and not a single week has gone by when I haven't stared at his heartless scrawl on the first page of *Border Crossing*. Obsessive? I'm willing to own that. After all, hell hath no fury like a woman scorned.

And I've been scorned.

THE IDEA CAME to me after rereading Agatha Christie's *Murder on the Orient Express* for the umpteenth time—a truly clever ending that never fails to impress—and realized that if Jake McFadden had screwed me over, he'd probably done the same to others. All I needed was a carefully curated cast of castoffs. Oh, not to kill McFadden. I may be obsessive, and you already know that I can hold a grudge, but I'm not a murderer. A bit of larceny to teach him a lesson? I'm not above that.

The first step had been to come up with a concept that would appeal to McFadden's attention-seeking ego, his pocketbook, and his love of downtown bars. I knew he was a regular at the Skit-Kat Club, where he enjoyed watching stand-up comics and occasionally did a bit of bad improv himself. Why not invent a venue where authors could read short stories or excerpts from their novels? The plan would need some embellishment, but hey, I'm a writer (now published, in case you were wondering). I embellish stuff for a living. Besides, it's not like we were talking about a real club or anything, it just had to seem real enough for McFadden to invest.

As luck would have it, Gigi—the bartender at O'Leary's—is also a woman scorned by McFadden. Not that he remembers wining, dining, and bedding her a dozen years back, she a naïve eighteen-year-old at the time. He'd been her Creative Writing instructor, and it turned out she'd been one of a long line of wannabe authors vying for his attention and getting it. Not that writing advice ever entered the equation.

"Jake's martini isn't the only thing he likes with a twist," Gigi had told me, her expression dark.

With Gigi's help I was able to enlist the aid of eight more authors who'd had the misfortune to cross McFadden's path, and, like Gigi, they'd been students, and in some cases, his clients. Turns out he has a very "hands-on" approach to editing, at least when it comes to women.

The "Last Chance Coalition"—that's the name our castoff collective had chosen to define our mission, mostly because we were all tired of carrying the weight of unfulfilled revenge—debated the best strategy. Despite McFadden's track record of not remembering me, I was reluctant to be the one to lay the trap. If, and it was a big if, it all came back to him, his suspicions might be aroused. That would never do. The other authors? McFadden had no reason to trust them. As a regular at O'Leary's, on the other hand, Gigi was someone he knew—not that he'd made the connection between the thirty-year-old barkeep and the student he'd once slept with. I expect her neon pink hair, multiple piercings, and full sleeve tats helped with that.

After careful deliberation, we decided it would be best if it was his idea to invest. We'd set the plan in motion two months earlier, Gigi telling McFadden how a Bay Street bigwig had been looking to start up something like a Skit-Kat Club for mystery writers. She'd made a point of laughing it off. Nothing worse than appearing too eager.

A month after that, Gigi let it drop that the Bay Street bigwig had nailed down the perfect space in the Distillery District and was now actively seeking qualified investors, wondered if she could recommend anyone who might be interested.

McFadden bit on Gigi's third casual mention. We hired an out-of-work actor to play the Bay Street bigwig, arranged to have O'Leary's closed for a "private function," and rehearsed our hearts out every night from midnight to mid-morning for the next ten days.

THE EVENING WENT off without a hitch. Gigi was convincingly nervous as she introduced "Mr. Lacroix" to the group, and the actor —I never did get his real name—played his part to perfection, pandering to McFadden without being obvious, while being just a tad bit dismissive of the rest of us.

It didn't take long. The more Gigi and our coalition of castoffs clamored to be part of Lacroix's vision, the more McFadden's interest was piqued. By the end of the night, he'd all but committed to providing the necessary start-up capital—but only if he could go it alone.

"Not a problem," Lacroix had assured him, so long as it was a private cash deal. He couldn't afford to dilute equity to subsequent investors when it came time to crowd source additional funding, which was sure to be required down the road. It was why he was only asking for three grand.

That wasn't the real reason, of course. In Ontario, anything less than $5,000 is considered petty theft versus the far more serious charge of grand larceny. We might have wanted to get even, but none of us were keen on going to jail. Besides, this wasn't about the money. Split ten ways there wouldn't be much left after paying Lacroix for his performance—and his silence.

None of us were surprised when McFadden stormed out of O'Leary's muttering insults and expletives. In fact, we'd banked on it. You see, we'd started having second thoughts. Oh, not about screwing McFadden over. It's just that the concept, we all agreed, could *actually* work. Asking for a lowball cash deal was bound to raise a red flag, McFadden would walk away, incensed at almost being duped by a bartender, and the Last Chance Coalition would figure out a way to bring the Mystery Mic Club to fruition for real. Our success, without him, would be revenge enough.

Opportunity came knocking a few weeks later, when an actual bigwig from Hollywood arrived in Toronto looking for innovative ideas for a new reality TV series (Ontario arts funding at its finest).

I'm not sure how Lacroix finagled it, but he got me a meeting with the Hollywood honcho. Well, me and a hundred other hopefuls. I saw McFadden in the queue, and he gave me that smirky smile. *Damn, had he known who I was all along?*

"What about making it a mystery mic night held at an actual night club?" I'd asked Mr. Hollywood when my turn came and, dry-mouthed and stomach churning, then proceeded to fill him in on the concept. No one was more surprised than me when he bought not just the concept, but O'Leary's Bar & Grill.

The Mystery Mic Club turned out to be a critical success and a ratings bonanza with the coveted 18-49 demographic, in large part because of "Mr. Lacroix," the club's debonair emcee, and Gigi, who stayed on as a wisecracking bartender with a heart of gold and a nose for talent.

And me? I landed the role of Head Screenwriter for the series (spoiler alert: reality TV is often scripted). Even ended up winning an Emmy Award, where I thanked everyone from the executive producers and director to the makeup artist, costume designer, set director, entire crew, and of course, the Last Chance Coalition authors who'd made it all possible, with a special nod to Gigi and Mr. Lacroix.

Darn. If only I'd remembered to thank the show's editor.

Maybe next time, Jake McFadden.

Maybe next time.

THE LINEUP

Christina Boufis: www.christinaboufis.com

John Bukowski: www.thrillerjohnb.net

Brenda Chapman: https://brendachapman.ca

Susan Daly: www.susandaly.com

Wil A. Emerson: www.wilemerson.com

Tracy Falenwolfe: www.tracyfalenwolfe.com

Kate Fellowes: http://katefellowes.wordpress.com

Molly Wills Fraser: www.mollywillsfraser.com

Gina X. Grant: www.ginaxgrant.com

Karen Grose: www.karengrose.ca

Wendy Harrison: www.wendyharrisonwriter.com

Julie Hastrup: https://hastrup.com/

Larry M. Keeton: www.larrykeetonwriter.com

Charlie Kondek: CharlieKondekWrites.com

Edward Lodi: www.goodreads.com/author/show/275844.
Edward_Lodi

Bethany Maines: www.BethanyMaines.com

Gregory Meece: twitter.com/GRMSenior

Cate Moyle: https://catemoylepens.weebly.com/

Judy Penz Sheluk: www.judypenzsheluk.com

KM Rockwood: www.kmrockwood.com

Kevin R. Tipple: https://kevintipplescorner.blogspot.com/

Robert Weibezahl: robertweibezahl.wordpress.com